A NOVEL BY

PHILIPPA STOCKLEY

PIMPERNEL
PRESS LTD
www.pimpernelpress.com

PRELUDE

*Z*enobia Crace was having her new house near the Temple decorated. The upholsterer, a silk merchant and his four assistants had finally left, after spending the entire morning measuring a suite of rooms.

The noon meal was over and the fresco painters were due to arrive, to talk to Zenobia's husband, John, about the ceiling of the great hall. Italian and supposedly the best in Europe, they were bringing sample drawings, and Zenobia, who had heard that all Italians were without exception handsome, was excited by the idea of being addressed as *Signora Contessa*, or some such foreign thing, and bowed to by vigorous young men with lustrous hair and swarthy skin. What a change it would make.

From where she sat by a mullioned window, watching the early afternoon light polish the planked oak table, she could see John in the adjoining chamber. Amber blobs bloomed on the gleaming wood every time the sun intensified or she lifted the heavy lead glass to her lips, while in a closet off the room beyond, stray rays tantalised the black lacquer of her husband's prized imported desk and turned its surface to oiled water.

Sweetmeats sat on a figured gilt dish, as well as plump mirabelles and gages, sugared and served in tiny glasses half-filled with fruit liqueurs, as enticing as emeralds and rubies. Zenobia felt part of the dancing light. Why stint herself these pleasures, a young woman of dazzling appearance – it was hardly a secret – stuck with an ageing man? And one recently afflicted by something his doctor did not understand, a strange smell that seeped from his skin without warning. She kept costly beeswax candles burning on tall stands far enough from the bed not to endanger its heavy tapestry curtains, for fire was a constant hazard. It was said that candles helped eliminate stink or at least distract from it. Some were scented with lemon and others with orris. But when the affliction struck, it was as if John rotted where he lay, propped on pillows embroidered with his self-important monogram. The taint came and went, often just the palest whiff, which because of his extraordinary wealth, people pretended not to notice. All the same, they looked at her, wondering how she could bear it. Young men with calculating pity in narrowed eyes: how long would the old man last and what would she be worth? She was aware of their thoughts. She had them herself with increasing frequency.

John Crace's body still worked well enough. He had always been energetic in business and particularly in pleasure. Now, though suffering from back pains that Zenobia scolded his physician were from staying in bed, he still clambered out and took meals with her. And to her disgust he clambered on top of her, too, his large, once-magnificent body like a weighted plate on a sallet. That aspect of his character had increased. But she was not yet with child, which made him alternately angry and demanding.

Crace was fifty-five, give or take. A good age. His new physician, Stoddart, was older, though, perhaps by dint of being ineluctably stupid, he looked younger. Zenobia was now on the cusp of twenty, and her husband had hinted that after near four years of marriage, perhaps he should exchange her for a younger and *fecund* bride.

It wouldn't be a novelty, she thought, refilling her squat-bottomed glass. He had already had two wives and two sons (though only the one he disliked had survived to manhood), so the question of her breeding was surely unimportant in the scheme of things. But age had increased his ambition. While for now her slender feet in their useless heeled slippers were firmly under the table, how long would that last if she didn't spawn the child that obsessed him? She knew he could do what he said.

After the Fire, crooked builders and other chancers who seized on London's desperation to rebuild the city had flourished. It was exactly what John Crace had done – and flourished spectacularly. Born Theocritus Koros, a young man of uncertain foreign origin who appeared fully formed from nowhere, he promised fast and delivered faster. Though he had told Zenobia little of his previous life, she knew that he had once been in shipping, plying a dangerous trade between London and the West Indies. The lifespan of most involved in that business was short, but for those who survived, the profits dazzled. Despite uncharted waters, storms, pirates, marauding Caribs, and unfamiliar, ravaging diseases, despite frequent losses of entire cargoes of clayed sugar or slaves, over the years he had amassed, lost and re-amassed a vast fortune.

Ten years after buying his first ship, wealthy and still hale, he considered the plague and fire as blessings. He changed tack and invested his blood-spattered gains in English stone, earth, sand and lime. He became a builder.

The fire's aftermath proved a godsend for men devoid of pity or scruple. Life at sea and in the new colony of Barbados had taught Crace the low price of humanity. His foremen, criminals plucked from Newgate, hardened sailors and returning overseers and buccaneers among them, were cut from the same cloth. Labourers on his building sites, brick-works, quarries and forges died at an alarming rate, but those who had lost everything took any job and his foremen only picked the desperate among them.

Sovereign contracts soon ensured his rapid rise, followed by the acquisition of a piece of land between Charing Cross and the Temple, a gift from the second King Charles. In just over three years, the man still known to the world as Theocritus Koros promptly erected an ostentatious house in the height of fashion, with a showpiece garden running down to the river. At which point the woman who proved to be his final wife urged him to change his name to something easier on the ear and tongue.

He balked at Zenobia's first suggestion of Cross; it jangled the nerves of a man newly perturbed by visions of a fiery, hellish death. Though he had escaped the real flames, their memory licked at the corners of his mind, proffering sooty grins and a burning embrace. Despite surviving both plague and furnace, as he approached his mid-fifties he had begun to worry about the final resting place of his soul, yet shrank from peering into the long-unlit pit of his heart. Now that illness had begun to dog him, he sometimes allowed Zenobia to influence decisions, which was to have repercussions.

For as things turned out, Crace did not have as long as he hoped to contemplate whether his soul went up like a rocket or down like a stick, for his wife, carrying what he was sure was a son, though still scarce bigger in her womb than a week-old rat, would be widowed remarkably shortly after he rewrote his will.

Had Zenobia known this, it might have given her comfort. As it was, loathing finished her glass, so she poured more of the fortified liquid, poured so haphazardly that some beaded on the table. She dashed the drop away with her palm just as she might, had he been an ant, have dashed away her husband. Glancing eagerly out of the windows in anticipation of the painters, she imagined how she would tell any future child about herself.

PART ONE

CHAPTER ONE

*Z*enobia had what was called an exotic, in other words half-foreign, background. London brimmed with foreigners. The city and docks bustled with merchants; thrummed with nations of every hue – spies, ambassadors, mercenaries, servants, sailors and slaves. Zenobia was none of those.

She was born in a roomy, dilapidated building at the north end of Smithfield, in a worthless part of London that the Great Fire inadvertently spared, to a Turkish father who traded spices and her unmarried mother, the girl who cleaned his rooms.

Hannah was beautiful, but in a thin way, as if side-on she might vanish, with hair the colour of flax. When the Turk first saw her, lit by a shaft of light on the stairs, carrying a bucket full of turds, he thought she looked as transparent as boiling sugar, which was how he imagined infidel angels to look. And that she needed feeding up, which idea appealed to him.

Even though he had made London his home and his last voyage to Turkey had been years earlier, he knew what good food was, because he missed it. He also knew places where Levantine Turks and Persians made dishes both sweet and savoury for any who could pay, with delicate leaves of gilded papery pastry full of the rich flavours and oils he craved. Just thinking about it made him taste them. As he looked at the girl he felt hungrier than he could remember, while his brain exploded with dizzying scents of cloves, cinnamon, and orange and rose waters, mixed with the salivating whiff of sugar on the point of caramelising, adding a faint hint of almond and a good dollop of honey to crisp buttery pastry.

'Come back at six this evening,' he commanded, trying not to smack his lips. 'There will be something for you.'

The girl shrank against the spine of the stair. Its massive length of Baltic timber plucked from a ship's mast hurt her back where she pressed against it. Her impassive eyes were like stone after rain. In that fair morning light, her brow showed so smooth and white that he wanted to lick it. At the same time, with the vivid imagination that both plagued and terrified her, she felt like a sacrificial victim tied to a stake, waiting with fatality for the death blow to fall.

Her fear communicated itself. Spurred by his thoughts of what he could do with such passivity, he smiled the wide smile which had melted every female heart he came across, and devastated those he had made a lifelong habit of leaving. Her inertia convinced him that it had succeeded yet again. 'Don't concern,' he beamed. 'Nothing bad. Only good thing happen. Come six, go home seven happy.'

If it could be called home, he thought in his own language, unsmiling and without interest. It was not apparent that anyone looked after her. He knew of her slovenly father, the caretaker. They huddled together somewhere in the basement of the cavernous building. There was a woman too, overblown, crouching, hideous. It was difficult to imagine such an inhuman object as the girl's mother, but since Hannah's lineage did not figure in his calculations, he did not dwell on it.

Hannah was fourteen and a half. The work she was obliged to do was too heavy for her. Her mother slapped her if she faltered. The small family shared two filthy rooms whose unwashed windows peered hazily at the back yard. Recently her father had been weighing her up in a way she disliked and she sensed that it was only a matter of time before he did something awful one day when her mother was out. His eyes darted like silverfish scurrying along cracks in the filthy boards.

When she went softly upstairs that early June evening she was full of trepidation. The Turk, which is what she called him in her mind, was powerfully set and dark, with oiled hair and sombre velvet clothes different from anything she had ever seen. He wore white linen and a collar embroidered with intricate strap-work, which her father had never done. His appearance commanded respect. She felt certain that he must be a merchant for in his two rooms she had seen and smelled boxes and bags of evidently potent spices. Hannah knew her life would be worthless if she overstepped the mark, so she never touched anything, though she would have liked to examine what it was that coloured the rooms with the pungent but also ravishing smell. But she didn't dare – which the Turk knew, because he had spied on her, too.

Throughout that day as she cleaned and swabbed up and down the building and in the festering yard, sniffing her armpits, debating whether to wash them at the pump before going up, she wondered what to do. His invitation could only mean one thing. If she turned him down, sooner or later her father would have her (an expression two tenants had used one day as she passed, then shushed each other). The thought appalled her. If she angered the Turk by refusing, he might rape her anyway, or accuse her of stealing something and get her hanged out of spite. It wouldn't be difficult: who would believe her? Her terms of reference were all tawdry, cruel or mean and there was nowhere to run except the streets. Since by comparison she did not find the Turk completely repulsive, for at least he smelled better than her father, she decided that her only course was to do what he said and make the best of it. Even so, she tucked a small folding knife deep in a pocket of her only petticoat, beneath her only overskirt. If he did anything abominable, she could always slit his gizzard, an expression her father liked to use.

The bells tolled as she went up. When he opened the door, it was the smell that struck her. From behind him, delectable scents flowered, bathing her in warm aromas. Orange, yes; and the pervasive, dark tang of cloves, which she had become accustomed to. But also . . .

'You smell them?' he asked, not concealing his delight at her delicately lifted nose, whose trembling nostrils, like those of a Carrara statue, glowed red like hibiscus water. 'Cinnamon, cardamom, vanilla, attar, orange, clove, pistachio, honey . . . figs . . . lamb . . . dates . . . ginger . . . you smell them all?'

'Yes,' she lied, even though most of the words meant little, not listening so much as obeying, breathing the air, tasting it. He wore a richer velvet robe than usual, picked out with gold, and a fringed sash worked with more gold. Behind him on a small wooden tilt-table at the end of the bed, which was covered with velvet prinked with silver thread, sat a majolica dish piled with tiny pastries of different shapes, crescents and triangles, from which these perfumes rose. Two pewter plates were set near. Light from the window turned a flagon of wine to ripe straw.

Ignoring her nerves, he made her sit, noticing how well she held herself. He served her and made her drink, which, once she had tasted the honeyed wine, she did with pleasure. He watched her eat, first with cautious fingers and then with greed that matched his own, eating for pure delight as he made her taste one delicious thing after another. He realised that he had no intention of letting her leave; not yet.

In this way and in the event willingly, without remembering the knife in her skirts because she was drunk for the first time, Hannah Golby became the Turk's mistress. A fortnight later, since her lover did not trust her father any more than she did, he moved her into his rooms, where she slept in the furthest room on a pallet in an alcove, save when he wanted her in his own bed, which was often.

Despite an almost complete lack of education, Hannah had natural intelligence and used it to her advantage. She kept the Turk's rooms spotless, for while it was obvious that he was enamoured, she sensed that she could not yet bear a child, and did not want him to lose interest and throw her out. Hoping things would soon change, she made herself useful running errands, dressed as a boy to avoid attention, which was easy with her narrow frame. And she decided to find out how to make the dishes he loved.

During his years in London the Turk had learned enough English to get by, but he could not cook. He would not allow Hannah to go to Turkish cooks to learn, saying that if they guessed her sex they would take advantage, for the ones who specialised in sweetmeats were men. She shrewdly suggested that even if she could not make the sweet delicacies he craved, it did not matter, since they had no furnace to bake in, but if he could buy a recipe for one or two dishes done in a pot, she would cook them over the fire. With perception that surprised him, she pointed out that should the dish deliberately lack an ingredient, his sense of smell and taste would identify it, at which – under his supervision, she added hastily – she would experiment until she got it right.

'I am at your service,' she smiled, crinkling her eyes in a way he found irresistible; 'my life belongs to you.' Humbly, but she meant it, for her life in those two high, light rooms, though illegitimate and on his terms, was spent with someone with a degree of culture as well as compassion and was infinitely better than the one she had left. Compared with her father, whose only clement act during her childhood had been to teach her rudimentary letters – no charity, he wanted an unpaid secretary – the Turk was usually genial, often generous, and some of his physical demands gave her pleasure. She had no intention of returning downstairs.

Her logic appealed to his brain and stomach and, since it contained no risk of her misuse, he allowed it. She learned to make a handful of dishes that brought him back each day with increasing anticipation. At last she began to swell, and so did the father of her child. When she was so large that she could scarcely move, to her astonishment he allowed her off her pallet and into his bed.

Hannah served the Turk as well as a wife, though without the name. In 1665 a baby, remarkable for having almost none of her father's darkness and by some miraculous flourish even more than her mother of blondeness, was born.

The approaching birth would have brought greater joy to Hannah had the plague not been working its way through the surrounding streets. Keeping to the Turk's rooms as the pregnancy progressed, she missed the ugly rumours of mysterious deaths around St Giles. She did hear that a few people had died contorted in agony and clotted with blood, black swellings in their groins or armpits. People discussed the symptoms as if gruesomely detailed knowledge was prophylactic. For a while the malaise had no name, but it came soon enough, and then she listened with one hand pressed to her mouth and the other to her stomach, in case the pestilence wormed its way there before the child came out. Some called it the wrath of God for dissolute living, others insisted that that was nonsense: it was gin that did it, everybody knew. For others, the turpentine-laden infusion was their only hope of prevention and they clung to it. If they were going to die – and, they said, surely most of them were – wouldn't it be better in gin-ridden euphoria? At which they drank faster and deeper.

For some time the Turk continued all errands to do with his trade, and he had necessary foodstuffs delivered. Not long before the child was born, his mood darkened; the ships that bore his spices were quarantined on the river, sacks mouldering in the holds. Everything was delayed and everyone was afraid. As trade dropped off, he sat sipping small glasses of Turkish fig liqueur, which he could still get off the ships by bribing the impounded crew. Now, even when spices came off, they were spoiled from delay and trade plummeted. During Hannah's final weeks, he began to disappear for days or, increasingly, nights at a time.

In July the King and court abruptly left the city. In the emptying streets people died in the open, lying where they fell or propped against a wall to wait for the burial carts. Some were thrown from windows, nightshirts round their armpits. The Turk had only told Hannah parts of this, though the rest was easy to guess, gazing down from the window. In her final month she half-sat, half-lay on a box seat, gasping from the searing heat, scarcely able to haul herself down to the yard to fill a pail.

A young man had recently moved in on the floor above, a cheerful tailor who claimed that what was now openly called the plague would never touch him, for he moved too fast. He fetched water for her and offered to do it as often as she liked, until the Turk made it clear that *he* did not like it and insisted that she went down herself.

As she watched out of the window, the extent of the epidemic at last became clear. Although Hannah could only see the opposite side of the street and a narrow stretch at that, there was first one corpse against a wall and then, the following day, two more, a man, woman and child lolling against each other. Next to their bodies the door had been nailed shut with a length of timber across it. The hammering had woken her.

As she watched, a man with long hair daubed a clumsy red cross with rapid strokes. The dip of his sodden maulstick in and out of a sploshing bucket held her spellbound. Gobs of paint, halfway to dried blood, splattered the flags and his breeches and shoes. He was so besmeared that he resembled a blotch-faced devil. From the expressions of passers-by, who gave him a wide berth, faces inside their coats, or with rags or herbs clamped to their noses, she knew that such terror swept the streets that the painter himself was an object of fear.

The following dawn the family of three was still there. The child had been savaged by dogs or foxes. One leg ripped off, its face was now a ragged hole from which a white arrowhead gleamed. Soon after sunrise they were thrown into a piled-up cart that creaked away down the street.

With neither mother nor siblings to hand, Hannah had little idea of birthing. Unconsciously she ran a finger up and down a faint line that had developed on her stomach. If she got any bigger, she was sure it would split like a fruit to reveal a small Turk dressed in velvet. She wondered whether the real one would come back in time to bear witness. Would he bring the plague with him when he did? Would he be there when she needed him?

On the day that the decomposing family was taken away, she had just eaten some bread and cheese with small beer and was sleepily smoking a pipe, when there came a light knock. Half-dozing, she had not heard footsteps, but recognised the tap of the tailor. She levered herself to her feet.

Samuel Welkin came in quickly and pushed the door shut, panting. Leaning on it to catch his breath, he watched her navigate slowly back to the box-seat, pale hair hanging to her waist in a clumsy plait tied with chewed orange ribbon that might once have been velvet. One hand gripped her narrow back, pressing where the laces were undone.

Only a few years older than her, Samuel was also thin and pale skinned, with greasy dark red shoulder-length hair and the delicate hands that often went with his trade. Dressed head to toe in darned black, with linen that was stained but not hopelessly shabby, he was, in a poor way, handsome. But Hannah hadn't noticed, for he had only moved in a month before, by which time she was focused on her insides.

As he stood there in his clumsy shoes, the colour returned to his cheeks in an uneven flush. She wondered if there were after all some grounds for the Turk's dislike.

'What is it, Mister Welkin?' she asked, warmth come to her own face, hoping he would put it down to the clamping heat that threatened to crush them. Her hair was plastered across her forehead and sweat turned it grey-green.

'What matter brings you here?' She knew she looked dishevelled, but a sudden grabbing pain made it difficult to care.

'You must get away from here . . . umm . . . Madam-the-Turk,' he said, suddenly more breathless, just stopping himself from using the name she went by in the building, which was The Turk's Whore.

Trying to keep calm for the sake of the child, she glanced down with a wry look that filled him with fear.

'Whatever do you mean, Mr Welkin?'

'What matter can there be?' she repeated, at his continued staring. But fear ran through her too, and her legs, stuck out like pegs, trembled. The pain came again, making it hard to concentrate.

'Your . . . umm . . . *husband*, ma'am,' he ventured. Then stopped as if he had said too much.

Although Hannah had only just turned sixteen, despite the pain, her composure outstripped her years.

'First, Mister Welkin, he is not my husband.' She did not wait for him to get a grip of himself. 'Whatever you wish to say, please spit it out.'

He ran the back of his hand across his forehead with an elegant gesture. His wrists were fine-boned, his fingers long and slender. How would they feel running over one's skin? But this was no place for a thought like that, ballasted with another man's child; a man who would, she felt, though she had no actual proof, kill both of them without difficulty or remorse. The Turk kept a twist-bladed dagger on him. She had watched him rub brown stuff off it. She pushed the thought away.

'Mr Welkin?'

'I have seen your husband in places he should not be,' he ground out. At her anxious look, realising that he frightened her, he took a few steps and came to an awkward halt at her side. To her further astonishment, he seized her hand. His grip was strong.

'I do not wish to alarm you. I rebuke myself. But I have seen your husband – the man who is not your husband . . . in the brothels near the docks, and heard him say that he plans to leave on one of his brother's ships at the first opportunity. I believe he intends to do it, ma'am – if he does not bring the pestilence to you first. For your sake – ' he blushed vividly – 'I do not know which is worse. If it please God, he could do both.'

Brother? She knew of no brother; but then, she knew so little of the father of her child. But what did that matter now he had abandoned her? Without thinking, she squeezed the warm hand: 'Go on,' she said, with a calm she did not feel. Samuel looked into her eyes with an expression she would never forget. Ducking her gaze, he took a deep breath and went trembling on, knowing that he confessed things about himself as well as the Turk.

'Those places are terrible, madam. You cannot imagine the depravity. People drop like flies. And that, madam, makes the harlots bolder. It came in by ship, that is what they say, and in those landing places it has taken an especially virulent hold. People behave as if they will not live to see another morning. The most godless things go on, bodies pile up as if – '

He let go, took another deep breath, and pulled a handkerchief from some compartment in his breeches. Seeing her eyes follow his every movement, flustered, he mopped his agonised brow and pressed his hands firmly on his lap.

'Forgive me. I do not know what has come over me. Perhaps I already have the fever.'

His face was the colour of ash, though still, she could not help noticing, fervent and handsome, with burning, beseeching eyes.

'It is all right, Mr Welkin,' she said, consumed by his fear, but determined not to show it, encouraged by the sign of his adoration. 'These are bad times. Despite being confined here, I have seen some small part of what is happening. I cannot control the man you call my husband and must rely on him while I await his child. There is nothing to be done except to hold fast and pray. Pray for all of us, Mr Welkin,' she concluded gravely, with a look so steady and clear that he, too, never forgot it.

He never forgot why, either, for as his hand was on the latch, a horrible sound came from the window seat. Between moan and screech it was his name, but not as he had ever heard it. The eyes fixed on him bound him to the young woman fallen back against the cushions, hands clapped to her stomach.

'Help,' she said.

During the week that seven thousand died, the Turk, who had gone to the docks, failed to return and missed the birth of his daughter – although he might have refused to acknowledge her, so translucent under her caul. When Samuel wrapped her in what later turned out to be a valuable sash, and held her up to the light, her skull bore the fluff of an albino fledgling. But when she smiled out of eyes like freshly oiled currants, the one legacy from her father, his heart was snared.

Hannah never knew what happened to the Turk. Given that the morning after Samuel visited her rooms she gave birth to her only child, she had no time to consider whether he died of the plague or fled. Life had taught her to be pragmatic and now there was a baby to feed. The fact was that he was gone. So, too, after the birth, was Samuel.

When Hannah eventually woke from a long sleep, as far as she could tell she was fairly clean, with a tiny creature tucked under one arm, deftly wrapped in some fringed stuff that she was too tired to recognise as the Turk's best sash. She remembered with embarrassment that Samuel had delivered the child and cut the cord with the panache that only a butcher or tailor would manage. But he was nowhere to be seen and she had neither time nor energy to wonder, for her daughter was making strident demands for food.

'Zenobia,' Hannah decided firmly, pulling the tiny creature up into the air. She looked at her for the first time, relieved that she hadn't suffocated. Looked in amazement at the eyes that glowered with short-sighted ferocity out of a head like a beet.

'Yes. Zenobia.'

Although in her exalted state she had no idea where the name came from, it was the Turk's mother's name. He had once told it to her, before he sailed out of her life. A queen's name, though she did not know it.

CHAPTER TWO

*D*ays passed and Hannah stayed locked in her rooms. A delivery of dry stuffs, the last thing organised by the Turk, meant that she had some rice, spices and a cloth bag of the lemons with which he savoured his food. The rice was in an ironclad chest, which protected it from rats, the Turk remembered from childhood. Perhaps because of this, and because Hannah used a great deal of lye, not to mention because of the pervasive oil of cloves, the apartment repelled vermin, unlike the rest of the house and those alongside.

Unknown to her, during those long summer weeks all but one other occupant of the building had died. Her parents had been the last, from whom Samuel caught it, which was why he did not visit again. He intended to, once a few days had passed and his awkwardness ebbed.

The evening after he delivered the baby he went to fetch water. At the landing, Hannah's mother stumbled up and clutched his arm, swearing in delirium. She dragged and clawed, sweat streaking her filthy face and chest. He prised her off and forced her away. Three days later, he woke feverish. Instead of visiting Hannah, hoping with no hope that it was merely a summer chill, he bent to his work table, each faltering stitch a prayer. The following day brought a tender swelling in one thigh and under an arm, and later, unable to move from pain, he fell on his bed to die.

By good fortune he had set the full water bucket down next to his bed. During the next two days he lay shaking in a violent fever.

With no food and no appetite, while the disease slithered his flesh with its razor-sharp tongue, in brief moments of consciousness all he could do was drink.

And as so many hoped in vain, he did not die. Now the only living occupant left in the building apart from Hannah and Zenobia, he staggered outside to search for food once he regained enough strength to get up. He had no idea how much time had passed. Filthy, his clothes hanging off him, he fell at once into the path of two body-carriers wheeling a barrow with a mottled corpse folded to fit. Shouting, they shoved him with their stout sticks, sailors casting off a disease-riddled hulk, and demanded to know who else was in the house.

Turning his eyes from their horrid load, Samuel was sure that Hannah and the child must be dead. It was not for lack of charity that he had not made certain, for he had fallen in love so badly that even seeing her swollen as a bladder and smeared with blood had not changed it. When he crept down the stairs past the bolted door he had paused, uncertain whether to call her name. At last he had tapped and waited, leaning against the wall to steady himself from collapsing, his heart thudding beneath his shirt, but heard no sound. Having delivered the baby of the woman he longed for, he could not bear to see them rotting or, worse, dying.

Weak from hunger and thirst, terrified, overwhelmed with sadness, he replied curtly that they were all dead, every one, God rest their souls. With this he turned sharply and continued on his way, crying his heart out.

The first Hannah knew of the scale of the tragedy was when the disbelieving men thumped up the stairs yelling 'Bring out your dead!' at the top of their voices. They hammered at each door, moving swiftly, for while nobody knew how the mortification travelled, hanging around corpses was never wise.

Not knowing what pestilence might be attached to the body-carriers themselves, Hannah leaned all her weight against the heavy door, Zenobia clasped to her chest. However, as the footsteps, which had proceeded to the floors above, started to descend, the famished baby let out a cry.

The feet stopped.

'Hear that?' A strong voice.

'You hearded it too? Sounded like a wean.' A fist struck her door once more, as if it struck her. 'Your dead. Bring. Out. Your dead!' The same terrible voice, this time directed at the keyhole, where its owner peered into the room.

One hand clamped across Zenobia's enraged face, Hannah knew her dark skirts blocked the view but still feared that fingers would creep through the lock and grab her. The latch twisted and rattled. Then, 'oh come *on*,' came a second voice, 'leave 'em to rot. They'll only spread it if they *does* come out. Let's get them others. *Them* dried up chitlins can't argue.'

Raucous laughter as the clumsy feet descended. For ten minutes, Hannah listened to thuds, swearing, rapid hammering, then silence. Gathering what the men had done, she was still too frightened to open her door. If plague remained in the building, would the door stop it, or did it seep through gaps? She stuffed her apron along the crack at the bottom.

There was a little water and a flagon of ale, which would keep them alive for now. Two days later, when everything had run out, parched and thinner than ever, carrying a pallid infant, she crept on to the landing. The dusty building felt cool, deserted; the window on the stairs cobwebbed. As she felt her way down, the treads gave out a hostile note. She did not know whether she would stumble into a corpse or her father. With no one to protect her, the thought of her father terrified her most of all.

In this state, when even the smallest sound was alarming, she discovered no one. The long, wide hall was empty but for a small hand-trunk ransacked by the recent visitors, its splintered haft levered off. Tucking Zenobia inside it, she tried the front door, but as she had guessed, it was nailed shut from outside.

Frightened at being locked in, she remembered the door on the landing above her parents' rooms, which opened to the yard.

More cautiously than before she felt her way down the dirty timber stairs, to the basement she hadn't set foot in for a year. For after a generous payment to her father when he first moved her to his chambers, the Turk had continued paying for what the old man claimed was the loss of a worker. She had not seen her parents since.

The key sat in a crack in the wainscot known to the tenants. Because the body-carriers could not open the door, they had not nailed it up. She pumped two pails full and lugged them upstairs. From below, Zenobia began to shriek. Hannah ran and gathered her up, before continuing to the basement.

Despite being sure that her parents were dead, repulsion gripped her. It was as much as she could do to move. Only hunger and Zenobia's whine kept her from bolting.

It was a shock to see the two rooms of her childhood. Filthy and low, even in high summer they were cold, for no fire had chased the damp from beneath the gappy boards for weeks. In one corner was the unmade bed on which her mother and father had died, which she looked at with horror; in the other, heaped with rags, her truckle bed.

In a wormy cupboard beside the food-encrusted spit she found salt, rush-lights, a half-full crock of flour laced with weevils and three sprouting onions. It would do for a day or two. A tin-lined box held the unexpected treasure of a fist-size grey lump of sugar, which she put into her apron.

Her father's secret hideaway was under a plank next to the truckle bed. He kept strong drink there; she had watched him when he thought she slept. It always puzzled her that he hid it, for surely her mother knew that he drank. It struck her that drink might keep hunger at bay and pacify Zenobia. Hardly breathing, in case some malevolent goblin seized her fingers or bit her, she felt inside. Almost beyond reach her searching fingers felt something cold and hard, and drew out a narrow, dusty iron strongbox a handspan-and-a-half long. She set it down, to come back to when she'd finished looking around.

Her father's desk occupied the other room. Next to the old Bible he had used to teach her to read were his rent ledgers, from which she learned the Turk's surname. It had taken long enough to understand that his first name was Mehmet. She contemplated the unfamiliar word written in her father's ignorant hand, the letters as thin and crabbed as he, as if she contemplated the Turk himself. He was gone, dead or fled abroad, never to return to her and the child, the miserable coward. What did his name matter? She would be damned if her child would ever bear it, and put it out of her mind.

Zenobia was flushed and restless. Deciding that there was nothing else of use, Hannah crammed her treasures inside the bag her mother had used for marketing. The iron box was too unwieldy, so she opened it. There were two mildew-spotted papers and a leather pouch, which to her astonishment held five gold sovereigns, as well as some small coin that could add up to as much again. She laid the pouch in the bag.

The first paper was the Turk's promissory note, which she ripped up. The other was the deed to the ramshackle building. Beneath her father's name, a witnessed note confirmed that if he died, all went to her.

It had never crossed Hannah's mind that the creature she had always believed to be a caretaker might own the building, yet so the paper proved. Perhaps the cunning old man had posed as a servant to avoid robbery and named her as some ruse in case he got into trouble. But it didn't matter now, for there was her own name, fair and square. She tucked the document in her pocket.

With Zenobia squealing in one arm and the bulging bag in the other, Hannah clambered upstairs to mull over this improvement in her fortunes. For not only did she now own a large rentable property in the north part of the city, but she had a sum that would easily support her for six months, perhaps a year. Wondering whether she and the infant would live long enough to enjoy their newfound status, she locked them both in once more.

CHAPTER THREE

*S*amuel Welkin's childhood had been hard. Born at the Auld Gate on the eastern side of the city wall, the ninth child of a jobbing tailor, from his first breath he was surplus to requirements in a household already splitting at the seams. The family survived in three nondescript rooms and shared an outside pump and foul gutter in a dark narrow alley with twenty other people, who included a baker and a money lender. There was also a laundry that served as a brothel, which was how his parents met.

Samuel's father, William, stitched from seven in the morning until seven at night, cross-legged on a table at the local tailoring establishment run by a man called Hobus Severin. Fortunately for the Welkins, besides being a good tailor, Will Welkin was an able cutter. When Severin's chief cutter died of the quinsy a month after Samuel was born, his job went to Welkin. The modest rise in income, not to mention reprieve from the blindness that so often afflicted tailors, meant that Mrs Welkin, who was now a laundress and boiler (in her previous trade of whoring her looks never brought much luck, though her grip was famously strong), did not suffocate young Samuel, or drop him on his head in the stone-floored washroom as she had planned to every day since his birth. Unwanted children were imaginatively murdered in those parts; the ever-rising population had to be controlled somehow. Nobody questioned grimy cloth-swaddled bundles ripped apart by dogs in back alleys, which appeared to contain butcher's off-cuts, or tossed into cesspits or furnaces, or rocked straight into the river.

Sensing the cliff-edge he clung to, Samuel grew up helping first his mother and then his father. At seven he swept lint from under the stitching tables, ran errands as soon as he could carry a bolt of cloth without one end going in the mud, then moved on to tailor's tacks, which he did at a table with its legs cut to stumps. His labour was useful to Hobus Severin. At twelve, Samuel was indentured as an apprentice. By sixteen he was as proficient at his father, whom he had watched cutting, and whose shears he took to the knife grinder.

Even though the atmosphere in a tailor's shop was unhealthy and the posture stooped, Samuel grew up lively and cheerful. He had excellent eyesight, nimble fingers, sinewy arms, strong shoulders, a good heart, spontaneous enthusiasm and vigour for which there was no explanation given his diet of chalked bread, watered milk, root vegetables and lard. Where his elder siblings, now reduced to four by the usual cross-section of fatal childhood ailments, were rickety and pasty, Samuel glowed. His red hair sprang from his pink-white skin and his sharp teeth were fairly sound. Sometimes Welkin senior wondered if the boy was his own, but he was too tired to pursue it, and besides, Sam was loving and useful. Then too, paternal pride insisted that someone so gifted in his own trade (if Welkin was truthful, the boy had already outstripped him) must be honestly descended.

William died when Samuel was eighteen and Sam stepped into the vacant position at Severin's without discussion. Shortly, Master Hobus's neck swelled from a spongy growth and Sam took over in all but name. After a botched operation some months later, Hobus bled to death on the cutting table with no one to succeed him and a suit ruined beneath him. Unexpectedly, he left enough money for the boy to rent a room for a few months and set up modestly on his own.

Samuel quickly found such a place in a rooming house north of Smithfield. Leaving his family behind, with gratitude on his mother's side for one less mouth, he settled quickly into the new lodgings, which is where the plague found him.

Sam's ability to think on his feet had served him well. However, by fleeing the plague-house, weakened and starving, he found himself in a city fraught with danger.

Given the likelihood of a foul and abrupt death, those Londoners too poor to flee took to the pleasure of flesh. While Sam roamed the streets on the lookout for anything to eat, he was unable to avoid strangers coupling in daylight, which revolted him so much that he was sure he could never love again. Racked with hunger and misery, he considered ending his life. Yet such a sin seemed impertinent to the God who had spared him. He wandered on, as carts shovelled distorted bodies into pits that pocked the east like running sores.

One such pit was just beyond Auld Gate, where Samuel went when he ran out of what he had scavenged. If any of his family was alive, they might have some food. In this poor disease-scourged area, business had ground to a halt and people protected what little they had. Most bakers were closed and prices quadrupled. Sam remembered the baker at the end of his parents' alley with little hope.

'Walk with me, master?'

The woman came up soundlessly and clamped herself to his elbow. About his age, she looked as haggard as his mother. A gummy grin in a dirt-engrained face showed just two large teeth. Hollowed by hunger, her breasts slumped in her bodice. She fondled one, a salmon's head in a linen-lined basket.

'I see where your eyes goes,' she exulted. 'Want some? All of me for a ha'penny, do what you will. Come with me.' She pulled him, putting all her strength into it. She stank of piss and vomit. And drink; she lurched in a halo of wood alcohol.

'Come on, master. You know you ain't going to live. None of us is. Have some fun. I'll do it for nothing with a fine man like you. There's a crew of us by the pit, join us. Us girls could use a strong cock to warm our cockles.'

Her padded hip ground into him to emphasise her intention. Despite himself, he was intrigued.

'The pit?'

'We does it right on the edge. When someone dies we jus' shoves 'em over. Couple was so hard at it the other day they fell in. You should of seen it. Straight in the lye! Flew up like snow and blinded my mucker Marigold. She was scrabbling so hard at the pain she fell in on top. Howled till we cried, we did. Couldn't be arsed to get them out.'

She mistook Samuel's look of horror.

'Got yer heated, aint it? Come on, come wiv me, lover. We're fucked anyway, so we fucks till we dies.' She coughed out foul breath.

When he shoved her, she fell with her feet in the air. For a moment, she lay like a startled cat, brown petticoats fallen back, naked beneath. He thought he saw swollen marks, but perhaps he was imagining it. He felt his face burn.

Wadding her skirts between her legs she got up. 'More fool you for not having some when you could of. God rot you, you bastard.' As she wove away, Samuel ran towards his parents' alley.

But rough planks had been nailed across the narrow opening that was no wider than a man's shoulders. He peered through a gap. Two decaying bodies rested against the wall in the darkness. He made out the profile of one of his sisters and was about to throw up when he caught a quick movement and a pinprick of light. From the murk beyond the bodies, a child with burning eyes darted and ran up to the planks. The boy looked like Thomas, born long after their parents thought their breeding was done.

'Sammell?' The child sobbed. 'Sam, I'm the on'y one left, and I can't get out the other end, it's blocked up proper!'

The bottom bit of wood was splitting along the nails. The street was so full of rubbish that it only took Sam a moment to find something to lever it off with. Thomas crawled underneath and clung to his brother's legs, crying that the bodies of their family and the other tenants were in there. Like Samuel, he too had survived, and once the fever broke he had eaten everything he could find, until there was nothing left.

Samuel's heart sank: there was no hope of any food here either, and his whole family, except Thomas, was dead.

'Hold my hand, little one.' From the dazed way the skeletal child moved, Samuel realised that without food he would soon die. 'We'll find somewhere to go before nightfall.' He put on a cheerful voice.

The gravity of their situation struck him. This part of town was used as a dumping ground by the rest of the city. Its shops and taverns were boarded up. Everyone who couldn't flee was barricaded in. It was a dangerous place to stay a moment longer than necessary. Certainly, Sam thought grimly, they must be away before dusk, for darkness gave criminals courage. If they stayed, they would be cut down where they stood. No wonder his brother, clinging to his leg, looked mad.

The brothers huddled in the boarded-up doorway next to the alley, shielding themselves from a sudden downpour.

'Think, Thomas,' Sam encouraged, rubbing his brother's bony shoulder. 'Are you sure there's nothing left? What happened to Tubman, the baker?'

Thomas was adamant that the Tubmans had both died, but he had been too scared to go inside the bakery because of rats running around when he'd looked through the window. The bakehouse was at the furthest end of the yard.

'So many of them, great big 'uns.' He demonstrated with his hands. 'Big fat 'uns! I reckon they'd got in the flour.'

Telling Tom to stay put and shout if anyone touched him, Samuel glanced around to make sure he wasn't being watched. The rain had cleared the dusty streets for a while. He squeezed under the plank and hurried past his dead sister and mother, whose downturned face was ghastly in the dismal light. Trying not to think, he went on grimly, picking up a spar of timber to serve as a club.

The bakery was dark, its windows sooty inside and out. He smashed a pane and undid the casement. In the fading light he felt sick with fear, but if he found nothing to eat they would both die. As he forced the stiff window, a few rats dashed across the bakery. Shouting, he pounded the wood against the window frame to frighten them and clambered in.

Dead rodents, droppings and flecks of sacking covered the floor. Any flour was gone. Stamping his feet to keep the creatures at bay, he saw the empty cupboards, ransacked by his own family or others. At the rear were two closed ovens, long cold. Right at the back of one was a tray of six small round loaves, burned hard. God knew how old they were, but he didn't care. Tucking three inside his shirt, buttoning two more inside his coat and throwing one at the rats to give him time to get out, he returned the way he had come.

'Look alive!' Despite the heat, the child shivered uncontrollably, but Sam didn't dare let him touch the burnt bread yet, with so many lunatics around who would kill for less.

Pressed to his chest, the loaves gave him courage. Soaked in water, they should be edible. He thought of the pump at his lodgings. Was there a chance that Hannah and the baby were alive? Even if she was, it would be impossible for her to manage. He was now appalled that, however weak he had been, he had left without trying to break down her door. How could he have been so callous?

The boy beside him had lost the energy to whimper. Hope rushed into Samuel's heart. 'Come, Thomas,' he exclaimed. 'We'll go somewhere safe and eat. Not long now. We'll manage. I'll look after you. You'll see.'

PART TWO

CHAPTER ONE

*T*he day after he married Hannah, Samuel Welkin had changed his name to Severin. Now a master tailor of some repute, he had raised Zenobia for as long as she could remember, and she thought of him as her father. Thomas, only seven years older than Zenobia, lived with them. Zenobia called him uncle, though while she was younger he seemed more like a brother.

Samuel's elegant clientele included many at court, for his skill at cutting was unparalleled. He conducted his trade on the top floor of a pair of joined houses in Smithfield where the family also lived. He had acquired one of this pair from Hannah on marriage; shortly after her death he bought a lease on its neighbour.

As Zenobia grew up, the history of Smithfield, its burnings and butchery, and now the slicing and slithering of stuffs which went on in her father's attic workshops, seemed all of a piece. Though precisely where the burning of martyrs and the jointing of bullocks ended and the shriek of silk cut by a tailor's shears began, she neither knew nor cared, except that in her young mind one inevitably led to another and they were all exciting and dangerous.

Samuel had married Hannah when Zenobia was two months old. Her real father, he told her, died of the plague shortly before she was born. A merchant, Samuel added reluctantly. He gave few details beyond this brief statement and something, some instinct, kept her from pushing, though she knew there was a piece missing, some lie, some anomaly, in his account. But she didn't care, because from a very early age she grasped that some things, such as her new father's name, were better changed.

This instinct, that a creative adaptation of facts can be a boon, an advance, seemed to Zenobia one of the most important truths of life itself, which she clung to and where necessary embellished.

She also learned that whether or not her father died of it, it was certainly because of the plague that her mother inherited one of the houses they lived in, along with a lot of money. And that her father set himself up with all this, once the sickness had left the city, and before the fire, which, coming hard on the heels of the pestilence, in many quarters finished the devastation that the plague had begun.

Helpfully for Samuel, many of his competitors' premises in the heart of town were reduced to ashes. This led to a rapid rise in the number and quality of his clients and a dramatic increase in his fortunes. Though within sight and smell of the heat and smoke in the conflagration's final days, the Severin house was in a part of the city that remained unscathed. After buying the next door property, Samuel knocked the lofts through to make a sky-lit workshop whose size and light were widely envied. The tailoring shop was called Severin. The same word flourished on the black and gold sign that stuck out further into the street than anyone else's and had a lot more gold on its swags and curlicues. All of which Zenobia found easy to understand when her father explained, as if anxious for her approval, that it was its appearance and sound that drove him to take it for their family name, for it was more elegant than his own, and in his business elegance was all.

Zenobia's shrewd hard-headedness was at odds with Samuel's aesthetic sensibility. Demanding and self-centred from an early age, to her it was self-evident that Zenobia Severin would take her much further than Zenobia Welkin. In this calculating self-interest, along with her black eyes, she took after her real father, Mehmet.

According to Samuel, her only source of information on the matter, her mother had met an ambiguous fate. As Zenobia could not remember her, when she was six or seven she asked him to tell her what her mother was like. He passed her a handled steel mirror and said they were more alike than seemed reasonable, except that Hannah's eyes had been grey, as subtle and changeable as fast-flowing water, while hers, snapping like an enraged scorpion, spoke of determination and earthy demands.

He did not voice the last part, but he thought it.

In those eyes, her growing passions and rages found imperious expression. Even as a little girl they felled him without effort so that he was rudderless whenever she looked at him. He pitied any other man who fell under their spell.

Where Hannah had seemed ethereal, Zenobia was a blade put through fire before being thrust into flesh. Unlike her mother's, her paleness concealed heat, which flamed from eyes jet black against white skin. This combined with almost luminous hair to ensure that from an early age she attracted glances from any man who came into her orbit.

Since he first recounted it, she never tired of listening to the story of how he had returned to Smithfield to rescue her mother.

'I was just a poor lad who sewed for a living,' he said, as her spellbound eyes reflected his. 'I loved her from the moment I set eyes on her. But I'd fled the house she was trapped in – *this* house – trapped there with you, a helpless newborn. I was afraid, but your mother was fearless, just as you are. Then, full of shame, I returned and broke in at the back. I knew where the key was kept, so I smashed the glass, and by God's great mercy she was alive. Without a care in the world!'

The final bit was an artistic elaboration, for Hannah had been cowering, thinking he was an intruder come to hack her to death and steal her money. A smell worse than fear had risen up to greet him.

'We never separated after that. Scarcely for an hour – not until her sudden death.'

He fell silent.

Zenobia waited until he collected himself but watched with the eyes of a starving kestrel. His last comment was nonsensical: they must have parted sometimes, but she let him carry on with the fiction.

'We had a year together, perhaps a little more. Then came that fateful day. I was working on an important commission for a wealthy noble.'

He paused to let this sink in, but however she begged, he never gave the name of the man, just implied considerable greatness.

'Two suits, each consisting of coat, waistcoat and petticoat breeches in the best silk and the finest embroideries imaginable. Pure silver and gold. Your mother left you here in the private part of the house with your nursemaid for she was going into the city. On the way back, she promised to collect a set of worked fronts for one of them. They were being done in metal, which as you know is highly skilled. She had made friends with the embroiderer who, unusually for such difficult work, was a woman. From time to time your mother performed such errands and enjoyed the companionship of her own sex. But it was a complicated design and there were still a few hours' work to do. She decided to help; they would finish it together. She sent me word. I worked such long hours and, as I said, she had begun to seek the company of other women. She said that this woman was an immigrant, educated. Perhaps she was Turkish, I don't remember. As far as I can tell, they finished late, or perhaps they didn't finish at all, for she accepted a bed in the house. It was the first night of the conflagration and they were sleeping at the top, a few doors from where it started. The wind was strong and as craven as the devil. It blew the flames from one house to the next as if it tossed skeins of orange silk across the sky. Those devilled flames leapt across the roofs and ran down the houses. Gigantic hands' – he demonstrated – 'fingers fashioned from flame, set fire to the timber laps, gouged out windows so that they popped and roared, consumed everything in their path like locusts.

'The house was stacked with Italian velvets and French silks, skeins of embroidery silks packed in boxes, and the air full of lint, which catches like gun-cotton. Tailors worked there too, so there were bales of cambric and cotton and wadding for breeches. The building was a tinderbox; a death-trap; a hell hole. It would have exploded . . . like that!'

He clapped his hands with a noise so stark that Zenobia jumped, even when she knew it was coming.

'Nobody in that house stood a chance.'

As she grew older, Zenobia wondered how her father could possibly know these details, or believe them, particularly the odd part about the embroiderer being a woman, and that being so unusual. It jarred when he first told her and every time after: a flicker in his eyes made him unable to look directly at her, however intensely she willed him. She knew he wanted to believe it and that he did not. She said nothing and stored it up. She had been very young when he first told her the story (for she was convinced that it *was* a story), but it suited him to tell it, and perhaps over the years he had come to believe it. Certainly, she thought, he must need to, for the alternative, given that he had gone back into a nailed-up plague house to save her mother's life when no one knew if you could catch the sickness twice, was horrible.

Whatever the truth, from the start, he and Thomas raised her with a lack of parental discipline that suited her perfectly, with all the peculiarities of a doting but frequently absent father for a pretty child, alongside the occasional interest of Thomas, a shallow young man, for a girl who for years, if he considered her at all, he thought of as a sort of toy.

Samuel wanted Zenobia to grow up a lady, even if it meant that one day she would look down on him. To this end he gave her a maid and tutor. To ensure that she would be in a position to marry well, he was determined that she experience none of the difficulties he and her mother had known. He saw his trade as an obstacle to her advancement, which was another reason to immerse himself in it; as if, by disappearing upstairs, a moneymaking engine, he would taint her less.

Samuel toiled from seven in the morning until seven at night, just as his own father had done. But unlike his father, by the time he was thirty, he had a dozen tailors and a reputation for the finest work. He was becoming wealthy and, at nine, Zenobia wanted for nothing except companionship and guidance. For her temperament, given to vivid flights of fancy, was liable if left unchecked to get her into trouble; a tendency that, as she approached puberty, her uncle Thomas recognised and tucked away for future use.

The next few years struck Zenobia as a tiresome ford on the way to womanhood, for as passionately as her father wished to make a lady of her, she was equally determined to make her own way in the world. Unfortunately, neither of them discussed their plans with the other.

During those years, Zenobia was put in the charge of various tutors, who did their job well. Intelligent and quick to learn, she suffered the frustration of all girls equal, if not superior, to many adults. Listening to adult conversation, there was no reason to disbelieve it: her studies had given her wisdom beyond her years. However, trapped inside the house and a female body, there was little she could do.

And so Zenobia, forbidden to set foot in the workshops, began to bend her pent-up energy on the only man in her orbit other than her tutor, her so-called uncle Thomas.

The little boy who had almost died of starvation had also benefited from Samuel's largesse. In as much as a maggot will become a strikingly coloured carrion fly, with flashy wings, swivelling eyes, and a habit of grooming on every occasion, Thomas had changed beyond recognition into a puffed-up piece of persiflage with the morality of a pig's bladder. When Zenobia turned thirteen and first began to take note of him, he was twenty, but looked younger.

Thomas's aptitude was figures and from the age of twelve he kept his brother's accounts. Able to do this with such ease that it did not fully occupy him, after a few years he took to loitering in the coffee houses at Covent Garden and around the great building site that was to be the new St Paul's. Sharp ears open to the conversations of the men rebuilding the city, he interested himself in the new business of trading and invested a little of Samuel's money here and there.

Thomas reasoned that there was no need to burden his busy elder brother with all the ins and outs of his own extramural activities or the increasing irregularities of his accounts, both of which he could easily hide. As the years passed, some small financial returns were made to his brother. Other larger ones were not. By this means, when he reached eighteen he was able to live in a style far beyond his allowance, just as a successful parasite enjoys a delicious life at the expense of its host.

His brother, having saved him, also housed, fed and dressed him. But additional perquisites – such as a gold snuff box, fine linen and laces, a new cloak, a sedan chair with an emerald green taffeta lining and runners on tap, a box at the theatre and the money to maintain an extravagant mistress – Thomas negotiated by dint of what he argued to himself were the fruits of his own labour.

Indeed, having made money behind his brother's back, young Thomas soon put enough of it aside to carry on under his own steam, which he did with increasing boldness and financial success. In the new world of stockbroking, he had found his metier. At twenty he had a private life Samuel knew nothing about, particularly as Thomas tipped his brother's servants handsomely to keep their mouths shut. There was a new mistress in the new Covent Garden, maintained in a bold new house in Bedford Street with staff he paid for, and a profligate lifestyle that included substantial gambling as well as investing.

All of this was clear to Zenobia, the one person in the house from whom Thomas had not considered it necessary to hide his activities, or to bribe, for until recently he still thought of her as attractive but infantile. With little to occupy her energy besides her lessons, she took a special interest in her uncle's business. Which, she observed, he had become sloppy at hiding. In the face of his older brother's apparent indifference, he paraded about downstairs as if he were the master and Samuel, hard at work on the upper floors running the business that paid for everything, his servant.

Though smaller than average, Thomas was slim and agile. His brother cut his clothes so well that his short legs seemed longer and his long arms, with their sharp-nailed hands, shorter. He wore two-inch heels and had his wigs made preposterously high, all of which brought him up to the lofty environs of five-foot six, so that with his energetic demeanour and darting eyes, people rarely noticed his height. Because of a pocked complexion he resorted, when at the theatre or shopping at the Exchange, to such copious amounts of powder and rouge that he presented a startling appearance, but his most arresting feature was a scarlet-painted mouth, which certainly distracted, whatever ribald viciousness it spouted.

It is hardly surprising that an impressionable thirteen-year-old girl would be fascinated by such showy attributes even if they were not aimed at her: the careless flicking open of the wrought-gold snuff-box; the quality of his heavy lace, as starched as a double doily; the meaty odour of rose attar pomade that trailed after him like a string of sausages; the clicking red heels of his Spanish leather shoes; and the powdered bruises she sometimes saw on his neck as he gave her what he explained was a brotherly hug.

Nor is it surprising that the repulsive young man, who soon felt that one mistress was inadequate for someone of his ability and appetite, and supplemented those pleasures with ad hoc expeditions into less salubrious purlieus than his mistress's apartment and person (in other words, the street and the molly house), was diverted one evening by the sight of his so-called niece in her night-gown as he crept like fog along the corridor, on the way to an assignation in town.

At this juncture in her reveries, when her absorbed recollection of childhood might have betrayed her lack of attention, Zenobia turned quick, sharp eyes towards John Crace. The Italians still had not arrived. Visible through his bedchamber doors, her husband had slipped down among the pillows, his large head cradled in a lawn cap from which firm grey tufts escaped. Even in sleep he was stern and commanding, though his sallow skin was paler than it used to be, with shadows under the eyes that rest no longer dispelled. But, given her excellent eyesight, Zenobia was sure that he was still fast asleep.

She poured a fourth glass of wine and continued her contemplation.

CHAPTER TWO

*I*t was not that Zenobia and Thomas did anything that evening that would outrage propriety or her father, for Zenobia was determined not to be bamboozled by an over-painted popinjay into ruining her chances through an unsuitable liaison.

On paper this was a contest she could easily win, for her mind was vastly superior. But despite her nimble perceptions, like any young person she was increasingly absorbed by an awareness of her body and impatient to test it. Now and then, her flesh stirred with sensations she had never known. Thus, while figuratively speaking scarlet above the waist but pure as snow below, that snow was perilously close to being sullied by the first person who trod on it. Moreover, on the question of unwanted or even wanted babies, none of her books told her how such things came about.

Studying herself naked in her new glass, a reckless extravagance Samuel had ordered from Baker's in Vauxhall, she could see that she was slim and agile in most parts but recently protuberant in others. She had learnt enough of the world from love stories recounted by her tutor and the sweaty look he got while he did so, that she had sprouted something worth having. The story of Helen of Troy proved that men valued beauty absurdly highly, but its idealism frustrated her: how could she capitalise on these assets?

Life with Samuel and Thomas had taught her how different men could be from each other. Where Samuel toiled day after day to amass a fortune, like building a house brick by brick, Thomas took risks that made or lost money very quickly. He loved telling her about vast sums lost and won in the hazardous West Indies. And while the brothers used different methods to make money, what they had in common with all men was that once they had it, they guarded it like a fox guards chickens.

Not having any money of her own had begun to grate, particularly as Samuel's fortune, and therefore that of his brother, was built on money and property left by her mother, which in her view was rightfully hers. So, since she possessed a body that was increasingly admired, Zenobia decided to put a high value on it and sell it. Despite her small social compass, she knew one person sharp enough to get a good deal, if he could be persuaded to work in her favour: uncle Thomas.

But not as a consumer, for not only would such a liaison perform as poorly as a short-term bond, it would also imperil Thomas's livelihood as a leech on her brother. He must be an intermediary and negotiator. Therefore, the thing was to put herself on show and see what transpired. But how, stuck at home at her books? Since even a prized jewel kept in a cabinet eventually dusts and dims, she was determined to get out.

Zenobia had been thrown a great deal on her own resources, without the balancing influence of ordinary, stupid children. Her classical education was far more masculine than her father would have approved if he had ever paid attention. Her tutor, Mr Russell, had been a naval strategist for Lord Albemarle against the Dutch devil De Ruyter, before the amputation of his left leg following a random shot at the raid on the Medway, where he had been a bystander on the Sheerness dockside. That freak accident, when Zenobia was still in leading-strings, made Russell seek an alternative career. Having capsized himself as a naval financier, for the past five years he had clung to the safer spar of tutoring. But a sea-dog never forgets its barque and once caught up in a story, particularly if swashbuckling was involved, he forgot the sex and age of his pupil. Thus, Zenobia thought more like an admiral than a delicate vessel destined to follow some passing masculine wind. Moreover, though she only knew the sketchiest details of her origins, at fourteen she was just as captivating as her mother at the same age. The look she spotted in Jack Russell's eyes when he described Helen of Troy's snowy buttocks in lingering couplets was the same look her mother had seen in the eyes of Mehmet the Turk the day she met him on the stairs with a bucket of turds.

'Uncle Thomas?'

His mind full of what he had just glimpsed through the open doorway, Thomas froze. The husky voice, unmistakably Zenobia's, that to Thomas's mind suited a professional minx rather than this over-educated person, was assured and even.

He retraced his mincing step. Zenobia stood in her night-gown in front of the mirror, radiant hair skimming delicate shoulders. In that otherwise dark room, by the light of sconces fixed to the glass, he saw the perfect outline of her body beneath the linen as if it had been snipped by his brother's shears. He shivered with anticipation. The evening had taken an unexpected turn.

'You look pale, uncle. Please come in,' the confident young tones continued.

More lecherous than a goat and as aware as Zenobia that they were not related, he could not believe what he had just heard and needed no further encouragement. He locked her door behind him with a practised hand. The iron key struck into the cleft of his breeches in a manner that he found pleasantly disturbing.

Zenobia did not bridle at the prospect of a flushed young man locked in with her, but stood firm, feet planted on the silk carpet as if on parade. Having tested the backlit effect of the candles earlier that day with the help of a second mirror, she knew how she looked. In respect of vanity and contrivance she could see her uncle and raise him.

'Like an angel,' he murmured, taking the thought from her mind and a determined step towards her. But to his consternation she moved adroitly out of the line of light and rapidly lit candles.

'*Uncle.*' She pulled on an overmantle that came magically to hand. 'I have interrupted you on the way to visit your mistress in Covent Garden, is it not so?'

He gaped. All heady thoughts of rape or even, failing that, the distinct second best of consensual pleasure, evaporated.

'I, ah – '

'Well, I would like to go too.' Smoothly, ignoring his expression. 'If you could obtain an evening dress for me, I will go with you tomorrow.'

'But – '

'It goes without saying,' she interrupted as if brushing off a flea, 'that this would be a secret pact between us. My father would not approve, as we both know. But if you do me this favour, I shall expect to do one in return.'

The look she gave him was so direct and molten, yet also so innocent, that his innards coiled. He made a conscious effort to bring his red lips together.

'A favour,' he repeated hopefully, leaning against the door and the tantalising key.

Like plague spots, her eyes were unblinking. 'Whatever you consider appropriate. You must guide me, uncle, for I am a mere girl, unschooled in the evils of the world. I rely on you to teach me how to repay your kindness.'

Given that in a naval and military sense she was out of her depth and playing with fire, the sorry scene that seemed likely did not occur. Not because Thomas did not want it, which he did so badly that he thought he would spontaneously combust. Nor because a scruple welled inside his crooked heart, for he would have thrown her down with the brutality for which he was known without a second thought. No: it was because he was late for a pre-arranged evening of more acute and perverted debauchery than merely raping a novice, which held little charm if accomplished without a struggle. What he looked for in his victims was anxiety, pleading, and at the last, when there was no hope of rescue, pure terror. None of which was evident in the girl before him. To cap it all, his new mistress was given to locking him out of his own house if he was late.

Born a plantation slave in the West Indies, but by her own insistence an African princess, this mistress inspired an intensity of lust in him that regularly held him between her knees. So, reasoning that he would have ample opportunity to savour Zenobia at his leisure, a spicier prospect than a too-easy prize, he agreed to her request, clicked his heels, and went to Bedford Street.

Two hours after dinner the following evening, Thomas tapped softly on Zenobia's door. Earlier, a flat box had been delivered; he had told her to expect something from an address in Covent Garden. Snatching it from her maid, Zenobia opened it straight after dinner. As well as the dress she had asked for – though not a new one, for it smelled of sweat and pungent perfume – there was a black silk domino and oval velvet mask to cover the upper half of her face, with tip-tilted slits for her eyes. On top, a card read:

Wear these.

The hand was bold, its letters aggressively formed – done, she fancied, by a woman who wrote with the confidence of a man.

The moment Thomas's fingertips touched the door, it opened to reveal Zenobia shrouded in cloak and mask. She slipped out, took his gloved hand and ran with him along the corridor and down the back stairs. Apart from a few rush-lights guttering in closed lanterns, the hall was dark; only the faint flames and a trace of moonlight coming through the door's immense fanlight guided them. The house slept; the doorman snored in his chair.

Thomas's coach was waiting and with her uncle's help, she sprang inside.

It was eleven by the clock. The narrow streets were dark, only softened by the sliver of moon. To excite as much as save her (for like all self-aggrandising egoists, Thomas was a coward), he pointed out the loaded coach pistols in velvet-lined pockets to each side, which he kept in case of attack.

Without warning, Zenobia grasped the nearest, pulled it out and ran her gloved finger along the length of its barrel to the trigger, exclaiming at the cold metal, before returning it to its scarlet nest.

Once Thomas had calmed his horrified breathing, the rest of the journey continued in silence, broken only by the clatter of the horses' hooves and their snorts of exertion.

CHAPTER THREE

*J*ohn Crace's strong voice snapped her out of her daydream. 'Zenobia! I have been calling for some time,' he exclaimed, not tempering his anger. 'Come here.'

Raised on his elbows, though he sounded refreshed he did not look well. Trying to hide her unwillingness, she hastened to his side.

'Interview the painters without me. They may leave whatever designs they have brought for my consideration, but once they have taken measurements, instruct them to produce new ones. They will remember who I am; I will not be fobbed off with another man's leavings. Though they come recommended by a duke, I am not the fool who took what his *lordship* rejected. Examine the designs closely, then explain that something superior is required and set them to work. Money is no object, time immaterial. I am wealthier than any duke and intend to have the very best. The *very* best, do you hear?'

You always do, Zenobia thought grimly, *and look where it has got me. Trapped in a noisome cage.*

She curtseyed.

Winded by the rush of talk, he stopped to regain his breath, then suddenly grasped her hand and pressed the palm to his lips, forcing her fingers back. She bit her lip not to cry out.

'I will dine alone. After that come to me.' Greedily kissing her palm, his closed hand pushed up her wrist like an iron cuff, burning the skin to the thick lace at her elbow. With strength that had not left him, he pulled her across the bed, her face against his. It was impossible not to recoil from his breath. 'Come here,' he repeated, his eye an inch away; then let go unexpectedly so that she stumbled and fell.

Managing a deep curtsey, she put on a smile and tried not to limp as she took her leave. It would only make him even more cruel later.

But once her back was turned, fury mounted. He owned her and displayed her – the silk she wore, the diamonds that outdid any at court, her carriage with matched bays. And the house. Who could forget the damned house? Everything that made other men want her came at the same cost.

At least, she thought bitterly, she had sold herself to a high bidder. Short of a prince, could she have done better? For Crace did not exaggerate; his wealth made him as powerful as any duke. Sometimes it surprised her that he had not been ennobled, though his foreign origin might account for it. Nevertheless, what would he do to her that evening?

But that was hours later, she told herself firmly. Meanwhile, she was beautiful, young and healthy. Out of his eyeline her heart surged and she walked as fast as possible to the long gallery, the pain in her foot almost forgotten, her heart beating.

As she walked, she glanced from the cloister's glittering windows at the gardens she had designed these past two years. They were establishing well. It had been a hot summer; the gardeners worked hard to make everything thrive and the results were beginning to show.

She had learned a great deal about plants since Crace first began to build the house on the Thames for her; she had plundered his library, made it her particular study. Had King Charles's gardener, Master Tradescant, lived longer, she fancied her knowledge would have surprised him – not only on account of the showy tulips and magnolia grandiflora (all acquired at ruinous cost), but also the rarer, more curious things. Crace was not interested in the theory of gardening, only the results. It was the method he applied to everything, which had always ensured mastery. But over two years, left to her studies and experiments, she had created a garden to confound him.

Nearest the windows in the square between the projecting wings of the house was an ambitious knot garden, set out to her sketches. Its box edges had thickened nicely, making complex patterns fluffed with fresh green growth. Within these borders the subdued tones of lavender and rosemary, thyme and sage played – though the sage struggled in the clay soil. The pattern, with its paved circle of benches interspersed with bays and dwarf trees, a sundial at its centre, was based on a painting of the zodiac in one of Crace's prized manuscripts. Scattered between the herbs were gillyflowers, marguerites, peonies, calendula, phlox and richly scented tobacco plants just in flower. She decided she would have gillyflower wine made.

This show had taken over from hundreds of imported tulips that had spurted and flamed, as if a court of beauties performed a masque to honour spring. Their florid stripes and frills, spilling, nodding and bowing out of four huge tulip vases shipped from Holland, had dazzled everyone and made John Crace despair. For though he never mentioned it, they cost almost as much as the house. Zenobia smiled at the memory. Served him right for keeping her snared, rather than give her the apartment at court she had asked for, where she could enjoy the company of other young people and feel alive.

To the side of the knot gardens, roses on the west-facing wing scrambled through apricots, greengages and a black Hamburg vine espaliered between the windows. The vine was a royal gift from the palace at Molesey. Despite its youth, a few bunches of still-small fruit hid beneath its leaves. Across the other side were the walled vegetable gardens, in which she had no interest.

In the garden's shadiest part near the north-facing wall, along which ran the cloister, a marble bench on lion paws was surrounded by monkshood, nightshades, lily of the valley and foxgloves to create a tranquil spot for John. She had worked hardest here, for he did not enjoy strong sunlight, but was fond of this great white seat shipped from a Medici palace. Across from it on the sunnier side its mate basked, dappled by a vigorous stand of castor oil plants spreading their palm-shaped leaves. Already higher than a man, with unripe clusters of inedible berries, she hoped it would soon provide John with welcoming shade.

From here, lawns sloped towards a Greek temple – really a pavilion, for, backed by a wall, its only pillars faced the house. It sat on a grassy rise near the boundary wall beyond which was the river and Crace's mooring. The rise was made from the earthworks of the house. Geometric paths crisscrossed these lawns, with Roman statuary at the intersections.

This fashionable garden was so large and ambitious that one forgot that Charing Cross was nearby and that, further north, Ludgate Hill and Chancery Lane transported building materials for all the new houses flung up to replace those lost in the fire. Crace's building projects had helped the city regrow, a giant insect that had lost one skeleton and was busy putting on a bigger, shinier one.

As the gold-tinged summer haze intensified, Zenobia revelled. How splendid the garden was, how she longed to share it with someone her own age, someone who exulted, as she did, despite her pale skin, in heat and sunshine. Someone who would not become breathless walking to the temple, where perhaps they would linger away from prying eyes.

But such thoughts were folly, for unless some accident befell him, her husband could live twenty more years. Despite this, she rubbed her cheeks, smoothed the lace over her bruised arm and tugged her stomacher to lift out her bosom, which, as she glanced down, rose and fell so fetchingly that she moved faster to increase the happy effect.

For a footman who had been patiently waiting had just told her that the Italians had arrived.

CHAPTER FOUR

'*T*his is Lily.'

'*Princess* Lily, if you please – Milord.'

Awed by the speaker's flashing eyes, from the depths of her borrowed cloak and mask Zenobia observed Thomas falter as if about to quibble, then think better of it and correct himself while executing a deep bow. All as if a kingfisher dipped across a sparkling pond an instant before a thunder clap.

There was no time to wonder. Huge double doors were briskly swung apart by two powdered footmen in velvet pasted with gold frogging, to reveal the princess on the balustraded landing of the staircase they had just climbed.

So far in Zenobia's young life she had met few grown-up women who were not servants and certainly never a black one in a cloth-of-silver gown and a wig from which ostrich feathers with diamond-studded quills plashed and sparked, giving her the appearance of having a fountain on her head.

As if watching a play from a box, Zenobia peered intently out from the domino.

'Child, do not stare.'

But there was an amused flicker in the mesmerising eyes.

'In the *best* circles, it is not considered *comme il faut*. *Signor* Severin will play at dice in here *avec les autres*.' Her voice was guttural, and her French, though not impeccable, pronounced with gusto. 'Come along with me so that we may get acquainted.'

'Ah, *que vous êtes si méchant.*' She rapped Thomas surprisingly hard over his gloved knuckles with a bone-splatted fan as he protested in a spoilt whine that he wanted to introduce Zenobia to the card-players.

Having tossed the broken fan over the balusters and mocking Thomas's thwarted expression, Lily pushed Zenobia upstairs and left Thomas to enter the room alone. As footmen reopened the gaming-room doors, Zenobia glimpsed card tables lit by flaming candelabra, decanters, and a side buffet cluttered with silver dishes. Upturned eyes were watching her: more eyes than she had ever seen except at church, savagely gleaming, whites flaming in candlelight; eyes of men and women packed like a slavering herd penned in Cowcross Street – then Lily tugged her away with a snort of contempt.

They entered a furnace blazing with too many candles; a room hewn from gold-veined coal. Extravagant black watered-silk walls set with gilded mirrors and sconces surrounded a bed hung in black velvet dusted with gold. Even the panes of the velvet-swagged windows glittered like old diamonds against the night sky. In the middle, Lily tore her wig off and kicked it with a curse. It skidded across the polished floor like the twin of the fat spaniel quivering on the bed. Short and shorn Lily stood, showing tightly cropped hair the like of which Zenobia had never seen.

Between the windows gold chafing dishes and two ewers stood on a buffet, all doubled by a ceiling-height mirror between golden pillars, while between door and bed a small table held wine and roast partridge. A large goblet brimmed with what looked like milk.

'For you.' Lily said. 'I keep my own cow. I learned to in the country. What else are these London back yards good for? Useless for crops, useless for flowers. You cannot drink the filth that passes in the street for milk. Watered chalk. Disease in a jug. Does your family keep a cow? Take off the cloak and let me see,' she continued without pause, undoing and pushing apart the borrowed domino, oblivious as Zenobia shrank back at the touch of her warm fingers. Her eyes narrowed in swift assessment. 'Thin – but you are young. This will fill out, here, and here.' She prodded up and down. 'The milk will do you good.'

To Zenobia's astonishment, Lily lifted one of her small breasts from the too-big bodice, weighed it in her fingertips as if it was a bun and put it back, arranged for better effect. 'Yes, they will get bigger, but you must play your part. Take that cloak off; you are not a bat. Sit and eat. Nature needs a hand, she cannot do everything unaided. Even natural philosophers know nothing about these matters – although there is a handsome one called Newton who knows a thing or two. Would you like to meet him? He sometimes comes here. He's clever, though mad: you ought to hear his daft ideas about fruit. You should marry someone like him, life would never be dull. Who cooks for you? Have a tart. What became of your mother?'

Zenobia drank the milk and ate a small tart of apple in marchpane. Though this was not the evening she had expected, the stream of words put her at ease and she found herself enjoying it. She told Lily what she knew of her parents, which in the telling she realised was little. Then she started to explain about Samuel.

'Yes, of course I know about him,' Lily interrupted. 'You are lucky, he has a good reputation, not corrupt like that idiot downstairs.'

Zenobia started, but the other woman took no notice and went on, gathering up the fluffy dog with a diamond collar, as if corralling beaten egg-white.

'Your father's skill is highly regarded. You should not be surprised. He has the best clients, and if you are patient, he will find you an honest husband among them. It is known that you exist, so what brings you to a place like this? Why in the name of the King would you want to mix with that riff-raff downstairs, particularly the one who, as we speak, is claiming to all and sundry that you belong to him? If you do not take care, he will ruin you without even touching you. Unless that is what you want? I cannot imagine it, but the world is full of such peculiarities. I should know. If it is –'

Seeing Zenobia's face droop, Lily smiled briefly.

'Ah. Fortunately, thanks to me, they could not see you properly, so for now his words cannot harm you. But watch him like a hawk.' She sank sharp teeth into a second pastry that was the faded green of an October leaf, and gulped a large goblet of wine. 'He is treacherous and his heart not kindly, mark my words. Not only that, but his interest is not really women, though he gives us a go when the whim takes him. He'll have whatever he can get his filthy hands on and stick his filthy person into.' She made a face. 'Have another, it takes away the taste.'

Suddenly she stopped, a tart halfway to her mouth, threw her head back and laughed.

Zenobia had always thought that her father had rather nice teeth, in that, though they were the colour of light amber, he had nearly half of them, and the front ones were shiny. Now she saw how pretty teeth could be.

Lily stopped. 'I'm sorry, I forgot. You know so little about me, whereas I have heard all about you. Is that not so? Your eyes are like a pigeon's. And you haven't seen anyone this colour before, have you?'

She turned her hands to and fro so Zenobia could see the pale palms.

'Here.' She thrust them across the table as if they were a pair of gloves for sale. 'Don't be afraid, have a good look. I did when I first met a white person, though it wasn't his hands. I thought it was painted. I made him wash it, to prove it. Anyway, for a start, it's true what I tell that buffoon, your uncle: I *am* a princess. But what difference does it make? Though you, with the name of a queen, ought to understand. My title means nothing here, just as your king's wouldn't where my family comes from. When I was six I was brought from the Barbadoes to become a lady's maid. They are beautiful islands far away from here.

'People think that because we're black we're stupid, but it doesn't follow. Fate landed me with a bored mistress who had an intelligent child my age. We took lessons together and read constantly. The library even had plays by Shakespeare. The couple were wealthy, and the woman's husband, who died shortly after I . . . er . . . left, fancied himself a scholar.

'I could recite Queen Elizabeth's letter to her sister from memory, though it was very long. *She* was no fool. All young women should read that letter. She wrote it when she was only a few years older than you are now, but it was the letter of a great diplomat, and it saved her life. Then, too, I learned a fine hand, spoke two languages, read Latin and Greek, and was a good seamstress, which was useful when the master's lack of discretion made it time for a change of scene.'

She swept crumbs violently off her petticoat front.

Before Zenobia could ask her what she meant, Lily winked and went on.

'No one needs to know any of that, of course.'

Taking a gulp of Zenobia's milk, she burped into her fan. 'Or wants to,' she added eventually. 'Most men don't want clever wives and they certainly don't want well-read mistresses.'

She stroked a pair of diamond and pearl bracelets, then rattled them like castanets. Zenobia jumped. Lily laughed.

'Shakespeare coming out of my mouth, word-perfect. Desdemona! Can you imagine their faces? They want me to be exotic, so exotic I am, and a great deal more than they could imagine. I can out-exotic a pineapple. It's a better living being an exotic madam than a clever maid. Much better.' She clinked her gilded goblet against Zenobia's glass.

'There's a pisspot in the corner,' she added, heading in that direction, hoisting her skirts, talking over her shoulder. 'Don't be shy, we're all girls here. In case you're wondering what *that* looks like in this colour, come and have a look.'

Raucous shrieks had been rising steadily from the floor below. At one o'clock in the morning, sprawled on a silk canapé, they took a dish of chocolate, which Lily said was more digestible than coffee. Lily did not sweeten hers, leaving the sugar scraps glittering in the silver bowl. She made a face. 'I have seen too much of it. White death. My family died for it. All I see is a bowl of blood.'

She shook herself. 'This is not what you expected, is it?'

'I don't know,' Zenobia began. 'My father is busy, so when I was young, I also read a lot. Although', she added quickly, in case Lily thought her ungrateful, 'he *nearly* took me to a play once, by Aphra someone. But . . . what are women like me supposed to do? The way men look at me isn't about my thoughts. They don't listen, they just look. When I heard about you, I . . .'

Lily snorted. 'You thought I sounded exciting. An escape. The exception that proves the rule, the goose with the golden egg. You wanted to see what I could teach you. But you also thought, she's just uncle Thomas's whore, so she must be dim. Whatever she does, I can do better. Carriages and fine clothes and excitement; intrigue and all sorts of amusements to replace the dull life you lead: that's what you thought, isn't it? I'm sure you're chafing to be mistress of your own house, too. So, because the only way is to marry a rich man, you want to get out into the world, and think this might be a good start. Am I right?'

Lily patted Zenobia's hand with an expression so unfeignedly warm that Zenobia stifled a sob.

'There, there, you remind me of me at your age, except that nothing has gone wrong for you. I don't blame you for wanting to see for yourself; it's bold. When I heard, I laughed, because I understood. That's why I agreed to lend the clothes. Not so you could carry out your scheme and end up a notch on that fool's bedpost, but to talk some sense into you before it was too late. Before you end up like me, before you expose yourself to damage you can't mend.

'You made Thomas do what you want, so you've obviously got brains. But that's also why I sent the domino. You've no idea what you are setting yourself up for. If only you knew how lucky you are at home with your books. Lord, what I'd give for a life like that again, the one thing I can never have. Dear girl, would you reject paradise?'

Coming from the mouth of a former slave who, by her own admission, was now a rich mistress, the words surprised Zenobia. Why would a freed songbird beg for bars?

'You're at a dangerous age, and it is late, so pay attention. Thomas will swallow you whole and spit out the pips. You've heard of Nell Gwynne? You're the orange, Thomas the blade. If you let him, he'll gut you.' The twisting of her hand made Zenobia recoil, but Lily went on.

'He's made it his career. He was born crooked, a swindler and a reprobate. If he touches you, you're finished: good for nothing, certainly not marriage. No one would so much as sniff your skirts, not at any price. Look how he lives off your father. I wager you've figured that out too, playing that thing – what is it called, the spinsteret. The spongers and hangers-on downstairs suck up to him because he pays. He's a faucet of gold. But wait till the tap dries, then watch the doors slam. Those droppings all smell as bad as each other.

'Child, don't envy me. We don't last. When I die, no masses will be sung and no children cry. A turn on the stage, a bounce in a royal bed, a ballad on a wall, then the pox and the poorhouse. One in a hundred bags a coronet, the rest die in their own vomit. All this?' In the glittering room, she flung her arms out and spat on the floor. 'The loneliest life in the world. I'd swap it like a shot, but I can't. My life depends more on men than any wife's. Thomas will soon tire, for my fascination is only skin-deep. Then I will start again, until the only one to embrace me will be Death. But you! The whole world to savour. Stay at home, obey your father, and marry the first wealthy man who admires you. *Then* do what you want. Not before. You can invite me to your marriage to thank me.'

Lily raised Zenobia's chin and searched her eyes. The girl might be as pale as milk, but there were no tears: she was tougher than Lily had first thought. With the right start, this one could buck the odds, and *might* bag a coronet.

But sympathy never made anyone strong, and Lily didn't need young rivals.

'I've shocked you? Good! But . . .'

She peered more closely, holding Zenobia so hard that the girl could not duck, though her eyes blazed.

'What on earth have you promised him?' Lily asked. 'You *have*, haven't you? That's what has made him do things for you.'

She let go as if tossing something worthless into the dirt, her voice harsh. 'Did he *make* you? Answer me! *What has he made you promise?*'

'Nothing!' Zenobia declared, for she was neither coward nor liar. 'It was I who –'

'Ah, you think it's a game, that you have some power. And he let you. Oh, he knew what he was doing. As God is my witness, I could wring his neck, that scrawny runt.' She paced about, eyes flashing, then sat down in a great puff of white and silver silk.

'What have you offered?' She cried hoarsely. 'The truth!'

Zenobia shook her head violently but covered her face with her hands.

'He should be *ashamed*!' Lily exploded, knuckles clenched, turning away so that Zenobia could not see her expression.

She rose so abruptly that the dog leapt off the bed. Her skirts knocked the chair over as she strode to the window, fanning rapidly. From the floor below came fresh shrieks mixed with crashes, laughter and a screech of pain. When she turned again, her words were short.

'Put the domino back on. Keep it, I have plenty. No one must see your face. You have not been here and do not know me. We will use the back way and my chair will take you home. Do not talk to Thomas tomorrow unless your father can hear every word. Lock your bedchamber. Don't open the door to anyone except your father or maid. Promise me that you will not be alone with him for a second. He will demand a reward for bringing you here and he won't waste time. *Listen to me.* Don't worry,' she added, seeing the fear in Zenobia's eyes. 'I will think of something.'

Lily pushed the corner of a panel, which sprang open to reveal stairs plunging into darkness. 'I will send a message through your maid. Just let me think. Now, child, give me your word. Quick, and mind your step; the treads are narrow. We must get you home to bed, before your father discovers that you ever left.' With which, Lily the courtesan kissed the schoolgirl's forehead with at least some of the tenderness of a mother.

CHAPTER FIVE

*A*t thirty-six, though still energetic, Samuel had filled out physically and shrunk morally, and his red hair had thinned like autumn grass. Since Hannah's death, the romance that gladdened his heart had cooled; had he been boiled sugar on a slab, he had set brittle. He filled his days with work to replace his lack of a wife and loved the girl he had delivered as much as if she really was his own.

If he had thought about it more often, he would have remembered that Zenobia was the most important thing in the world, but as it was, such thoughts were so rare that he had begun to forget that, too. More beloved pet than daughter, until now she had always responded to his whistle. He took her so entirely for granted that he scarcely noticed her changing.

After her first night out till two, Zenobia did not come down for breakfast. Since Samuel only saw her at breakfast and supper and rarely between, these meals were such important rituals that even the idea of her absence would have thrown him into great consternation. He did not like surprises. He felt he had had enough in life and none of them pleasant. Zenobia's unexplained absence was as unusual as a comet, and in his narrow existence as portentous. He had reason to think so, since the only time he had ever seen one was in the year she was born. He considered the comet a sign of the plague and was convinced that it had brought the fire trailing on its tails the following year, and so destroyed the woman he loved.

Since then he had made his life orderly to the point of regimentation. Apart from the illustrious clients shown up to a room beneath his workrooms, the only people he regularly mixed with were his cutters and tailors, who were loyal, conscientious and pedestrian – but whose conversations as they stitched swirled with lurid fantasies. Not surprisingly, Samuel's imaginative scope now rarely stretched beyond his gift for creating any garment a man could desire. What refinement he once had only lingered in the clothes he made. When he did imagine something beyond this sphere, it was now, like his tailors, with the commonplace horror of a scandal sheet.

He had pushed himself into the background and allowed himself to fade with the idea that Zenobia, unfettered by a tradesman father, could shine brighter. The final card he had to play was that she was not even his daughter, so any lingering associations could be brushed aside, discarded like the shell that has borne the pearl.

When she did not appear for her dish of scalding coffee, which he poured even though there was a maid to do it, and a piping hot buttered muffin, which he took great pleasure in passing to her, his first thought was that she was dead. The next was that the same comet that had stolen Hannah had come back and snatched her daughter.

He was pulling his hair and ringing the bell in such an agitated fashion that the cook wondered if he was suffering a fit, when Thomas strolled into the breakfast room.

Despite a peacock brocade morning gown and tasseled cap, Thomas, erratically powdered but as yet unwigged, looked much the worse for wear. Having had one man under a card table and two women on top, then a blazing row about Zenobia followed by a violent fight with Lily, at dawn he had let himself quietly back in, tipped the doorman to see to the carriage and slipped up the back stairs. He bypassed Samuel's chamber, which was on the other flank of the building, but passed Zenobia's, which he stood outside, not only listening, but also repeatedly trying the handle.

'Have you seen Zenobia?'

Unprepared for the very question running through his brain, Thomas, whose head throbbed, although more from the black eye Lily had given him than from lust and alcohol, stared.

But Samuel was too upset to pay much attention to his brother's expression, or to the extraordinary amount of face-powder he had used in an abortive attempt to cover the bruises on his cheek.

'Zenobia?' Thomas stammered. 'Why should I have seen her?'

At last taking stock of his appearance, Samuel considered the glaringly white face before him. Thomas had got into fights before. Once, he had explained that he had been defending the impugned honour of a lady. Samuel told himself it must be the same explanation this time. For by his own repeated declaration, Thomas maintained the highest principles, and while Samuel did not entirely believe him, for rumours had begun to percolate even to the workshops, it was more conducive to a peaceful life to feign ignorance.

But Thomas's silence was too much. Samuel waved towards the empty chair. 'Because she isn't here! Are you blind? Do you suppose she has come to any harm?'

'Have you asked her maid? The pretty one?' Thomas signalled for hot toast, which he proceeded to demolish with relish. 'I daresay it is just one of the childish tantrums she has been having lately.' He downed his coffee in one draught and signed for more.

Samuel put his knife down.

'Tantrums?'

Wielding a steel blade on a kipper and coddled egg with the vigour of a surgeon, Thomas felt hot food rush into his stomach and blood course around his body. He had heard blood described that way in the coffee shops, and he was no slouch when it came to adopting scientific advances. His spirits rose and with them the ingenuity of his brain. '*You* are too busy to notice, brother. These past weeks, the child has not been herself. It is her age. She will not be a child much longer. Thanks to your neglect, she stays in her room doing what she calls studying, week after week. In truth, she is languishing. It cannot be wholesome for a young girl poised on the threshold like a dove for flight. Haven't you noticed how listless she has become? A shade of her former amiable self. A wisp. I believe she is sickening. She has no air, no exercise, and no diversions. Sometimes when you are not there, she is seized by a sort of frenzy and has – there is no other way to put it – a tantrum.'

Ignoring his brother's aghast expression and starting to enjoy himself, he hurled the sucked kipper bone at a slops basin.

'I wasn't going to tell you this, I did not want to worry you or express too close an interest in our dear child. But I am gravely concerned over her state of mind. In my view, she is perilously close to madness. A hair's breadth,' he added, attacking a third tremulous poached egg so violently that yolk spurted as if he had slit its throat.

'Then we must do something, and at once!' Samuel pounded his napkin. 'I had no idea. The child seemed so contented. What do you advise? A doctor? A surgeon? Should she be bled?'

'A surgeon!' Thomas scoffed. 'Pray, when has a surgeon ever done anybody anything but harm, apart from that Pepys fellow being slit from gizzard to hazard and laying a stone the size of an egg years ago? You may as well call for the undertaker. Keep those quacks away if you wish to save her.

'No, dearest brother,' he went on smoothly, decorating his tale more rapidly than the finest of Samuel's workmen frolicked across a pocket, 'all that young lady needs, if she is to survive, is fresh air and diversion. It will transform her. She has been shut up too long. I have it on the best authority that such a thing may prove fatal at her age. Abandoned to her own devices, she has become deceitful and cunning, letting you think that all is well when all is quite the reverse. What she needs is a lively shaking. A vigorous agitation. Like a fire in a grate that has grown sullen, a good rattle with a poker and *tra la*, all will be merry and bright. Doctors! Pah. My intervention will set her on a new path and her horizons will expand, I vouch for it.'

Samuel sat back with admiration. 'You are perceptive. I have neglected these matters. They are not the preserve of a father. My poor child lacks motherly guidance. She said she was happy and I took her at her word. How could I have been so foolish? It had not struck me that she had become peevish. But my hands are so full. Why, this very morning, an urgent order has come from Lord –'

'Let me arrange everything,' Thomas broke in, a tiny cutlet in his sharp-clawed fingers, stripping the flesh with the filthy teeth of a hyena. Thought of exercise always gave him an appetite. 'Put her in my care and I will guarantee a change. Do agree? It may take one day, even two. But you must leave her entirely to me.'

Samuel had a great deal to accomplish. Securing this particular client was tantamount to being made official tailor to the King. 'I praise the day you were born,' he said, shaking his brother's grease-spattered claw. 'Who could have a truer friend? Do whatever you think best, she is in your capable hands.'

CHAPTER SIX

en minutes after this exchange, a jug of steaming hot chocolate whisked with cream arrived in Zenobia's room, which she assumed Samuel had sent. Though he had never done such a thing, it did not seem unusual because her head throbbed from staying up late and the room swirled and plunged so violently that she was convinced she would die.

Her maid said there was also a note, but Zenobia waved it aside. But Jane could not read; the handwriting was not Samuel's, and the note had not come with the jug, but been left at the back door by an unknown man, who had gone off towards the stables to a small closed carriage with a gold fleur-de-lis on the door panel. All facts that the maid, trained as a servant but not a detective, did not think her place to mention.

Sitting up gulping delicious cocoa, Zenobia tried to remember Lily's words. There was something she was absolutely *not* to do, and also something Lily said that she herself *would* do; and that very morning to boot. But which was which escaped her, furling through her brain like the lazy curls coiling from her cup. Rather than her head clearing, she grew drowsier, and shortly could remember nothing, which did not seem to matter at all.

When Jane returned for the tray, Zenobia lay across the bed, a second, half-drunk cup of chocolate strewn on the sheets and the silver pot upside down on the floor. Under instructions to report to Thomas, who had told her that Master Severin was not to be disturbed on any account, Jane ran to find him, in terror in case her mistress was dead and the fault pinned on her. Servants hanged for less. She did not have to run far, for Thomas's rooms were just along the corridor, and he had been waiting with the door ajar ever since Jane had knocked to collect the breakfast things.

'You did right to act so speedily,' he assured her, making a mental note to extract recompense at his convenience, striding in behind her to a shocking scene that did not seem to surprise him. 'Your promptitude will surely ensure her survival, and no blame attach itself to you. Though it would be prudent to keep it from her father, in case he leaps to the conclusion that you *deserted your duties*. You know what fathers of only daughters are like.'

Pressing his advantage, he was about to tell Jane, who had turned whiter than the sheet, with the hangman's noose already burning her neck, to leave him with the patient, when he noticed the still-unopened note on the tray. Even at that distance, from the stabbing black letters which resembled the work of an angry scythe, he was sure it was Lily's hand.

'Clear this up.' Harshly, he gestured at the upturned chocolate pot and rumpled sheets. As Jane went terrified about her work, Thomas, pretending to listen to Zenobia's pulse, whipped the note open, read it, and thrust it furiously into a pocket. But, scrubbing the floorboards with her apron, weeping, wondering whether there was time to let her mother know she was about to be hanged, which would be difficult because her mother lived out at Ratcliffe and she herself could not write, Jane hadn't seen a thing.

'Nothing to worry about,' Thomas declared cheerfully to the girl's bottom, mashing the note in his doublet as if it was Lily's face. His experience as a jobber had taught him to think fast; and oh! Lily would get her come-uppance much more speedily than she expected, he thought, grinding his teeth. How dare she cross him? He paid her bills, for God's sake. She belonged to him. But she was no longer a novelty; it was time for a change: he would cast her so far down that she would never come up for air again.

Despite his gusting fury at Lily's interference in his plans, he forced himself into a semblance of calm. 'There is no need to disturb my brother. Take this and off you go. I will stay until your mistress wakes. She has merely fainted. When she comes to, I shall take her for some fresh air.'

He thrust the tray at Jane and shoved her out of the room with such a twist of her buttock that it left her in no doubt about the way she would have to show gratitude later on.

The moment the door shut, Thomas bundled Zenobia into the discarded black cloak and crammed on her slippers. Leaving her in a chair, he rushed down the back stairs, dashed to the coach that the note said was waiting, and pressed the two men he found there into his own service with half a year's wages apiece.

CHAPTER SEVEN

*I*nside a fast-moving closed carriage, with her new domino mysteriously on top of her nightdress, Zenobia came to with a splitting headache. Despite the penetrating scent of rose, violet and civet, surely it could not be the carriage that had brought her home? As she tried to clear her head, it pulled up in what sounded like a cobbled yard.

Before she could unfasten a blind, the door was yanked open. A sweaty man grabbed her, pushed her cloak over her face and slung her over his shoulder. He carried her up some wooden steps to a landing. A second man clumped along the rough planks, while the first cursed at her weight. They unlocked a door and took her inside.

She struggled to free her face, but one of them slapped her through the cloak, so she fell quiet, fuming. Then she was thrown on to a bed in the cold room, too stunned to cry out.

They left, locking the door from the outside, and Zenobia leapt up. The tall windows were shuttered outside, but daylight came through the gaps, and a hand-span space at the top dimly lit a room ten-foot square. There was the dirty bed with a threadbare coverlet, plus a small table and two chairs. A pitcher of water on the floor and a chamber pot under the bed. Garment pegs were fixed to the grubby panelling. The table held a jug of what looked like claret, two chipped glasses and a candlestick with a new candle, but no way to light it. A small fire had been laid, but there was no means to bring it to life. There were no mirrors, pictures or books, and the boards were unswept. It was the grimmest room she had ever seen. She could not imagine its purpose, nor why anyone would bring her here.

She clambered on the table to look over the shutters, but they were too high. But the rumble of coaches, clatter of hooves and voices calling about lading and victuals told her that she was at an inn. Once a woman's voice guffawed from somewhere.

It was impossible to tell where she was or how far from home. Although she hammered and shouted, nobody came, and hoarse from calling, she gave up for a while.

The light faded. She was cold and hungry. The domino was thin, so she drank some wine. Thomas said it put fire in the belly. She supposed she had been kidnapped, but had no idea why. Though certainly comfortable, her father was not rich; they only ate off pewter, and she had no jewels. The whole thing was perplexing, but since it looked as if she was going to be in the room overnight, she started a renewed battery at the door, first with her fist and silk-slippered foot and then with the candlestick. When there was still no sound of rescue and only a sliver of fading sky between her and utter darkness, she became downhearted.

But the courage Lily had noticed did not desert her long. Scolding herself, she finished the wine and climbed into bed wrapped in the domino. Praying not to be molested while she slept and vowing to herself with a ferocity that she did not feel that if she survived the night she would escape in the morning, she at last fell asleep.

A sound woke her. Perhaps footsteps on the planks; then the door handle suddenly rattled. She sat bolt upright, her heart as loud as a clock.

Someone hurled themselves against the door. At the third attempt the lock splintered and a man in a dark cloak strode in, swinging a lantern. The lantern cast eerie shadows on his face, and his hat was low over his wig. Yet his gait and stature seemed familiar.

'Father in Heaven, my dearest girl!' Uncle Thomas flung himself on the bed and gathered her up. 'Who on earth has brought you to this dreadful place, to kill you or take you for a slave? We must leave here at once.'

He lifted her and staggered towards the door. However, given that Thomas was neither tall nor strong, he set her down again. 'My carriage is below, can you walk, leaning on me? We must escape before your kidnappers return. Hurry! There is no time to lose. You are chilled to the bone, you will catch a fever.'

Swaddling her so tightly that she could scarcely see and hugging her so that she could hardly breathe, he dragged her down the stairs. For the second time that day she could not look about.

From inside his carriage, whose window covers were fastened, he called up to the coachman to fly with all speed and insisted she drink some brandy from a flask. 'It is the best thing for shock,' he said, 'drink as much as you can.'

He pressed it to her lips, spilling some.

Exhausted, weak from hunger, faint from wine, Zenobia drank the scorching liquid as the carriage tore along in the darkness. After a little while she felt drowsy and Thomas put his arm around her and undid the fastening of her cloak. Having thrown his hat on the floor, he drew her close. Through her nightdress his cloak felt rough. She let her limbs relax for the first time since her capture.

Following these kindnesses, he kissed her neck, and then, moving lower, kissed it again. Then he began to kiss her breast, at which she protested.

'You are intoxicated,' he murmured. 'You do not know your own mind.'

She began to remonstrate but found she could not, for his mouth was on hers. 'There is a long ride ahead.' He pulled away enough to loosen his own garments with one hand while keeping the other over her mouth. 'Let us get comfortable.'

As the carriage thundered noisily through the streets, Thomas set about her.

CHAPTER EIGHT

*O*n iron rims, the carriage hurtled west. Jolting in the cramped space that smelled of fear and sweat, Zenobia pushed Thomas off, but the more she struggled the more determined he became, and her cries met with exerted breathing mixed with brandy and rotting teeth. Though he forced her down, the strike of wheel against stone repeatedly threw them apart. At every setback he redoubled his assault, pulling and pushing, tearing at her clothes. She knew that though they were the same size, he was much stronger and would soon win.

Even as she tried to hold him at bay, it was as if she watched them grappling. A blade of moonlight struck through the gap by the blind and sliced Thomas silver. The flash revealed a frenzied face, eyes that saw nothing, a gaping mouth and flared nostrils. Had she held any hope of reprieve, his expression told her he would never stop. When his hand grabbed at a part of her that she did not know existed, she realised that whatever he intended would happen as soon as they reached a smooth patch of road.

Freeing one arm she scrabbled blindly for the side pocket. At last her finger touched metal. She pulled out the half-cocked, loaded pistol, rested the muzzle against Thomas's cloak, cocked it fully as he had shown her, shut her eyes and pulled.

The retort smacked her hand back against the side with such a bang that she dropped the pistol. Burning smoke filled the carriage.

A screech came from Thomas's open mouth. He looked at her in surprise, his eyes swivelled and his hands let go. The carriage went up and sideways and the horses screamed as if they had been disembowelled.

Zenobia knew nothing more.

When she regained consciousness, her nostrils were clogged with the smell of gunpowder. She was uncertain and disorientated, for just above her head, through an open side-door, the Pole Star pricked the sky. Her mind cleared and she remembered. With difficulty, she hauled herself up and out of the opening into fresh blackness.

Clambering down over the jammed wheel, she ran to where the coachman, Pentreath, sprawled in the shallow gutter, his heavy cloak splayed like a moth. Afraid he was dead, or of hurting him if not, she gently shook his shoulder. He moaned but did not open his eyes and lay as if sleeping. He did not appear to be bleeding and the ground to the side of the road was soft, so she left him. The velvet darkness was lit only by a quarter moon that came and went behind cloud.

Uncertain buildings loomed everywhere. Terrified at being alone in this unknown spot she crept to the trembling horses and leaned against their powerful sides, hoping they would calm her. From the comfort of their heaving heat she glanced about nervously. Anyone could lurk nearby. She might be murdered, or abducted once more. Resting her head against the hot flank of one huge animal, she felt its heart surge. The horses were afraid, too; their breath sent giant white plumes against the sky.

As Zenobia's own breathing steadied, she looked again at the street that curved away to the right. High above, the star shone steady, so the street must head north. Its buildings began to look familiar. Hadn't she travelled this way just the day before, in the same coach, on the way to Lily's? Yes: it was Cow Lane, now she was sure of it – which meant that Chick Lane and home must be at the far end.

Wrapped in Lily's domino, heart in her mouth, she ran beside the brooding, overhanging buildings, trying to look like a shadow, expecting at any moment to be grabbed or robbed.

But nothing happened; in the blackness, nothing else moved; nobody was about. Reaching home, Zenobia crept softly upstairs, barefoot to stop the stairs creaking, and climbed into bed less than twenty minutes before Pentreath arrived.

CHAPTER NINE

'*O*h, no sir. He isn't dead. Not for the moment, at any rate,' Jeremiah Butter added lugubriously.

Samuel's butler, and his senior by some years, Butter had been in Samuel's service as long as he owned the house. Butter, who sometimes spoke as familiarly as a father, had gone straight to Samuel's bedchamber as soon as he and Pentreath had carried Thomas upstairs, wrapped in his cloak to stem the blood that still welled. They had dropped him once, but Butter left that part out. What was done was done. In Butter's decided opinion, Thomas was a vindictive little shit at the best of times and deserved to die.

Samuel contemplated the body of his younger brother. Shot halfway down one thigh, his shirttails were soaked red, and there was so much smeared blood that it was hard to see the wound. Butter was busy tying a fresh tourniquet to prevent still-oozing blood from soiling the valuable bedlinen. He said that Pentreath had been thrown clear when the horses reared.

Luckily, he went on, a water trough had prevented the carriage going over completely. When Pentreath looked, he had found Thomas slumped in the footwell next to a spent pistol and reported that the smell of gunpowder was very strong.

Pentreath had a gravel-filled gash on one side of his face, his shoulder was out and his wig had vanished. Samuel was surprised to see that the coachman's cropped head was already grey, for he was surely only thirty years old. He told him to sit, noticing that, though wounded, Pentreath brushed the back of his coat with his hand to avoid smearing mud on the silk of the chair pad.

The coachman didn't know how long he had been unconscious. It was one o'clock in the morning, there was little passing traffic and the drovers had not yet begun to arrive from the provinces with cattle to sell at Smithfield. It was fortunate that the accident had happened only a short walk from the house, he said. The horses were all right, he added, no bones broken. That had been his first thought, he continued. He did not apologise for this, though Butter glared at him.

The water trough had stopped the carriage from dragging the horses down, which could have killed them, Pentreath explained, and the door fell open on that side, which braced the carriage against the trough. Once certain that he had broken no bones either, he unharnessed the horses and rode one home, running the other alongside. He said they'd be stolen otherwise.

He had prayed that the master wouldn't die while he was away, he added hastily at another, much darker scowl from Butter; but the Lord knew, you couldn't get that dead weight up across a frightened horse without risk of killing Thomas or of injuring yourself. The beasts were terrified and had no saddles. On returning, with Butter's help he had brought the master back on a home-made stretcher. The two nearside coach wheels were so bent that they left the rest of the carriage there till light, for though valuable, the doors were emblazoned, and it would be hard to steal it without attracting attention.

'Who shot him?' Samuel flared, not remotely interested in Pentreath's care of the damned horses, Pentreath's health or Thomas's damn carriage for that matter. 'Where had he been?'

Pentreath didn't answer until Butter threatened him with his livelihood.

'He wanted me to take him to . . . a place he sometimes goes,' Pentreath muttered from the splendour of the gilded chair, not looking at Samuel, but glancing uneasily at Thomas, prostrate, blood-clotted breeches cut away on one side. His skin was as pale as a winding cloth. Bound to die, Pentreath thought grimly, chewing his lip. That wound was liable to go bad before you could shake a stick at it. Good riddance to bad rubbish.

'What place?'

Samuel longed urgently for sleep, but this fool of a coachman was dithering. Normally kind to his servants, he had a good mind to sack him on the spot. But the surgeon, Abercorn, still hadn't arrived to excise the bullet – though as far as Samuel could judge, there wasn't much the doctor could do that Butter had not already done.

It was impossible to tell whether the ball was still in the flesh or not, it looked so torn. The thought that Thomas's leg might have to come off made him shudder. Butter said the ball had gone right through and missed the bone. He had considerable skill, having been apprenticed to his father, a butcher, before service, and he still trained the staff at jointing. Knowing how familiar he was with lumps of meat and how handy with a knife, Samuel almost told him to get on with it, for it would be quicker than waiting for the surgeon. Besides, Abercorn was a renowned drunkard who blunted his knives hacking up corpses. At the very least, Butter's were razor sharp.

Samuel had no idea whether Thomas would live or die, but now that the butler was no longer scowling in the background, he repented his temper and told the coachman to speak up.

'An inn, sir,' Pentreath blurted, gripping the chair arms for courage.

Thomas had always been adamant that if ever Pentreath let on where they went, he could expect to end up in the river with his throat slashed. Pentreath was under no illusion that his master would carry out the threat. To his certain knowledge at least one woman who had gone to the inn for fun with Thomas had ended up taking the only bath in her whole life in the Thames. A very deep bath indeed. Pentreath shuddered. For as well as coach guns, Thomas had a smaller one, plus as a vicious filleting knife, which he kept about him and knew how to use. But since, in

Pentreath's horse-predicated opinion, Thomas looked set to die, he might escape such a horrible fate if he unburdened himself as Samuel bade.

'He kept a room there, sir, where he took women. There was one *partickuliar* one as he used to take there, though he hadn't for some time, not since he bought her a house –'

Samuel jerked awake. 'A *house*?'

The coachman's expression was increasingly unhappy, but at Samuel's abrupt movement, he went on.

'Well sir, I was told to wait in the yard. After a while, the master come out with her all wrapped up in her cloak and they got in the carriage. When he went to that place I always stayed on the box and minded my business, so I done the same last night. But I'm sure it was her, sir. It was her cloak, I's seen it before. And I know her size. She i'n't very big, nor bigger than mistress Zenobia. It was she all right, sure as my name's Pentreath. I could smell her, too. She has a most *partickuliar* smell. I'm buggered if it ain't her. Sir.'

He brought this lively nugget out with the flourish of a paper of fish.

Samuel started, but contained himself. 'Then what happened?'

'I doesn't know, I swear as plain as my nose, sir. I was on the box. He had a'ready told me to go to her house in Bedford Street, so that is where we was headed. You can't hear nothing up there, not when you're driving fast and mindful of the road. Nothing from inside the carriage, not unless they hang out and shout and not always then. That route is tormentuous, what with the building works round the new cathedral, and we was going at a fair clip. It's dangerous enough when you can *see* the road, sir, so many stones lying about. Coming up to the turn from Snow Hill to Ho'burn, just down there –,' he gestured out of the window, 'well then, there's a loud noise; really loud: *Bang!* I near as flew off of my seat, I could hear *that* all right. Knew it for a pistolier the minute I hearded it. And whoa! Straight up goes Sammy and Tommy – begging your pardon, sir, but them's their names. It wasn't my idea to call them that –' (this was a downright lie) 'well then, Sammy and Tommy rears right up against me like that, *bam*! I thought I was a goner. Sammy's seventeen hand if he's one, and there he goes with his great black arse uprearing, shining like a coal face. And just as I thought, 'this is it, my lad', over we go sideways, and I don't know nothing till I come to in the ditch. Jus' *exacterly* as like what I sayed earlier. Sir.'

The courtesy held more than a degree of resentment and reproach.

Gloomily, Pentreath glanced towards the door from under his brows. He longed to pick the grit out of his cheek, which stung as if a hot knife was scraping it. It was the rasping tongue of Death, there was no doubt about it. What did the master care about a mere driver? He'd seen horses die of cuts like this. It started as an ordinary cut, then before you knew it, it was pus-cloaked curtains.

Samuel interrupted.

Of course, the master *could* interrupt, Pentreath brooded, imagining his cheek swelling with the mordancy and blood-threaded green gobbets slithering out. *But* Samuel was the master. *He* could do as he pleased. Oh yes.

He shivered. The outlook was not good.

'Now, this, umm, *lady,*' Samuel pursued carefully, with frequent quick glances at Thomas as if he expected him to flip over and start a silly addle-pated conversation the way he used to do when he was a boy, as if none of this nightmare had happened.

'This . . . ah . . . lady. Are you quite sure it was her? Would you swear to it?'

'I would if I had to, sir. Like what I said, I didn't see her face, and I've been taught to look away. It's worth more than my job otherwise. But like what I 'splained earlier, I could smell her. I recognised that all right, that thick smell, rising up off her cloak. I've smelled it plenty. And we were going to her house. And he told me that it was her what gave him the pistols, sir, so in my view she'd know how to fire them.'

He warmed to the theme. 'What sort of lady knows how to fire a pistolier? Not Mistress Zenobia, who would scarce know which end's which. That *woman* must have got out the other side, the one as was tilted up. Climbed down over the wheel. Not stayed to help. Found her way home. *That's* guilt for you, sir, if I ever seen it. No other words for it. Shameless. The other thing…' He tailed off and looked about like a dog about to be struck.

'Go on.' Samuel felt in his pocket. He had been too hard on the man, he saw that now. 'Here's a guinea. Take it, take it, before we go for the magistrate. What else is there? Speak up, don't be afraid. You're a bright fellow.'

Galvanised by the bright glint of a third of a year's wages, Pentreath found his voice. 'There was a note in Master Thomas's pocket. I took the liberty of seeing if he had a handkerchief to staunch the wound. He had not, but I found this. Now sir, I can't read more'n a few letters, and my own name, Lemuel. The word looked a bit the same, so I made her name out – Lil or Lel, it must be – and – well – there's the same smell on it.'

After rubbing the crumpled scrap on his breeches he passed it over, triumphant. 'Excuse the blood, sir, but you can make out the words.'

Come to me. You know the place.
Lily

That was all the stained paper said.

'Yes,' Samuel said wearily, 'indeed I can. Thank you, you have done well.'

Once Pentreath had shuffled out, Samuel sniffed the scrap of blood-blotched paper before letting his hand fall to his lap.

'By God, should my brother die, when I have made out the owner of this stinking hand, this murderous, cowardly, dungheap of a whore who has done this, whoever she is, will most assuredly hang.'

CHAPTER TEN

*Z*enobia bundled the domino into a sticky clump and pushed it and her muddy, blood-marked slippers to the bottom of a chest that held folded skirts and bodices. Locking it, she replaced the key on her pocket chain. After a few hours' sleep, more tired than she could remember, she went to breakfast. As she trod softly down the wide, polished oak stairs, it occurred to her that the night before was a dream and that as usual uncle Thomas would be there, attacking his food with customary spiteful vigour.

Samuel sat grey-faced at the head of the table. Thomas's chair was empty.

Now certain that he was dead, Zenobia opened her mouth to confess her crime, but before she could make a sound her father spoke.

'Child, your uncle has been attacked. He lies gravely ill upstairs. I did not want to wake you. Sit by me, you are startled. You look unwell, as if you had had a presentiment.'

As usual he poured her sharp black coffee, chafed over a small flame on the buffet, and passed it. His hand shook slightly.

'Is he . . .?' She collected herself. If Thomas came to, would he say that she had shot him? What if he already had?

Her father was studying her with an unfamiliar, intense expression.

'Is he . . . awake? May I see him?' She struggled to keep her voice steady.

'You are considerate, but he has a fever and is unlikely to wake for some time. If –' he failed to steady his own voice, 'if he wakes at all. The surgeon has given him a great deal of laudanum.'

'What is the matter with him, father?'

Her heart pounded so loud that she was sure he would hear. It was almost impossible to get the words out; the fist of her heart in her throat kept the words back. Surely her bullet had been fatal? She had seen his eyes roll and there had been no sound afterwards.

'An attempt has been made on his life. He has been shot. An arrest will be made today. If he dies, his murderer will hang.' As Samuel hissed the vehement words he looked directly at her with the same intense, anguished look. Her heart stopped.

The delicate shell of fragrant liquid raised to her lips slipped from her fingers, bounced against the table edge and splintered on the polished floor.

This was it. Now he would accuse her. Death stared her in the face.

'There, there, child. You must not take it so hard. After all, it is not your fault.'

Not the words she expected. He patted her hand.

Samuel was glad to have someone else's grief to think about. Thomas, the very man who only the day before had been so concerned about Zenobia, was now close to death himself, while this sweet angel, the child he had personally delivered, was only concerned about her uncle. How strange life was, how full of mutability. What a noble spirit she had.

The thought flashed through his mind that if Thomas survived, he would give Zenobia to him in wedlock. His heart filled with magnanimity, a golden glow descended. It must come to pass, God willing he would make it so. The dear girl would be so grateful. In the circumstances, what match could be finer. And they were not related, which made it perfectly respectable.

He swelled with pride at the cleverness and subtlety of the idea, but only for a moment, for the chance of Thomas surviving looked slim. Surgeon Abercorn had wiped his blade on his breeches in a very dismissive manner.

'Ah, now, do not weep,' Samuel continued anxiously, mistaking her tears of temporary relief. 'The physician is not without hope. The ball passed right through. The wound is severe and he has lost a great deal of blood, but he may survive.'

He did not believe it.

'But', she started cautiously, bewildered, 'his assailant . . . who was it?'

'My child, you will be astounded to learn that it was a woman. Hard to believe, I grant you, but Pentreath recognised her.'

Complacently, Samuel pressed her icy hand, already thinking of getting back to work. However sick his brother was, life must go on and money be made.

'Yes indeed, he recognised her. A woman who . . . a woman of the kind that . . . Well, a woman your uncle knows,' he concluded feebly, rising in order to nip any more awkward questions in the bud. Zenobia had no business wanting to hear about women of that sort. Particularly as Thomas was soon to become her husband, whether she knew it or not.

'Pentreath knows her house and the watch is on the way to arrest her. Trouble yourself no further. Take some more coffee and go back upstairs. Butter will let you know as soon as you can see him. God bless you for your loving devotion to your uncle, dearest child. If I have any say in the matter, Heaven will reward you for it.'

CHAPTER ELEVEN

*B*ack upstairs, Zenobia waited for Thomas to come to and accuse her of attempted murder. Clutching a volume of Chaucer without reading a line, she stared out of the window and waited for the hammer to fall. Clearly, her father was unaware that she had left the house, which was no surprise, for he never saw her during the day and often worked through supper, leaving her to dine alone. Particularly busy at the moment, he had not missed her. But if Thomas woke, all that would change. She felt as if she would go out of her mind.

At noon, Jane brought cress soup and told her that according to the other maid, Mary, who prided herself on nursing, Thomas was still unconscious. Mary said he looked much worse. Shaking her neatly dressed head, Jane said that he was in a high fever and his leg was swollen and inflamed.

'Issuing,' she whispered darkly. She had no idea what the term meant but had overheard Pentreath say it to the cook. She fancied that she mimicked his intonation well. Butter had told the servants to expect Master Thomas to die, though he had sworn them to silence. This in an even more conspiratorial whisper. It was more than her job was worth to repeat it.

Pacing round the Turkish carpet, Zenobia recalled her incarceration and the carriage ride as intently as if it were happening all over again. Would she go to hell for hoping he would die, she wondered – and without regaining consciousness, so he could not accuse her?

Could Thomas have had her shut in that room? But with him fighting for his life, who would believe it? She would be locked up for a lunatic, which was almost as bad as being hanged.

The fact that he had attacked *her* now seemed irrelevant. No value would be put on her account, she would be accused of leading him on. Besides, if she said he had molested her, it proved she was in the carriage, so unless she pretended that someone else had entered, she would be tried for shooting him. And since Pentreath knew there was no one else, she was caught in a trap. The only thing that could free her was Thomas's death.

But who was the mysterious woman accused in her stead? Was her father playing catspaw, to force her to confess? She recommenced pacing.

As the afternoon lengthened she became convinced that she had been sent to her room to repent, to admit her offence, before being handed over to a magistrate. She wrung her hands.

In the crooked street below, the morning rush of cattle was long past, but people still went about their business. Soon, all that she once took for granted would be taken away: this beautiful room with its books, its comfortable bed; her table and writing things; her clothes, her maid. The life that struck her as boring and prison-like; marriage to an enlightened man; the chance to do something worthwhile: all that had meant so little now meant so much. All was lost. She would be taken to a sordid, stinking place and thrown among murderers and thieves, then dragged out, tried and hanged.

At the last part she wept, her small hands round her neck. A glance in the mirror brought a fresh bout of sobbing. In the rush to chase after excitement she had thrown away everything of beauty and value. Lily had warned her, but she hadn't listened.

What if she could find her way to Bedford Street, she thought, seizing on a glimmer of hope. Lily would know what to do. But she was not allowed out on her own, and even if she managed to slip out, she had no money for a sedan and could not wear the bloody domino at the bottom of her trunk. Gloom descended.

Thinking about the domino caused fresh alarm; she must destroy it at once. If she threw it out of the window, someone was bound to see. It had to be burned. She rang for Jane to light a fire against a chill. 'It is from worrying about uncle,' she said more boldly than she felt, ordering tea, despite having no appetite. 'Bring me news as soon as there is any.' Jane said that the surgeon would return at eight.

Just when the fire was gaining strength, there was a loud knocking at the front door. The footmen of her father's clients did not hammer like that, and fittings only took place in the mornings. Cursing, she crammed the domino back in the trunk.

Thomas's room was beyond the top of the stairs and the door was closed. Jane had told her that he still slept and that Mary sat with him.

From the turn of the landing, Zenobia could see the hall.

A tall, powerfully built man stood below, back turned. He was dressed in dark clothes: a cloak; a hat with a sweeping brim. When he removed the hat, Zenobia saw not the heavy-bottomed wig she expected, but coarse hair cropped in a severe style. After handing them to Malkin, he looked up, straight into her eyes.

Even though Malkin was about to show him into the large receiving room, the stranger made such a brusque gesture that the footman stepped back with the outer things and disappeared.

The stranger's face matched his body. Large, chiselled, with swarthy skin, a strong nose, a firm mouth. In youth perhaps austere, now he was striking. Grey eyes looked at her without wavering. Lines across his broad forehead spoke of troubled intelligence. His hands were large and broad, the hands of a labourer who no longer worked. One thumb bore a heavy signet ring. Even at this distance she could see that, though perhaps fifty, he could kill with a blow. His suit, while plain, was expensive. It was impossible to be the daughter of a tailor and not judge a piece of cloth at thirty paces.

'Ah,' he said, his voice carrying as if it would fill a much larger room and spill into a second, 'the daughter.'

A statement of fact that he did not expect disputed. He gave a cursory bow, but rather as if he was used to having people bow to him, young women in particular.

She curtseyed, but when she looked again, his eyes were still riveted to her, so that she was unable to look away.

'Your father is not yet come,' he informed her matter-of-factly, still talking up to her as if it was normal. 'You will entertain me. I do not wait. Come down.'

With the pat of his leg he would use to a gundog, he turned on his squat heel and let himself into the drawing room, while Malkin hovered anxiously behind.

When Samuel hurried into the hastily fire-lit room, Zenobia and the stranger sat opposite each other in high-backed chairs. Between them, the still-catching fire in its vast surround appeared dwarfed, crumpled. The man surveyed Zenobia fixedly and she returned his look. Chess pieces locked in mortal combat, or a couple so long married that they had turned to stone.

'Sire!' Samuel gasped, as if he had run down the back stairs from his workrooms two at a time, which in fact he had. Zenobia had never heard him sound like that. She broke the spell to look at him in wonder.

'Forgive me for keeping you waiting, your honour, but I see that my daughter . . .'

'Introduce us.'

Samuel bowed. 'Theocritus Koros, Zenobia Severin, my adopted daughter.'

'Ah. Then despite her heathen name – a fine name – she may sit with us yet.'

He pushed his stockinged legs out as if in his own parlour. Zenobia noticed mud on his coarse shoes. He must have walked. They were not the feet of a gentleman. She toyed with the word heathen, and with his lack of manners.

'The woman who shot your brother, Lily Boniface,' the visitor continued flatly, as wine and food were quickly brought, 'is at my house. I will consign her to Newgate after I have questioned her. I am not yet satisfied.'

A flat silver dish heaped with Thames oysters was placed beside him on a small table, along with a small half-cut loaf, a muslin-wrapped lemon and a bone-handled prising knife. He waved the salver away but tossed back the wine and held his glass out to fill.

His authority fascinated Zenobia. From the lowest servant to her father, everyone was in awe of this man with the strange name, and he seemed to expect it. Every word, every movement implied that he was in charge. But he had mentioned Lily Boniface. What made him think that she had shot Thomas?

There was nothing for it but to speak out and absolve Lily. Yet, for a reason she could not fathom, she said nothing and continued to contemplate him, unable to look away whenever he looked at her, watching the power in those great hands, his broad shoulders, his stout legs set as if stamping his right to the air between them.

'The woman will deny the accusation. Will absolutely deny it. What else can one expect.'

He glowered, first at Samuel and then at Zenobia, where his gaze settled. Making himself comfortable he pushed himself towards her, his immense torso leaning forwards as if he might crush her. His eyes did not flinch. 'She will deny it,' he repeated, talking straight at her as she struggled not to look away. He caressed his ring with powerful fingers in a way that horrified and compelled her.

Perspiration sheened Samuel's forehead. He got up, thought better of it and sat down again.

'My brother looks likely to die,' he began in an uncertain tone. 'The coachman is adamant that he knows this woman, he recognised her and knew her scent. He will swear to it,' he added more firmly.

'*Recognised* her?' The magistrate sat up. Zenobia saw how he would stalk anyone who crossed him until they yielded. He would root out an untruth without mercy, relentless in pursuit of whatever he wanted.

'He saw her face? A distinctive face that one would not forget. But he is a mere servant. Is there any other witness?'

With this he looked at her, hard, unremitting. Despite the roaring fire, she felt cold. What had Lily said when she denied the charge. *What did he know?*

Samuel rubbed his palms on the dun-coloured silk of his breeches, leaving a darker mark. Zenobia knew how badly he lied. 'No,' he began, slowly. 'Pentreath did not see her face, she wore a domino. But he recognised her scent, and her size . . . And he had taken her there before.'

'Domino, scent, size.' Koros chewed each word. His deep voice vibrated inside Zenobia's chest. There was the edge of an accent she could not place. As the sound rang through her, she felt her body jerk like a clapper from Tyburn gallows. Her own palms began to sweat, but fire ran through her too, nothing had ever disturbed her the way his voice did. Yet his words brought her to her senses.

'Is it enough to hang for, Zenobia? To *swing* for? An *odour* recalled by a coachman? Shall I try her for murder?'

She returned his gaze. He could not possibly read her thoughts, and surely Lily would not have told him about the domino. Besides, he said he had not yet questioned her. He had come straight from the house where Lily had been taken. He hadn't spoken to Pentreath, either; and the only person who knew the truth, apart from her, was unconscious upstairs. Yet she felt as if he knew her every thought.

'Surely nobody will hang unless my uncle dies?' Her black eyes challenged him. 'For there has been no murder yet?'

The magistrate held his glass out once more and stroked his jaw.

'That will depend.' Quietly but not softly – the reverse of soft; his eyes made her feel more violated than in the carriage.

'Depend?' Samuel was poking the fire. 'Depend on what?'

Koros emptied his dregs into the flames and rose with a powerful movement, lithe despite his bulk, towering so that he almost blocked out the fire. He gazed down at Zenobia with a ferocity that annihilated her. Life and death were cupped in his hand and meant nothing to him.

'A clever daughter.' He gave a cursory nod in Samuel's direction.

'You will show me out yourself, Severin,' he ordered. 'We have matters to discuss.'

PART THREE

CHAPTER ONE

*T*he Italian wore his own long glossy black hair, exuberantly curled, and a black cloth suit fastened with boisterous clumps of green silk ribbons with shining silver points, which rampaged up his chest like blown cabbages. A strong smell of lemon-rasp came off him. As Zenobia walked the length of the gallery, he unrolled a parchment on a gilded walnut table with florid legs and a liver-spotted top, one of a pair that John Crace valued very high.

The two men with him must be Italian too, Zenobia thought, although before she reached them they had bowed and set off to join two of her own servants, who waited with ladders and rules at the end she had just come from. They began to measure the ceiling.

Having patted out the parchment as if it was priceless, the Italian anchored one side with a bronze inkwell Crace prized even higher than the table, and the other with a massive candlestick, each of which he handled as if they were his.

He had said nothing, or at least, not with words. For from the moment Zenobia entered the great hall and spotted the knot of three men, she was aware that every step was commented on. Not because she heard – and besides, she could not speak Italian – but because their lips moved in what she took for appreciative murmurs.

The assistants had cropped hair and work clothes, so she hardly glanced at them. But in addition to his flamboyant appearance, the artist's eyes were the colour of fresh hazelnuts, with green rims and bright whites. They examined her so boldly as she stopped that she found herself almost, but not quite, unable to return his look.

'*Signor.*' She lavished the rich extent of her Italian on him in a superior tone to counterbalance his smile and the insolent way he appraised her.

'Signor*a.*' He grinned and executed an accomplished bow with a jaunty spring, and a superfluous flourish of his fingers, as if shaking fluff from his puffed breeches.

'*Signor!*' Firmer now, with a curtsey nowhere near as deep as his bow. She was mistress here and had bestowed the honour of his own language on him. Despite which, he had looked at her in the same insolent way that he handled her possessions. It was almost as if he handled her.

'*Signor-a!*' He yodelled with unbridled enthusiasm and more than a whisker of amusement. It was impossible not to notice that his curved lips were sardonic as well as full. The words flew out so rapidly that she struggled to concentrate. She could not drag her eyes from him as he serenaded: '*E l'affascinante signora italiana?*'

She had no idea what he had just said. If he had not been so handsome, he would be excruciatingly irksome.

The challenge in his grin was increasingly exciting.

'Could it be possible, madam, that –' Suddenly using faultless if glottal English, he strode round the table, showering her with scent. Had he plunged her into a lemon grove and ravished her beneath a tree, the sensation could scarcely have been more intense. 'Could it be that you are under the misapprehension that I am *Italian?*'

'Do you claim that you are not?'

'Assuredly not, madam. It pleases me to say that I come from Holland.'

With a rap on one ribboned cabbage over the region of his heart, he bowed again, but this time normally.

'Through and through. From the same land as the world's most exalted painter, Rembrandt. Not that of van Dyck, so dearly beloved of your *first* King Charles. Perhaps you have heard of them? Most assuredly not from the birthplace of *Tiziano*.'

Lingering over the word he stared at her bosom, which from many tugs on the way, was as much outside her dress as in.

'My name, ma'am, is Hendrik Snyders.'

As he kissed her hand he yanked her very close to his doublet, and also close to the unrolled parchment.

Whatever nationality this smug imposter held and however he had come to mislead her husband, the drawing was very fine: in all of Crace's collection she had never seen anything like it. If this were to be painted on the complicatedly coved ceiling above them, the effect would be magnificent, heavenly. His description of vigorously sailing figures was masterful, the foreshortening as well done as by Michelangelo – of whom she *had* heard, so she was irked that he had not asked her *that* question.

It was as if he not only understood the house, but her, too – even though that was quite impossible.

In sketchily indicated colours, the middle section depicted a great battle for mankind's soul: evil set against good and truth and beauty. Round this central cartouche an azure sky changed subtly to the pale pinks of dawn at one end and dusk's baleful ink at the other, indicating, she supposed, the inevitable passage of time.

Was it to do with Catholics and Protestants? Not only a dangerous subject but one that bored her. She left politicking to her husband. But as she inspected the design once more, hotly aware of his eyes upon her, she glimpsed a trefoil motif in the puffy clouds.

Of Crace's original religion Zenobia knew nothing, just as she knew nothing of his family. But recently he had begun talking about his soul. As a magistrate, he stoutly avowed the religion of the King. She knew that the duke who had recommended these painters was a Catholic. However, with Catholic King James already clashing with his Protestant nobles, it might be imprudent to nail such colours to something as hard to hide as a ceiling. At least, unless one was sure which way the wind would blow. For as everyone her husband's age knew, they could blow your head straight on to a block. Just look at what happened to the King's father.

This thought worried her, though not regarding her husband: his head bent for the axe gave her the same pleasure as a fly under a swat. But despite Samuel Severin's Catholic-sounding name, she had been raised Protestant, in line with Samuel's true name of Welkin. She had no intention of dying for a painting, however breathtaking.

One glimpse showed that this sublime confection had wings that could, allowed the right political and religious atmosphere, and should King James blow kindly on it, soar her ceiling, her house, and by inference her, into empyrean heights of royal favour – even into the history books; into immortal fame.

But what did that matter, because whatever wings the design had might as well be made of lead. The only flapping they were going to do was as they curled up in flames and soared up the chimney, poked into a frenzy by her husband, unless she could change his mind to keep them, and persuade the painter to alter the pattern in the clouds.

'What lies beneath the inkwell?' Zenobia asked. She leaned across to move it, treading firmly on Herr Snyders' foot at the same time. Drawing in his breath sharply, he gave her a sideways look, but his foot remained beneath hers. 'Should I tread you in return, madam? One kiss will confirm it.' His eyes taunted her.

'Only one.' He put the nail of his finger delicately to his cheek. 'Just here.'

Though she glared, she kept him pinioned.

'Ah, let me help, I cannot bear to see you struggle.' He clamped his warm hand over hers on top of the gilded ornament just in time to stop it crashing to the floor.

Instead of speaking, Zenobia pressed her arm firmly against his.

Through her silk skirts, his long leg found its way behind hers and pinned it to the table. A hundred feet away, up ladders, the assistants had their backs turned.

Hendrik Snyders suddenly let go and bent to retrieve something from the marble floor. But on his return, the hand that had been flat on the drawing was stuck through the pocket slit of her skirt.

Her heart lurched. Then again, he was Dutch, they probably had their own way of doing things. She pushed herself against him and the edge of the table to help his manoeuvre, her arms on the table as a support, not caring, as her heart quickened, if the drawing tore to shreds; praying that the servants, should they look round, would not notice the telltale sway of the silk bell of her skirts, unable as she was to control it.

Flushed faces fixed on the drawing they leaned over side by side.

'My husband wishes me to inform you that he does not want this,' she panted some moments later.

'Ah! But you are a great artist,' she gasped, leaning on the parchment as if she examined it closely, and to get a more pleasing angle against him. Bent across it, the constriction of her stays, their ivory buskin pressed like a sword against the edge of the table and her ribs, made it hard to breathe and turned her whisper to a groan.

All the time his fingers were busy.

'Oh! For the love of Our Lord,' she gasped, rising up on her toes. 'Stop that at once. Surely you could do something else to please me? Something . . . more . . . substantial . . . than this?'

Abruptly, he withdrew his hand and took such a rapid step back that if she had not been leaning on the ripped drawing she would have toppled over.

'I am at your disposal, ma'am,' he announced loudly, with a bow, in which she noticed, with a renewed glare, that he sniffed his fingertips as he flourished them.

'My God,' he went on so that only she heard, 'your husband is an ungrateful peasant and a bloated toad. Let me stamp on him and toss out of a window. I will crush him with my bare hands. Let me throttle the arrogant old fool and have you in ways you have never dreamed of.'

For the benefit of their servants, he added: '*May* we go somewhere to discuss matters, *Signora*?'

'Follow me,' she declared in the ringing tones of an absolute mistress.

She straightened her gleaming skirts with one firm sweep while Hendrik smoothed and rolled the broken drawing.

They finished their discussion on the stone floor of a service passageway whose entrance was hidden behind a tapestry.

'From Holland also,' Hendrick noted as he shoved her back out towards the gallery, his big hands fire in the small of her back. 'Very good with the fingers. Very adroit, Signora, would you not agree? When may I come at you again?' He added politely as they re-entered the gallery.

'When your English is vastly improved and you have something more to offer,' Zenobia flung over her shoulder, moving quickly ahead. Without looking at him again she walked past his assistants high up on a precarious scaffold made of a plank set between tall ladders.

I am going back to report on the afternoon . . . She forced herself not to look back, heading towards her husband's chamber, feeling her twisted ankle again . . . *And later* . . .

But she refused to dwell on later, for Master Snyders would surely return in a few days and whatever John Crace did to her that night, or any other night for that matter, now meant absolutely nothing. Because even if it was true that her husband was slowly dying as his doctor claimed with an increasingly long face, as far as she was concerned, since this afternoon he was already dead.

CHAPTER TWO

'For the Lord's sake, you must leave him. This is not a game.'

Slanting between the pillars of the temple, indolent light turned a wide strip of Hendrik's brown skin bronze, then gold, which Zenobia, always alabaster, found disturbingly attractive. Slowly, she traced the raised vein down his forearm. That arm was stronger than the left, the hand more powerful.

Sitting up abruptly she gave his hand back like an unwanted gift. 'Leave him? Have *you* taken leave of your senses?' She smoothed the crumpled taffeta of her lustrous shot skirts and retied the garters of her white stockings just above the knee. Ignoring his interference, she forced on embroidered shoes, snatching one from his grasp as he tried to hide it. The heat from his skin, its healthy smell mixed with lemon oil, was such a relief after the sickly smell that dogged John. If only she could bathe in this to cover that, for no amount of scrubbing would remove it, and sometimes she felt as if it permeated her own body. But John would notice if she did. Had he already? She was under no illusion about his jealousy. She prayed he had not.

Sighing, she looked at Hendrik at last. 'How could I? I am married to him and he is dying. He will take himself off in due course, then all will be natural and easy. Then we can do as we like. Have patience. Besides, I'm not a monster.'

'You *say* he's dying.'

'You don't say I'm not a monster.'

Hendrik smiled broadly then laughed, showing crowded teeth. He made himself comfortable on heaped cushions and poured more wine. 'I observe no sign of his imminent departure to a better world. I have been working here more than a month and there has been no change at all. If anything, he has improved.'

She did not reply. There was truth in what he said, but she had avoided thinking about it.

'Invigorated, even,' he added, thoughtfully. 'Not by the blinding beauty of my work, though God knows it would be enough to send any ordinary mortal into transports.'

She looked him over curiously. 'What evil idea has taken such a black hold of you?'

'Perhaps nothing. But the other day when he invited me to dine I had the feeling he knew something. That he watched us. And that he wasn't afraid. Rather, it was more as if . . . as if it brought him to life; a challenge.'

'Mere fancies.' She dismissed him, smoothing a final wrinkle on her calf, twisting a curl with licked fingers. 'You are a foreigner, you scarcely know him. I saw nothing of the sort. Besides, what could an ill old man do to you?'

'It would be foolhardy to make light of this, my love.' He caught her hands and kissed them lingeringly, before gently pushing back the muslin cuff of one puffed sleeve and continuing up her forearm as if they had all the time in the world, as if sufficient kisses could protect them, garland them from evil.

'You know full well what that man could do. It isn't me I was thinking of, though I would not willingly put myself in his bad graces. He could have me killed without a thought, but –'

She stared. 'Come, come. You cannot believe that he would ever harm me?'

'It is you that I want.' Hendrik grazed his lips, which tasted faintly of wine, across hers, silencing her. 'I want you to stay alive, as do I. Without doubt I am the greatest painter this revolting country has ever seen and a great deal greater than it deserves, and I fully intend to be recognised across all these northern states, including my own. It would be enough for many, but not for me. Without you it is worthless dust. Most particularly, I want you. But not like this.'

'What's wrong with this?' She rose like a brocaded cobra. He soothed her with his voice, with a touch.

'You are the most remarkably stubborn and unnatural woman. You speak like a man and when you feel like it, you fuck like one. Nothing is wrong with that, except that it is not enough. If you were normal, you would know it without being told, you would accept the gifts I strew before you instead of trampling them.' His eyes flashed. 'I want to lie with you in soft linen, without being stabbed by your bodice hooks, lacerated by your stays, given an ague by cold stone, and always looking over my shoulder in case that crook rises up behind us and strikes us dead.'

Colour drained from her cheeks. He shook her playfully. 'Come, do you know how rough that tinsel on your bodice is? Every time we lie together is like going into battle. How it scratches and scrapes, a thousand fiendish knives lacerate my heart. It is impossible to come at you without injury. When you belong to me I will dress you in simple stuff, like a peasant, and keep you out of sight of the world.'

He drew her into the curve of his arm.

'And for the love of our Saviour, Zenobia, he is so old he is practically Tudor. How can you bear him near you?'

She put her fingertips gently over his mouth, trying not to caress his lips, though their softness made her want to. But there was no time. However carelessly she had answered, she did not believe her own words.

'You are a spoiled child, a petulant boy. Six, not twenty-six. We both understand how things are. I could bear it before I met you and we must both bear it now.'

'Why? Once this painting is done, come home with me and he can be damned. I may not be as rich, but I am richer than most, with every prospect of a great deal more. My star is rising, my country is as fine as this. Not only that but your beliefs are the same as mine. *Why* stay? Do you hold something back?'

'I said hush.' Speaking with finality, no longer his mistress but his master, she rose, leaned against a pillar and stared across the lawns towards the distant house. Half concealed by the gentle swell of the ground, only its upper windows were visible, sparkling like the string of table-cut diamonds she wore in her hair. A present from John, a priceless rope around her head that could too easily slip to her neck.

Just across those sere, landscaped lawns, he lay. She sensed him as powerfully as if he strode into sight with the untiring long steps he used when she first knew him. Then he walked for miles, his energy boundless, nor would he ever stop until he achieved his aim. He might be distant, but he was everywhere. Eyes burning, she searched for trouble, her narrow back turned so that Hendrik could not see her expression. 'I have told you I can bear it. If I can, so must you.'

She spoke to the sky, whose grey-blue haze off to the west threatened a late summer shower; spoke too to the smoke threading up from the chimneys in the wing behind the house. Preparations for supper were under way.

'Get up. If we delay longer, I will be missed.'

CHAPTER THREE

*W*as that true about needing to bear it, she wondered as her woman, Agatha, cut her out of her dress. Crace had not asked for her, though these days he sent messages at any hour of the night with unnerving frequency and deprived her of sleep.

Nor was it entirely true that she had borne it before. She was already sick of him when the painters arrived, but meeting Hendrik crystallised it. If he had not come, perhaps she could have gone on until Crace died. Now every moment was agony. That was the difference.

But she would just have to carry on, she concluded, lying at last in her high, sweet-smelling bed, drifting towards sleep. Once dawn broke in a few hours she would find an excuse to examine the ceiling and catch a glimpse of him, find a trumped-up reason to speak, however briefly. He came every second or third day, but there were ways of finding out which those were. Her girls gossiped about the handsome Dutchman, discussed his clothes, whispered about what outrageous thing he had said to one of them, and she encouraged them.

That he was an unstoppable flirt had not escaped her. There was even a rumour, quashed as she entered a room, that he had had the kitchen maid that past week. They said the maid had had no say in the matter and been left in a state, perhaps with child. But men as handsome as Hendrik could have whatever they wanted, she thought. If a servant attracted a master's attention, they got what they asked for. And the rumour, which she lost no time reporting to John, deflected attention from her own business. The kitchen girl, despite being as round as a pudding, with breasts like two unbaked dumplings, could never offer any competition. Hendrik was just letting off steam from his frustration at how little time he spent with her, so as far as she was concerned he could have all of them, one after the other. Enjoying this thought in a way John would punish her for, she fell asleep.

Carrying a covered lamp, Agatha approached the bed, her face tart. It was three in the morning and she had been roused out of the arms of her lover, one of Hendrik's assistants who slept in so they could start at dawn. Zenobia was awake before she reached her. There was no need to ask what the matter was. Silently, Agatha held out a robe.

When Zenobia returned less than an hour later, walking slowly, there was no need to speak then either. A glance was enough. Beneath the furred overgown draped round her shoulders, her night-gown was torn, a patch of blood on the back. Depressions on her neck looked like thumbprints and one cheek had been struck.

Agatha had the fire lit and hot water infused with calmative herbs brought to bathe the bruises. She knew a great deal about medicinal plants. Once the sleep-hazed servant left, she removed Zenobia's night-gown. Zenobia was able to lift her arms, though she winced. But when Agatha saw her back, she failed to smother a sound. Thank God the chambermaid had gone. Her mistress had been struck with more than a hand, one weal had broken the skin. Agatha drew a deep breath, pursed her lips and kept her eyes lowered as she washed and patted Zenobia dry. She smeared salve on the damaged part, trying not to cause further pain. Nor did she look directly into the face turned towards the licking flames, for she knew that if she did, she would speak out of turn. A servant had no right to comment on anything her master did. Whoever did that was dismissed, or worse.

She smoothed Zenobia's hair, brought a fresh linen gown, and lowered it over her head.

'Thank you.' Zenobia's voice was colourless, her face quite dry. She looked unblinkingly at the fire. 'You may go now.'

Agatha had been Zenobia's maid since her marriage to Theocritus Koros, shortly before the world knew him as John Crace. She had not served his first wife, Maria, who had had two sons, of whom the elder, Matthew, broke his neck while playing on a wall with his younger brother, Balthasar.

Balthasar was now at court, financed by his father – though the boy made light of this, as if gold stuck to him. As mud to a pig, thought Agatha. The young man blamed his father for his mother's death, for which lack of filial piety he could easily be disinherited. Two years before, in front of the King, he had declared that he never wanted to see his father alive again, except on that man's death bed. Had he been a day older than thirteen, and less ignored by Crace, which was the true source of the grievance, he would not have got away with it; but as things stood he would still inherit everything, bar what Crace set aside for Zenobia – unless she gave birth to the second son he tried so hard to produce. Agatha was sure that Balthasar understood the threat Zenobia posed very well.

Nor had she served Crace's second wife, who died after seven months, also in childbirth. The women who attended that lying-in had disappeared.

Agatha loathed her master. Zenobia knew nothing of this. It was important to be circumspect, for Agatha knew that the spies who reported her mistress's movements back to Crace would not hesitate to include her too, in which case she would never see her thirty-seventh year.

From the day she first saw Zenobia, she had belonged wholeheartedly to her and not to Crace. There was nothing she could do to change the instinct of her heart, for the girl moved her. Not just her beauty, but even more her spirit. Here, Agatha thought, observing the girl look so directly at men that they flinched, here is someone who might prove a match for that monster. In which case, in whatever business, she was entirely at her disposal.

Agatha quickly grasped the affair between Zenobia and the Dutchman, and from that moment her terror grew, for despite hiding it well, they did not hide it well enough. How could she tell Zenobia that her every movement was spied on and that, more jealous than a civet, Crace would kill for much less? Some of this she felt sure Zenobia must realise, but whether she understood the mortal danger she put herself and her lover in was another matter. These thoughts had agonised Agatha for the past month, but her position left her powerless to speak.

Yet the young woman's suffering enraged her so much that if anyone could have read her mind at that moment, they would have found it to be very black indeed.

CHAPTER FOUR

*F*ather and daughter were unusually quiet over supper. The magistrate had left, snatching his hat and cloak from Malkin's grasp as if the footman was an imbecile. Thomas's empty place at table cast a pall. Not even a piping-hot *fricassey* of spiced lamb with the promise of a syllabub to follow shook their despondency. Samuel had a soup plate of meat broth sent up to his brother, but Thomas had not woken since the morning, and it stayed untouched. The long oak table, fully inhabited with three persons seated and two serving, felt barren with one less body in the room.

Zenobia found it hard to swallow. Before supper, her father had spent fifteen minutes in his study with the disturbing magistrate. Unable to hear a word, she was out of her mind over what had passed between them. Unable to bear it any longer, she laid her heavy silver spoon beside the untouched dessert, whose nutmeg bubbles reminded her of Thomas's pocked skin.

'Shall you tell me over some brandy what the magistrate said, father? I know how anxious you are about uncle Thomas. You need to invigorate your spirits. You must not allow yourself to decline.'

Taking the small stemmed glass, its brimming bowl little bigger than his thumb, Samuel gave her an uneasy glance, as if he found it difficult to look at her directly.

'Did he – Magistrate Koros, that is – did he have anything further to impart?'

'He is in no doubt about the guilt of the creature in his charge,' Samuel began with an increasing frown. The small glass untasted, he gnawed a fingernail. Alarmed, Zenobia watched; for he kept his nails impeccable, so as not to snag priceless silk and ruin a garment worth as much as a house.

'He assured me that he will interview her tomorrow and bring matters to a swift conclusion . . .' Samuel tailed off and looked about as if for an escape route.

'Conclusion?'

'That she will hang at the first opportunity, which could be very soon.'

Zenobia clutched at her skirts. 'Hang? But as I asked the magistrate, is that not hasty, given that uncle is alive, and shall, I fervently hope, so continue . . . and that his lordship has not yet interviewed the woman . . . and that there has been no trial?' She struggled to keep her voice steady.

Although fairly sure that no one knew she had left the house, she was horrified to hear that Lily, whom she had liked, and who she was sure meant her no harm, might hang because of her. Worse, that nobody would lift a finger to stop such a miscarriage of justice, or even question it, because Lily was nobody: a worthless madam and a black one to boot. She was the only one who knew the truth, the only one who could save her new friend – even though, if uncle Thomas died, it might cost her own life.

'Why do you concern yourself with the matter?' Samuel was unusually terse. 'What can this harpy be to you? Nothing! It must be so. From what I can establish she is a person of the most vicious and degenerate sort, a reprobate, a leech who has made a career feeding on society. A bane, a curse that the world will be better off without. The mere mention of such a creature can only bring shame on your reputation.'

His face was scarlet. 'Whether or not my dearest brother, my only living flesh, dies – which I heartily beseech God he shall not – she is still guilty of the crime of attempted murder, is she not? Can there be any doubt? Pentreath will testify to her identity, in which case, should his lordship consider it so, he informed me that it may, at the pleasure of the jury, carry an identical penalty.'

At the careless way he spoke about Lily Boniface as if she was a piece of driftwood that he intended to snap and toss aside, Zenobia felt herself pale, her mind in ferment. The man before her was not the mild-tempered, kind-hearted father she knew. Her thoughts at once turned to the magistrate. He had poisoned Samuel's mind; sewn these fatal seeds.

Remembering what she had read about the law in long hours of study, Zenobia roused herself. Perhaps there was some gain to be had now. 'As I understand it, there must be an arraignment before there is a trial.'

She handed him his neglected glass as carefully as her shaking fingers allowed. If she spilled it, he would see her distress.

'Is that not what the magistrate said?' She was determined to bring Samuel back from wherever the other man had led him: 'That she must go before a grand jury, who may not even send her to trial? What if there had been some dreadful accident, or a robber entered the carriage, someone as yet unidentified?

'Even if she was in the carriage, what evidence is there that she tried to kill him? Might she not have fled in terror at the entry of an uncouth assailant, fearing the very situation you describe: that given her occupation; her colour; without supporters and with the automatic opprobrium of the world against her, she would be found guilty of a crime she did not commit, for which she would hang or even burn?'

At the mention of burning, Samuel emptied his glass at one go, which she had never seen him do, despite the small amount it held. He was a light drinker at the best of times. But although she had seen him tipsy on less, it was not the case now.

'Master Koros said you had a sharp brain. He expressed a considerable degree of admiration for your . . . how did he put it, promising depths. Only a man of great perception would grasp so quickly what I have long known; though hearing you speak it impresses me afresh. But my dear child, for that very reason, we may rely on him to judge aright in his own domain. Even were there a grain of truth in what you say, someone must be brought to justice, and the magistrate – the magistrate, no less! – is certain that that harlot is the culprit.'

With a softer expression, he put his hand to her cheek. 'Let me set your heart at rest on one point, to show you that he is a man of wisdom and consideration. When I told him about the inn Pentreath mentioned, he decided to send constables there at dawn, in case it throws any further light on the matter, before he interviews her. You see, child, he does not take matters lightly, but intends to investigate. Not many would do so much for one so worthless. In a case that involves my family, I consider it a mark of respect.'

Zenobia gulped her drink as soon as she had renewed his, glad that he was too distracted to notice her pour her own much fuller. 'The inn?'

'The place where Thomas evidently had an assignation to meet the vicious creature.' Samuel concluded placidly. 'Now, child, off to bed, it is very late. We must be at Thomas's side the moment he wakes. Let us not disturb him now, he is well attended, and Butter says he sleeps peacefully.'

As early light began to mitigate darkness and the first doomed cries of animals coming to market reached her ears, Zenobia sat awake as she had all night, tapers flickering and the shutters open. She had long ago learned to sleep through those desperate sounds, even with the windows closed tight, but now the dull, restless shuffle of the animals, their dismal groans evidence of a deep-seated foreboding of their imminent fate, chimed a sonorous chord with her own sense of doom.

The magistrate Koros: what did he really believe? Did he even care, as long as someone hanged and what he called justice was served? How could she let him try Lily for a crime she had not committed, when all Lily had done was to try to avert another crime; one whose likelihood she had foreseen? Lily was the only heroic person in this sorry tale.

During the past three days there had been little time to think about what had really happened. Now, bolt upright by the open window so as not to fall asleep, Zenobia tried to work out how she had ended up at the inn. She remembered being bundled out of a small carriage, which she was sure was the one Lily had sent her home in, for Lily's heavy scent, which Pentreath noticed, had been strong.

But how had she got into it? Now she recalled her terrible headache and the pot of chocolate. After that was a blank, until she was imprisoned at the inn. Now she thought about it, Samuel never sent her chocolate, but since Jane said it came from him, she had not questioned it. What if it had been drugged? And if so, since she was in Lily's carriage, had Lily done it?

Zenobia discarded the idea. Why would someone so determined to protect her against Thomas kidnap her? Perhaps to ensnare her in her own business; but Lily had argued vehemently against such a life. Zenobia scolded herself; even having the thought made her as bad as the magistrate and her father. She had believed Lily when she said it and she believed it now. She was sure that Lily was not to blame. Besides, how could Lily drug her without an accomplice? The answer must be closer to home, and the more she thought about it, the more obvious the answer: Thomas.

But that didn't explain why Lily's carriage had been there that morning – unless she was trying to send Zenobia a message, which she had promised to do.

Exasperated, Zenobia knew that the only person who knew the complete truth, who was responsible for this horrible muddle and could soon also be responsible for an innocent woman's death, was Thomas, sleeping peacefully nearby.

Just before dawn, still dressed, Zenobia went to her uncle's room and calmly told Mary, who was dozing next to the bed, to feed the fire and then go and rest.

She had never set foot in his room. Unwilling to go near the bed, in case he rose up and attacked her again, her heart beat so fast that she had to lean against the door. Faintly lit by two solitary candles, Thomas lay in a room stuffed with costly items. His bed hangings were blue camlet diapered with gold and silver. A table crammed with gold and crystal bottles glinted with gems and pearls, while an enamelled silver box spewed jewellery. His best wig was ready to powder on an ebony stand, and a large new portrait over the fireplace flaunted his newest suit. There was a pier glass even more costly than hers, and a small garderobe to one side. She saw no books, not even a Bible.

Among this opulence, Thomas lay comatose, on top of the linen because of his leg, waxen and wizened despite the roaring fire. In place of his wig, a cap rested on his too-large ears, emphasising the puny head on its weaselly neck. Thomas usually concealed his prominent Adam's apple with torrential lace. A big nightshirt of Samuel's engulfed him, the blood-soaked leg protruding from a neat slit, and a fur coverlet dozed at the end of the bed like a large folded ferret.

Never having seen him without a cake of powder and rouge, Zenobia had no more idea what he really looked like than of the colour of his hair. His skin was pocked and what hair he had was black. Strands protruded from the cap in uncombed tufts, and from his chin. With his eyes tight shut, purplish and sunken, and his usually painted lips deathly pale, he was a strange and horrible sight, a scrawny fledgling with its claws folded together on its chest – though clearly alive, for its beak was open, and a faint whistle came out of it.

Here was the man who had terrified her, so capable of harm, so bent on it. She looked at his bony blue hands and his dirty chewed fingernails with contempt.

Having observed all this and discovered that her heart had calmed, she took a deep breath. With the same strange feeling of observing herself that she had had in the carriage, she removed a small feather pillow from beneath Thomas's head, held it over his face – and then replaced it in a more comfortable position. Exhausted by a sleepless night, she sat in the chair, leaned back, closed her eyes, and fell into a deep slumber.

Moving slowly so that the creaking boards and the hasps of the trunk did not betray her, Zenobia retrieved the stained domino and shoes and folded them into a bundle small enough to carry beneath her cloak.

It was still early, just before six, when she crept down the stairs. Letting herself out of the front door, she headed towards Hatton Garden, where she knew, having extracted the information from her father, that magistrate Koros kept his establishment.

The lead-covered portico curving above the wide front door looked like the hooded head of an executioner, face bowed in deep shadow. Zenobia faltered. If she turned around and retraced her steps, no one would know she had ever left home. It was still only just dawn.

As she debated, the clear, still-cool air was pierced by warning bird cries. A sudden commotion erupted in a bush across the dirt track behind her and a one-eyed cat exploded from beneath it as a lark catapulted from the dark glossy foliage, rocketed upwards and blazed shrieking to freedom. Then it was gone. Hissing at Zenobia, the cat slipped back into the undergrowth.

Zenobia glanced at the barred basement windows. Somewhere in that dank recess, Lily was held captive. The windows were shuttered inside. Any hope of slipping into the house and finding a way to release her, which Zenobia had imagined on her journey, was crushed. She had been childish; that sort of thing only happened in plays. The only way to free Lily was a direct appeal to the magistrate. For although Samuel had been impervious to the way his eyes devoured her, she had not. Surely that look must mean she had some power.

She took a deep breath, mounted the scrubbed stone steps and lifted the heavy knocker. The thick ring, clamped in the iron jaw of a glowering sea monster, fell from her grip with a thud as forbidding as its owner. Such terror struck her that she almost turned away for the second time.

As the gonging head reverberated, its bronze face fixed in a snarl, she shivered. Everything about this man was imposing, from the newness of the stone pillars and the shine of his windows – each, it seemed, freshly washed, though all she could see through them were more closed shutters – to the gleaming floor as she was shown in by a footman, who surveyed her from a great height and asked her business.

Shrinking back into her cloak, aware of the bundle pressed to her side, she mustered herself.

'A matter for your master. Show me to him, or where I may await him.'

He led her to a hall chair, one of two crested rows as accusing as if they were jurors and she on trial. After a few minutes a second footman appeared and asked her to follow him upstairs.

Koros stood in the middle of his dressing room next to a glass on a stand. She caught her breath.

The high-ceilinged chamber was large and the scent of rosemary rose from polished oak boards. Deep-red silk damask figured with pomegranates covered the walls. As the footman opened the shutters one by one, it turned to blood where light skewed squares across it. As the shutters were folded back, colours sprang to life. At the far end an immense post bed began to glow. A bronze candelabrum on a chain gleamed from the ceiling. There was a Turkey carpet on a table and imperial-red bed hangings, black-edged, as imposing as their owner. His bleached white sheets were still unmade, as if he had leapt out to stand before her in his shirt and breeches, his cropped hair wet from a bowl over which a cloth had been tossed. On tall stands, his wig and robes reminded her of his importance. Profoundly dark with crimson-pink linings, the robes frightened her, while the grey heavy-bottomed wig, its curls carved from ashes, glowered, not caring whether they held his head or not. In these robes he could shorten her life to a hand-span.

What had she done in coming here? How could she have been so stupid? But it was too late now.

His right hand held an open razor. Carelessly, he did not move when he set eyes on her. A flash ran up and down the blade with a blinding slither.

She blinked but did not flinch. She had never heard of a wealthy man shaving himself. Her father, though expert with razor-sharp scissors, would never dream of such a thing. She took all this in at a glance as he waved the footman out. The man pulled the great doors to behind him.

Without turning, Koros studied her reflection with the same piercing look as the evening before. Strengthening sunlight made his eyes glow. 'Put back your hood,' he said, weighing the razor as if he weighed justice, whether to chop her head off or not. Through the mirror, light again seared the blade-edge. The way he held it so lightly was mesmerising. 'Show me your hair.'

She pushed the hood back, heart hammering in case he ordered her to take off the cloak as well. And God knew what else.

'Go over to the light and stand still. No, to the left. Yes, there, near the bed, very still, where I can see you. If you move it will distract me.'

The blade rasped against his chin. He took his time, seemingly looking only at what he was doing; yet she knew that he watched her reflected: the way she held herself, how the light bleached her hair white; made her eyes glitter blackly. Involuntarily screwing her face up against the glare, she determined not to look down, not to appear meek.

Chin up, she stared back. This was what it would be like to be brought before him, knowing that he held one's life and was so indifferent to it.

He placed the closed razor next to the bowl, patted his face with the cloth and threw it down, but still did not turn. Yet the robes and wig might as well have been him. If he put them on, everything would be lost.

'You delay me, but I will hear you,' he said, as if reading her thoughts.

He continued through the mirror. 'What have you come to tell me?' The unexpected question surprised her more than his wanting to see her hair and almost made her lose her resolve, but she steadied herself.

'Madam Boniface is innocent of my father's charge,' she replied. Quietly, but still keeping her eyes fixed to his through the glass, not daring to blink. 'She most certainly did not kill my uncle.'

'Ah.' Without warning he moved towards her, so that she found herself backing towards the bed. Then he is dead? Has he died?' he insisted, gripping her thin arms through the cloak. His hands burned through to her skin. For a second, she was sure he would throw her backwards and strip her clothes from her. As he grasped her she stiffened, aware of what was pressed to her side.

A change came over him. She tried to shrink into herself, but it was too late, his interest had shifted, his fingers discovered the bundle.

'What is concealed here?'

She brought it out slowly. Her pale green silk slippers, one toe brown with dry blood, fell to the floor. The domino flowered in her hands, a lustrous black poppy. She tried to gather it up, but he had already seen what it was, and took it, felt the blood-stiffened part, put the slippery silk to his nose and sniffed. As the stuff unfolded, Lily's warm attar, violet and civet scented the air, enclosing them. It clung like flesh, united them.

'I was wearing it,' she blurted, hardly caring what she said, for he bent over her, not blinking, concentrating so utterly that there might have been nothing in the world besides. The domino hung limp from his hand as if cut down fresh from the gallows.

'You,' he echoed. He dropped the domino. It lay between them like a stain. 'This means nothing,' he said.

'Sit.' He took her cloak from her shoulders and gestured towards a tilt table where food was laid. Small peaches, which she had never tasted, uncut black bread, and patted butter stamped with his monogram. The dozen white-and-red peaches on a blue-and-white platter must have been costly. It struck her that he lived in a singular way. He poured pale, watered wine into a glass whose double-twisted stem was so fine that she scarcely dared hold it in case it snapped.

'*You* wore it,' he repeated, separating each word to consider it from every angle. 'Explain.'

He took her glass back and drank it, even though her lips had touched it.

He did not look as old as he had the night before. His throat and chest showed under his still-open shirt, which he made no movement to fasten. He did not care whether he insulted her. Most certainly he was not like her father.

His chest gleamed, she saw the hard muscles. It reminded her of the carcasses of cattle hanging at the slaughter yards near Cow Lane, or piled on carts afterwards, jerking away to market, legs dangling. He looked as powerful as that, except that he was alive and only a few inches away.

'Madam Boniface sent it to me two days ago,' she forced out. 'I wanted to meet her and my uncle drove me to her house, to satisfy my curiosity. The next day, I was taken to an inn somewhere against my will.'

'An inn? Where?' Koros interrupted.

'I don't know,' she replied.

'Who drove you?'

'I do not know. The carriage was closed. They covered my face when they took me out of it.'

'They?' he asked.

She heard herself answer that she did not know that either. As she spoke, panic rose. This was how he tripped people up, how he turned words inside out and discarded them. It would be her fate, too, unless she kept calm. She could hear that he did not believe her. As she listened to her own breathy, high young voice, to what she had just said, she understood why, and fear ran through her with the cold scald of fire.

'You do not know where you went, you do not know who took you, yet you say without a shadow of doubt that your uncle was responsible.'

'Yes.' The taunt surprised her. She was even more surprised that, instead of going on, he peeled a peach as carefully as he had shaved, using a heavy steel-bladed silver knife that dwarfed the fruit. It was as if she had vanished. She watched the precise movements of his hands.

'I will ask you again.' Softer. He sliced and ate the peach, piece by piece, off the glinting steel, never taking his eyes from hers as soft morsels vanished between his lips: 'How do you know you were at an inn?'

He poured another glass of watered wine, but this time watched until she drank it, then refilled. She had never had wine in the morning, only small beer, but she did not dare disobey. She drank every drop.

'I heard voices and horses. I heard what people said.'

'Then?'

'Then they left me there.'

'Then?' There was no time to think.

'It grew dark and I was afraid. I was locked in a room. With a bed.' She could see the room clearly, but she could also see that he was about to ask another question, to interrupt again, not giving her the chance to make her story solid and true, so she rushed on, knowing that her voice rose in something like panic, but not caring, for she must be allowed to speak.

'Then I was asleep . . . and then my uncle rescued me. At least, that's what he said: that my life was in danger, that I might be killed or something much worse. He put me in his carriage. But then he began to do things that should not be done. Unseemly things.'

'Go on.' A husky sound in the magistrate's voice made her even more fearful.

'I shot him,' she concluded flatly, folded her hands in her lap and looked at them. She did not want him to see the tears that threatened to roll down her cheek.

He turned aside and drank another glass of wine, then another, as if it was a process of thought. The wine jug was mounted in silver, its handle the body of a crane twisted towards a long beak. The empty jug glittered.

He started to raise himself and from the way he moved she was afraid. She steadied herself.

Someone knocked at the door.

Though he ignored it, he settled back. Zenobia's heart pounded so hard she thought she would die. He took her hand. How insignificant it was, how he could crush her. She did not flinch. She must not.

'Let me see if I understand,' he said slowly, one finger just touching the skin of her thin wrist where the veins showed. 'You claim that the woman Boniface, a notorious whore, a blackamoor, did not shoot your uncle as your father states and the carriage driver corroborates, but that you did?'

He turned her hand to and fro. Lightly; yet she knew that if she withdrew, his grip would become iron, that if she was to make him believe her she must allow him to do whatever he wanted.

'With this very hand, you cocked and fired a heavy pistol into your uncle's body, with the intent to kill him?'

Tears blurred her eyes, she tried to see what he saw in her small hand, to stop them spilling.

'No!' Her voice surprised her as much as Thomas's pistol firing.

She tried to wrench herself away, but he had her fast. 'No! I just wanted to stop him. He was hurting me. I thought he would kill me.'

Still encased, her hand clenched like a musket ball.

'Very well: Your uncle attempted to molest you and in desperation you defended yourself. Is that it?'

'Yes,' Zenobia said dully.

He released her.

'Yes. Shall I hang?'

Theocritus Koros pushed back his chair and studied her, so lit by sunlight that she flared. Her eyes flashed; he noted that she forced herself to keep them open despite the stabbing brightness. The room was deathly quiet. Whoever had knocked had gone away.

'What a remarkable young woman,' he said. 'I told your father as much. Since I have been a magistrate I have seen many surprising things, some revolting, some clever, most idiotic. Human nature in all its forms, mainly too inconsequential to recall. I have watched men and women and learned the different ways they think and behave. The different ways in which they tell the truth and the many more different ways in which they lie. But I have never come across anything like you, who would throw her own life away for someone so entirely without worth. Your father is a fool to let you out of his sight. If you belonged to me I would lock you up so that no one else could set eyes on you. I knew you would be trouble.'

She said nothing.

His eyes moved over her, up from her slippered feet to linger at her bosom. 'May I take it – from what you say – that your uncle did not succeed in his aim?' His voice had become hoarse.

He peeled another peach with the stained knife, but the blade gouged the flesh. A lump of fruit dropped on to his breeches.

Three glistening drops of pink liquid like beads sank into the black damask. He threw a napkin across his leg, but she had seen.

'No, he did not,' she said firmly, beginning to understand, wishing she could run away, knowing that she could not, for if she did, Lily would certainly hang.

'No.' She repeated louder, so that there could be no shade of doubt. 'But he was determined to, I am certain of it. That is why I killed him.'

He walked to the window and sat on the sill, legs out, square-toed shoes enormous, studying her from further off, but still as if he thrust himself against her.

'You did not kill him.' He dismissed her in a level voice. 'You did not kill him and you know you did not,' he repeated, as if convincing himself.

He looked out once more and the look turned into a stare. When he spoke again, all emotion had vanished and his voice was as cold as steel.

'You dare come here with this absurd claim, to save the life of a person you scarcely know. You even bring the very garment she wore to commit the crime. By all accounts she is nobody, nothing. Were the object of your misguided attempt of any quality whatsoever, your action could seem almost admirable. But she is not, and furthermore it is not true. Everything you have said this morning is a lie.'

'But –' Zenobia heard panic in her voice, but he talked over her. 'You want to believe these lies because you are young and innocent. You have no idea of the horrible danger you put yourself in. *Do you understand*,' he ground out, a raw edge sawing at his voice, 'that if I accept your words I should be obliged to put you before the sessions? You would be at the Old Bailey within a week. The grand jury is not interested in what you claim that your uncle tried to do, the fevered imaginings of a spoiled child playing games. You even admit that you have not been hurt – so what do you complain of? That is how the jury will see it. A jury deals with facts, and the facts are plain: you shot your uncle. That is what you will say, for you freely admit it. Do you even begin to grasp what the penalty for that would be, how deadly the game you are playing is?'

'Sir, it is no game!'

He silenced her with such a violent pass of his hand that it was as if he struck her down. 'Thank God I know the truth. This Boniface is well known and not only in Covent Garden. That is by no means the compass of her activities. Her misdemeanours are substantial and the house she runs disreputable, whether your uncle backs her or not. She is a parasite on society. You should never have gone there. It was inevitable that something of this sort would happen to one as unprincipled, as abnormal, as that woman. She gave your uncle the pistols. She had them made and knows how to use them. She owns an identical set. While your attempt to take on her crime is noble, particularly given your age and sex, it is foolhardy, and all it does is confirm her guilt. She will go to Newgate this afternoon and thence before the grand jury at the next quarter sessions. There is no doubt in my mind that they will find against her, either on a charge of attempted murder or of murder itself. In either event, given that your uncle was her protector, the outcome will be the same. She may burn for this. Jurors do not take kindly to such a simulacrum of *petty treason*.'

He got up and started to push her backwards, and his voice deepened. 'Now, as for you –'

But before he could finish the sentence, as her spirit sank so low that she could scarcely hold herself upright, sure that she would faint, there came a much louder knocking, and a footman entered without permission.

'Your lordship.' The man bowed to avoid the hideous scowl on Koros's face. 'It could wait no longer, lordship. The prisoner has escaped.'

'And you delayed telling me, you *imbecile*!' Koros roared. The look he gave the man was enough to kill him. 'Run for the constables. You are stupid but fleet; I will deal with you later. Send Petter to Master Severin, the royal tailor. Tell him his daughter is here and that I will send her home in my chair. Go, before I kick you all the way to Chick Lane.'

When the terrified servant had fled, Koros turned back to Zenobia. Though rage flared across his face, she knew that for the moment she was safe from harm.

'I will not allow myself to believe that you came here to distract me while my prisoner escaped, nor that you are an accomplice – even though you may have intended her to wear the garment you brought as a disguise.'

He put his heavy hand up once more as Zenobia, astonished by the false accusation, opened her mouth.

'Not one more word. You have caused enough trouble. Thank God in Heaven that you came to me before blurting this nonsense to your father, when it would have been harder to save you from the consequences.'

She bent to pick up one of her dropped slippers, then thought better of it.

'May I go now?' She was more exhausted than she had ever felt.

The request appeared to distract him. For a split second she glimpsed indecision under the rock-like surface. Then it was gone and he was invincible once more. 'Home . . . yes. You will go back to your father, for now. *For now*,' he repeated, violently ringing for a footman to take her to the sedan that waited in the side entrance, ready to take him anywhere day or night. He scribbled a note and gave it to the man with strict instructions to hand it only to Master Severin.

'I will call on your father this evening. Make sure you are there to receive me once I have spoken with him, for be in no doubt but that it concerns you closely.'

He bowed curtly, turned his back, and began to enrobe.

CHAPTER FIVE

*I*t took Koros half an hour to find what he was searching for among all the discarded furniture and piled-up trunks. He had not been in the attic since the house was built a decade earlier. Spanning the immense five-bay building, it comprised one huge room, its steeply angled eaves punctured by dormer windows on both sides. Had the house been smaller, the servants would have lived here. The space was in neat, though dusty, order. He opened several trunks before finding the right one, of faded hide, and smaller than he remembered.

Obscured by two other boxes, pushed under a casement, the trunk was smothered in dust. Paying no heed to his clothes, he knelt and felt along the metal rim that bound its hinged lid. Fingering his way round, at last he removed a small key and inserted it in the lock.

The trunk's black-painted interior held papers that he tossed back one by one, until he came to a parchment folder. Bound to the set of deeds inside was a faded letter tied with a ribbon, the seal long broken. Throwing the other papers carelessly back in and relocking the trunk, he sat down in a rush-bottomed chair and opened it.

A small oblong of parchment fell from the folded letter, an ink drawing of a naked black woman with high breasts, done with skilful pen strokes. Neat cross-hatching modelled her protruding belly and round thighs. Her elbows and knees were dimpled; there were small plain rings in her ears, and some sort of collar round her neck. She held an infant in the crook of her arm. A few lines of minute writing had been carefully inscribed beneath her with the same pen.

Flicking the drawing to and fro, Koros peered out of the window. Through thick dirt, four pigeons sunned themselves on the leaded parapet, their plumage the same lead colour, touched here and there with opalescent pink. The one cooing loudest bulged its iridescent neck out and waddled on top of another.

Koros rose, stooped to avoid hitting his head on a beam, ripped the head off the drawing and tucked it into his watch pocket. Crumpling the remainder, he tossed it on the floor and strode from the attic.

The moment his shoes had clumped to silence, a curious tremor passed over a dingy calico cloth that covered the triangular bulk of a spinet opposite, then the cloth moved aside a cautious half inch. This subtle movement could easily have been overlooked. After a pause, in which throbbing noises continued from beyond the window, a small hand slipped out and pushed the cloth back, and Lily crawled from beneath the instrument.

Careful not to knock anything over, she listened intently, every muscle alert. Her shorn hair was covered with a lilac night-cap and she still wore the now-filthy linen shift she had been arrested in, along with shoes and stockings that a servant had thrust into her hands as the constables dragged her away.

Cat-like eyes narrowed, head down, strained for danger, she continued to listen. Satisfied, she relaxed on her haunches and looked about. After gently removing her shoes, she padded over to the hide trunk, picked up the crumpled paper, and examined it. She smoothed and folded it three times, tucked it carefully in one shoe, and put the pair neatly on the chair that Koros had so recently vacated. 'My foot on your arse, you bastard,' she murmured.

Opening one trunk, then another, much as he had done, she soon found one full of discarded clothes that had been folded and interspersed with now scentless lavender. From it she selected a pair of old-fashioned breeches to fit a twelve-year-old boy and a coat to match. Plain-cut, grey, the everyday suit was badly worn. There was also a shirt, patched at the armpits where sweat had rotted it, of similar size, with a launderer's mark, MK, in fine stitches in the neckband. She could find no stockings; her own soiled ones would have to do. There was also a pile of folded chintz bandanas from which she selected the four plainest.

Dressing quickly in this suit, she rolled and tied a bandana round her neck, set her neatly folded shift at the bottom of the pile and soundlessly closed the trunk. Padding back to the chair, brushing at the floorboards with her cap to blur any footmarks, she tied her buckled shoes – for the morning of her arrest she had planned to ride – inside one bandana, and twisted two more into a strap. Fixing this crosswise over her chest to hold the shoes against the small of her back, she unfastened the casement window, stepped on top of Koros's trunk and eased herself out. She pushed the window shut smartly behind. As she had hoped, the catch slipped back into place.

The parapet stretched the full width of the house, and her window was close to the place where Koros's roof connected to that of the neighbouring house, which, being less important, was set a good six feet lower. Since Lily stood just under five-foot tall, she looked down with calculating interest from her crouched vantage point.

This smaller house also had a pitched roof with dormered casements, but a narrower parapet and gully. Not as wide as its grander neighbour, the building only had three windows. Though she would have preferred to wait until nightfall, she did not dare, for surely Koros would order a search at any moment.

There were still few people about and no carriages. Only the stone coping stood between her and a sheer plunge to the new pavement far below, where one or two tiny people moved. If she missed her footing there would be a horrible mess. Never afraid of heights, Lily continued to appraise the scene calmly.

Not looking down again, holding on with strong fingertips, she eased over the stone ledge, hoping that her toes would find the lower parapet. But it was not the case. Unable to pull herself back up, telling herself that it was far better to die quickly here than on Koros's rope, encouraging herself that it could only be a matter of inches, she uttered a brief prayer and dropped. In that moment, though falling less than a foot, she knew what it was like to hang, and vowed never to let it happen. Her landing was awkward; for a terrifying moment she staggered backwards, off balance, arms flailing, sure she would ricochet to the pavement; then her fingers found the coping behind her. She righted herself and crouched quickly down once more.

Elated, panting, dirty, Lily rested while her heart calmed and her breath steadied. And waited to see if any feet thundered up the stairs: but there was only silence.

'Oh, it would surprise you to see me now, you monster,' she muttered again, grinning to herself. Turning adroitly in the narrow space, she inched towards the first of the neighbour's three attic windows.

Just as in Koros's house, they were only lightly fastened. Peering round the frame of the first, she saw a servant's bedroom. Three narrow beds with thin blankets, tidily made; otherwise the room was empty. From a pair of boots by the closed door she supposed it to be the bedchamber of footmen. However, the window was latched and would not give.

She crawled onwards to the middle window. Rotting leaves made the gully wet and slimy, and the knees of her new suit were sodden. This window also belonged to a servants' chamber, this time with two beds. As she pushed and pulled at the fastening, she froze. The door opened and a maid entered, laughing to someone behind. Dropping flat on her stomach, Lily wormed gingerly along the gulley, praying that neither had seen her. To her horror, the latch above her back was undone. She pressed her body flat into the foul lead. 'Gorn, chuck, it out!' a voice cried. The window pulled to again, there was silence. Lily inched along, her legs now soaked in urine. The whole parapet smelled of piss. Her own servants must do it too, she reflected, nose full of the stench, rather than carry slopping pots down to empty in the yard.

Using her elbows, she worked her way grimly to the final window, which gave on to an empty small room. It was her last hope, and it was barred.

There was no house beyond and no other window to try. Ignoring a lurch of despair, she turned back doggedly and crept to the middle window once more. The maids' room was now empty and its casement had not been properly latched. Prising it open, she clambered in.

The room led to a corridor that spanned the back of the house, with stairs at one end and a door with 'Fire' painted neatly on it at the other. Opening this a crack, she saw a storage room and a small, bolted door that she hoped led to a way to the ground. But just as her inspection was complete, several voices rose up the stairs at the other end. She dashed across the room, wrenched the door, swung out on to the wooden platform, leapt on to the ladder and pulled the door to in the nick of time.

Gripping the ladder's thin iron bars, she descended rapidly, noiselessly, to the courtyard below. If anyone looked up now, her fate was sealed.

Crouching in the patchy shadow of young trees, Lily caked her silver-buckled shoes with manure to hide their gleam. Her clothes reeked, but there was nothing to do about it. Having taken bearings from the sun she set off, eyes downcast as befitted someone so lowly. Her heart heaved with jubilation as well as fear as she picked her way slowly east. She planned to skirt round the Wall, then cross Moor Field, to just beyond the Auld Gate, before heading south and losing herself in the cut-throat anonymity of Wapping. It would be a long day.

Her greatest fear was passing through Chick Lane on her way to Barbycan. She crept past Zenobia's house with her head tucked into her chest, knowing that she might be recognised and seized at any moment. But it was still early, and even when a black leather sedan stopped outside Severin's and the runners helped a young woman out, who stumbled with exhaustion on the steps, no one paid attention to the grubby lad in his hand-me-down suit, frayed bandana in place of a collar, shrinking against the walls on the other side of the street like a snivelling shadow. Many grand houses employed such novelties to run errands – toys, they were called, whether boys or girls, usually imported from the West Indies, chosen for their looks. If they grew up handsome, they might become footmen or maids, but most worked as dogsbodies until they were thrown out or were returned to the plantation that had sent them. Most never saw eighteen.

CHAPTER SIX

*I*n a clump of abject dwellings in the midden of streets north of the magistrate's mansion in Hatton Garden and of Severin's in Chick Lane, a dilapidated printer's shop clung to life in a dingy yard off Mutton Lane. Tall, narrow buildings either side enclosed the narrow yard further. As night approached and the shadows lengthened, Knapp's Yard was a pathetic, tumbling, defeated place. Human and horse dung hung thick on the hot air. The stench rose from packed dirt between the inhospitable houses to compete with the smell of rotting vegetables, all jumbled into the acid bite of poverty.

Sunk so deep in boiling intention that he was oblivious to his surroundings, Koros stamped through the squelching muck as if he would crush its neck. Closely wrapped in his customary dark cloak, his broad-brimmed hat low over his brow, no one recognised the illustrious magistrate who had just walked to the yard from Chick Lane, but he certainly recognised the place.

Rusted stairs like a starved horse's ribs clung to the building at the far end. Off an iron platform at the top, a peeling wooden sign stuck out over a nondescript door on which faded but tidy letters said: Joachim Knapp. Printer.

The bell jangled a lurching, pathetic sound.

It was searing hot under the eaves. Knapp put down his loaded stick of type beside the cage, wiped his hands on the flanks of his doublet and with ink-stained thumb and forefinger brought the scrap of paper up to his nose.

'It appears typical rather than actual.' He studied the small pen drawing of an African face dubiously. His voice creaked from little use, but there was intelligence in it. 'Does it resemble the party . . . ?'

Koros's face silenced him. The magistrate pulled a bag of coin from his breeches to bulge on his palm like a toad. 'Will you do it or not?'

Thin and pale from long, unsociable hours, Knapp's face took on a faint look of irritation, but he buried it as soon as it came. He ran bony fingers through his lank hair. His moulting wig hung on a peg on the black-spored back wall. He could not afford to turn work down and they both knew it. Knapp had been a gambler as long as Koros had known him, though these days he stuck to cocks and dogs rather than cards. Koros owned the freehold that had once been his, not only to the print shop but the entire yard. He often threatened to sell it and turn Knapp out to rot.

Before he had lost everything, a bright future had stretched ahead: hopes of a wife, children, happiness. The thought came unbidden now, as it frequently did. What a fool he had been. Just one toss of the dice twenty years ago; his unborn child's lifetime ago. That was all that ruin took. He sighed. His stomach hurt. It only hurt when Koros was nearby. Mustering a vestige of remembered dignity he took the drawstring purse without looking inside. But against his will his hand was shrewd. He weighed it. It was no more than the going rate, which added to his burden of gall, but there was no choice but to accept. His printers, working in the shaded light beyond, must be paid. The magistrate might as well have fucked him, he thought; the disgust would be the same. He had fucked so many one way or another, that was his reputation. What difference would one more make? The pouch disappeared somewhere in his rusty-looking garments.

At an ink-grained worktable, Koros caught up Knapp's pen as if it was his own. He drew strength from owning people as a leech from blood. His arm moved rapidly. In the otherwise silent room the scratching nib was a torturer striating flesh. 'Here, the words.' He crossed and rewrote one, a firm line beneath it.

'Tomorrow, at dawn – throughout the city, mind, and make sure they are thorough in the east – I shall see that face everywhere I turn, or you will find yourself looking for new premises. And believe me, Knapp, I will turn.'

Knapp did not doubt it.

Koros indicated the three other men. 'Get these shiftless creatures out into God's air to do some real work for once.'

They did not look up under the insult. One, hunched over a smaller press, hunched further; the compositor's fingers kept moving at the same even pace; while the proofreader, the thick-rimmed spectacle that pinched the bridge of his nose making an inflamed mark, continued to squint at a still-damp proof-sheet by the light of two caged candles. No flame was ever left unguarded here, for fire was their greatest terror.

As old as Koros and as poor as Knapp, the men's lives depended on the magistrate as much as their master's, perhaps more. They listened without seeming to. Rage and destitution are unhappy workmates.

Knapp bowed. If he could have killed the man in front of him, if he had only had the guts, he told himself he would have done it. What would it take? A dagger, yes; but surely even a humble compositor's rule, loaded with type, brought down hard on the back of the head with a lifetime of pent-up rage behind it, would do the trick? For a gilded moment, this happy vision blocked out the dingy room, the hundreds of sheets of printed paper drying on thin, taut ropes on pulleys above their heads, and his own feeble body swinging from a tree. Maybe even if that happened it would be worth it. He would die a man. The man standing before him had sapped and sucked him, destroyed him. Blood surged in his head, then quieted.

He must set and stamp the bill as quickly as possible, while some vestige of natural light still hung about the room. Ignoring Koros, he beckoned over the smallest of the other men to make the woodcut and waved him back to his desk with the scribbled paper.

With a final effort, he shook himself into a semblance of professionalism. 'Of course. All shall be done as you desire.'

CHAPTER SEVEN

*A*s the afternoon lengthened towards dusk, the Ratcliffe Highway was busy, thronged with curious faces. Having crossed the city, skirted the Tower and headed east again along East Smithfield until it turned into the Highway, Lily was desperate to turn south as soon as she could, to lose herself in the maze of slums and docks of Wapping. From the length of time she had spent tramping, the position of the sun and the increasing screech of gulls, she felt fairly sure of her direction. At last, when she had all but given up hope of reaching the river by nightfall, picking her way along the north flank of scrubby pasture-land where incurious cows lay belching in the heat, she veered right, down Old Gravel Lane. A chandler assured what he took for a mud- and sweat-streaked boy that he was heading towards the river.

Wapping seethed. Those in transit; scroungers; bottom-scrapers tied to menial work around the docks; as well as plenty hiding from the law: this teeming ribbon of restlessness roiling along the wide river's bank welcomed and hid dregs and sinners alike. Indians, Malays, Tartars, Chinese and blackamoors swilled and shifted in its grit and sand. If only she could merge in and rest a while, at first light she would pay for a passage down-river; small boats swarmed at all the steps to hop from one to another.

But first, she had to sleep. Her feet were bleeding from tramping for hours on end and her body ached all over. She normally never went further on her own feet than the mounting block at Bedford Street when her dapple was brought round. Limping drew unwelcome attention. She had thrown away the torn stockings, bloodied at the heels, and picked out a stick from a hedgerow, quickly stripping the leaves. She didn't fancy her chances if she stayed outside. While she could fend for herself in Covent Garden, it was not the same dressed as a poor boy in a place where all tastes were catered for and all crimes ignored. Once darkness fell, anything could happen.

At the first opportunity, she had exchanged her silver buckles, rubbed clean, for a sum now tied against her stomach with two bandanas. The warm coins were reassuring against her skin. She'd been lucky to get anything, she thought grimly, glancing about cautiously for a sign for a room. Had they been snatched from her grasp, had she been accused of stealing them, where would she be? She had got far less than their worth, but at least she was still free. Now, instead of the useless buckles, a string-tied packet in her elbow held a faded, patched servant's skirt and a jacket that would just about fit. There was a pound of black bread, too. She had not eaten all day; she had not dared to stop.

Where Gravel Street turned into Wapping Wall and the gulls shrieked over a caul of fish entrails spattered on the nearby wharf, she noticed a paper propped in a basement window that said 'Beds.'

Outside a mean, narrow house in a row of equally nasty houses constructed of timber and lath sat a person of indeterminate sex and age. Each overhanging first storey vied with its neighbours in dereliction. These pitiful structures had been beyond the rage of the fire.

In a once-dark hat, the weather-beaten person sat by an open, planked door whose bottom was rotted to a fringe. A stained clay pipe was clamped in its yellow jaw, artfully lodged between the muddy gap in two brown teeth, as if the tide had gone out and left markers.

'A bed for the night. How much?' Lily dropped her voice and jerked her thumb at the sign.

The woman, for by her voluminous skirts so she was, peered out of half-closed, milky eyes buried among scarred, shining flesh, pink and yellow where the pigment was missing. Lack of lashes and eyebrows added to the shock of her face. She extended a tobacco-stained hand, which Lily, trying not to shudder, took.

Dry fingers held her own as she failed not to shrink. 'You sound young. Young hands, too. Not used to labour. Pure white, ain't they, I dare say? Snowy?' The voice sounded wistful.

At Lily's silence she paused, still holding tight, then raised her face. Lily stared at the almost closed blank eyes submerged in their blistered web of skin and wondered if any light lay at the bottom, whether they saw anything at all.

'I'll have no trouble here,' the old woman continued flatly as if nothing was amiss. 'Nor women, neither. Penny on your own, ha'penny to share.'

Inserting the exorbitant sum into the bone-dry cup of a hand, Lily slipped past and went along the filthy hall towards the stairs to the basement.

She woke to howling gulls. The sparkling gauze of mist had already evaporated from the glittering river, its ruffled waters threaded with row boats serving ships chained midstream, tethered ducks fattening for the table. Exhausted from walking, she had overslept, for though there were two beds, the other had lain empty all night, the house silent. Lines of white fire now blazed between the shutter-cracks.

Any chance of slipping out under cover of early morning darkness and buying passage down-river was gone.

Cursing her stupidity, she leapt fully dressed off the straw mattress, caught up her bundle of clothes and climbed the narrow stairs to the hall, past the bolted back door on the turn.

Short of the head of the stairs she pulled up sharp. Round the turn, the wide-propped street door sent a carpet of light towards her. Lily shrank into the shadows. Outside, black against the morning dazzle, were not only the dirty skirts of the blind woman in her chair, but two sets of strong calves wearing coarse boots, a pair of stout sticks idling patterns in the dirt next to them.

She recoiled, but listened as intently as if her life depended on it.

'Have you seen this face, you foul old devil? Anyone like it here?' Demanded one pair of dark-stockinged legs. It was the voice of authority, of a watchman.

'How can *I* see, you puffed-up, pea-balled bleeder,' the landlady countered with scathing contempt. 'Can't *ye* see that I'm stark blind? Gaze into these fine darting eyes and eat your hearts out, my stout-stockinged fellow. Oh, what I could do with a pair of thighs like that. No. I don't allow no women here, there's on'y a lad on board, and that no more'n a child. Don't take my word for it, go and see for yerselfs, if ye've nothing better to do. He was out cold last time I looked in on him. He won't hurt a fly, he couldn't bugger more'n a midget.

'Leave me this fine paper if you like. I'll enjoy smoking it. Tossers,' she spat loudly at their departing backsides.

Lily stayed motionless on the unswept turn of the rotten stair for a lifetime. In the gloom beside her the yard door was bolted top and bottom with great, rusted bolts that looked as if they had never tasted oil. She had taken a good look when she came in, in case of the need to escape. If only she had drawn them then. If she tried to ease them now, the woman would hear them grate. Maybe she would call the watchmen back, too.

She took a firm breath and sauntered out of the front door.

The old woman was settled back in her oak rocker as if she had slept there. Head back, shapeless man's hat pulled forwards against the sun, only now with a bloodied gull feather tucked into it at a rakish angle. One hand held her pipe from which smoke drizzled, its chewed, broken end dirty amber. In the other, clawed in her lap, arthritic knuckles clutched a bit of paper. She had fallen asleep. Lily started to walk silently past.

'Not so quick my lad, is it? Keen to go and see Execution Steps, ain't thee? Wait a while. Take a look at this with those fresh young eyes of yours.'

She jerked up and caught hold of Lily's grey breeches, pulling her towards her. '*Sounds like* it tells of a runaway. They're on the hunt, those fuckwits. Read it to me, there's a good lad.'

Shoving the paper forward, she grasped Lily's arm between wrist and elbow and flapped one side of the hat's brim up to reveal a hairy wrinkled ear.

The parchment in Lily's shaking fingers was only a little longer than her hand. Below the stark **REWARD** was a crude woodcut of a black woman's face, which might just as well have represented the head of a round, shining beetle. The size of a small nut, it had been drawn at speed and quickly printed, for the cheap blackish ink was smeared and blotted, and still gave off a strong odour.

Below that, Lily slowly read out, so quiet and halting that in the salty air her words were hard to catch:

+++

A *substantial REWARD* is offered
***for information* Leading to the Capture of Felon**
and *Murdereff*
LILY BONNYFACE
Self-titled African *Princess* and Undoubted *Harlett*,
Laft seen in The Hatton Garden
at Six of the Clock on the Firft of this Month.
Any Perfons aiding or abetting the Said *Boniface,*
Shall they also be *Apprehended*
and Tryed for MURDER

+++

So close to the bottom edge of the paper that the tiny words almost missed it, in the smallest letters that could be struck, was printed, as it had to be by law, the name of the sponsor of the bill. Had Lily not had excellent eyesight she would have struggled to make it out. Above the name of the printer, Joachim Knapp, there were two names: *By the order of Master Samuel Severin and Magister Koros.*

✣

'Murderess, eh!' the woman interjected, her gravelled voice keen, as Lily faltered for a split second before going on.

The old skin flushed in hectic blotches.

'Aiding and abetting, is it,' she added, piercing as a gimlet, almost triumphant.

But as Lily finished, hardly able to breathe, knowing that if anyone passed and saw her stricken face now, in men's clothes or not, then all would be up and her life as good as over, the other woman's voice suddenly changed.

Low, hoarse, almost gasping, the words came fast. 'But wait on a moment. *Koros*, did you say? Repeat that word to me, child. Take your time over it, so there can be no mistake. Spell out the letters, one by one if you will. *Magister* Koros, did you say? K-O-R-O-S?' Her fingers clutched and clasped as if she did not know what she did.

'An odd name to be sure,' she muttered. 'A rare one, indeed it is. Very rare. Koros. Koros. Indeed.'

The paper was crumpled into a small lifeless ball in Lily's hand. Struck down with the terrible import of what she had just read, the smoking danger her life was in, the other's words registered only dimly.

'Pasting them things up all about, they are,' the old woman continued, a little stronger, rearranging her hat as if a fit had passed, setting the feather upright, like a mast.

'While you were at your good young sleep there with your bundle against ye, I heerd them at it, clattering up and down with their pails, boasting to each other. This *Koros*, and the other one whose name is marked down there, whatshisname; slavering they were, how they wants to get this Bonny-person very bad indeed: yes, *very* bad, I'd say – wouldn't you agree, child?'

The scarred eyes swivelled, the old head crooked so far sideways on its wrinkled neck that surely one small push would snap it off.

'*Very* bad.' The voice went on more thoughtfully. 'But it don't mention what the reward is? They seem to be keeping that to themselves, for now. More's the pity.'

It was all Lily could do not to rip herself away and run for her life, but instinct told her that her only chance was to stay where she was. The aged voice held a quality she could not fathom, but which seemed to be saying something else. Besides, the shock of what she had just read, the certain knowledge that she was being hunted for murder with a price on her head, hunted by the magistrate, along with Thomas's brother Samuel, when she had no idea who she was meant to have murdered, let alone why, made it impossible to move.

During the brief time she had spent in the magistrate's house, no formal charge had been brought, and when she asked the arresting constables what it was, they laughed in her face and said *she knew full well*, so she assumed that she had been dragged to Hatton Garden for procuring. It had happened before, and the terms of release included service in the magistrate's bed. Throughout the city from the Strand to Holborn, his appetite was known to everyone in her line of business. To be taken in by him could mean many things, but usually included satisfying him personally before being flung out again. Koros never paid for it. Yet, when she was manhandled into his basement and saw the barred windows, and heard the stout door slammed and locked behind her with the weighty turn of a strong iron key, which had never happened before, she knew that something was very wrong indeed.

Had she had not been so deft at picking locks she might have learned the charge against her; but from the tenor of this handbill it was one she would not care to face. She shuddered and pushed that thought aside. Whoever she was supposed to have killed, whatever nonsense this was, would have to wait. Because one thing was certain: her life was in very real danger.

'Sit by me a moment.' Breaking into her thoughts, the old voice forced her to pay attention. 'There's a little stool just in there, in that parlour to the side. You won't run off now, will you, and leave an ancient body all alone? Yes, that's the one. Settled, are ye? Now then, what do you make of it all, my boy? I told them there was nobut here but a youngster, scarce more'n a child, a lamb, no bother to anyone. Did I do right?'

Crouched low on the stool, hidden from the street by the old woman's skirts, shrinking behind her as much as possible, Lily lifted the flaps of her stolen doublet and slowly unknotted the fold of coins around her waist, never taking her eyes from the profile above. The square of jaunty printed cotton held everything she had in the world, and every hope, too, for without money there would be no escape down-river.

At the unmistakable chink, albeit dimmed by cloth, the cocked ear cocked further and the rheumy eye narrowed with what, in anyone who could see, would be a dreamy look.

'Yes. Indeed, you did right by me, madam,' Lily murmured, accustomed now to the strangeness of the deformed face.

One by one, she pressed each coin into the cupped hand that magically appeared again. She noticed that most of the little finger of the woman's right hand was missing, as if it had been sheared off. She watched the old fingers feel the coins, then bury them in her lap.

Without haste, making sure that nobody was abroad to see, Lily continued counting.

'Is that all?' Bright and sharp, with the hard ring of intelligence that she had noticed at the very first.

'Understand that I don't care nothing for the law. Less than nothing. I despise it, just as it once despised me. It brought me to this place and this situation, unfairly and unjustly. Oh, Lawd knows how I despise it. But even worse than that, I don't care to be cheated. I've a horror of it, a passion. And I don't care to be involved in no abetting, neither, not at my age. I'd sooner abet the devil to trounce those benighted God-rotten carcasses, but I won't abet unwilling, and that's a fact. Nor won't I swing for no other person, neither. You follow, child?'

'Yes.'

Still huddled on her stool, Lily glanced quickly down the long street in case the watch was anywhere in sight. She sensed there was more of the story to come and decided to hear it. Besides, the old woman could still yell to frighten the dead, so where could she run to? Not thirty yards before she would be brought down in the dirt like an animal, her back stamped on. Men like those stopped at nothing. The reward would see to that. They both knew it.

'If you are sure that is all,' the woman continued in the same intense tone, 'then pour us a good measure of this' – a flat, dark, stoppered bottle appeared from deep inside her half-undone stays as if from the hold of a ship – 'and I will tell you something worth hearing.'

'My given name is Elizabeth,' she began, 'but I have not heard it spoke for a long, long time. I have lived around here all my life and expect to die here.'

Smacking her lips, she held out her emptied blue glass. 'When I was a girl, my father imported and sold fine stuffs, mostly silk, though I have never worn it. We had a better house than this, just up there. There was a counter. And a yard, with a fine mulberry tree.' She indicated the way Lily had come, towards King Street. 'He worked hard. My two brothers helped him and I helped my mother. Our family thrived. When I was near thirteen, my father had made enough to move closer to town, and we was about to do so. All our goods were packed and loaded, ready to set off fine and early in the morning. He had chosen a house not far from St Botolph, near Aldgate Without. It was to be a new beginning. I was excited; we would trade with a better sort there. My elder brother had married some years since and moved to York, where he built a flourishing business, but Edward stayed at the docks with us. We both lived at home. It had long been understood that he would take over from my father. Everything was arranged. In a better house, I hoped to make a good match, perhaps with a silk mercer, for I had an eye and feel for the business and fancied that given encouragement I might even make a pattern drawer.

'I will never forget the morning we moved. It dawned as bright as today. We was all up at the crack, with a loaded handcart as well as a horse-drawn one. Edward took the handcart and set off on foot, for he was lusty and bold, and that morning he sang for joy. My parents and I clambered into the other one and followed. Edward soon fell behind. He waved cheerfully at me where I sat right at the back, dangling my legs without a care in the world. I loved my brother as dear as my own life. He was so handsome and strong that he gladdened the heart of any girl. But that was the last time I saw him like that.'

Despite her problems, or perhaps to escape them, Lily was drawn by the throb in the old voice. 'What happened?' she asked, refilling the greasy tot glasses, misted and bubbled as their owner's eyes. Her bread was long gone, she had had no breakfast, and now she had no money to get any. There was little to do but to sit and listen and drink the numbing gin, hidden for now behind those dark skirts.

'He was pressed. By sods just like those two, in a gang. Could've been those bastards' fathers. They'd seen him toiling with the cart and come up on him, behind him most like. At sixteen he was a fine figure, of middling height but so broad of shoulder you could of built a house on him. Made to last he was, like a bridge. Despite his load, he was striding out, proud to show his strength to any as cared to see. He made himself a sitting duck. I heered of what happened. That was all. Heered it from them as saw with their own eyes that those bastards saw him and took him. Took the goods too, the most vallible things we had. All the heavy furniture was on the cart, and all the lighter, littler things, the vallible ones, were safe in his hands. Or so we thought. Pressing's one thing, though it's bad enough, indeed. But outright theft is another. It happens down here, partickler along the wall. Even in doss houses like this. When they feel like it, the captains pay them to raid, and woe betide any what puts up a scuffle. It mainly happens in ale houses, like the Cow, or the Pelican, just down there. When they need men they take 'em, and they're paid well for it. *Someone* paid for my brother and got a good bargain. I didn't see him again for ten year, not till I was nearabout twenty-five. When I finally did, I wished to God I hadn't.'

Her voice took on another note, so tragic, with such anger and sadness mixed into it that despite her own dreadful predicament Lily was determined to hear the story out. It occurred to her that the woman, who had not betrayed her when she could have done so easily, might help her yet. She sat on.

The drink was almost gone.

'Fetch another bottle, quick, lad. Back there. That cupboard by the hearth.' A key appeared. 'There's a bit of larded cake, too, in a pie dish. Bring it if you want. You paid for it.'

Hungry, Lily did as she was asked, and waited to hear the rest.

'It did for my mother and broke my father's spirit. There was no one to hand the work on to. They gave up. When the news came, they went straight back and stayed in the old place till they died. Every day they hoped he would return and every night my mother wept that he hadn't. The business failed. My father's heart gave out for sadness. When my mother died, he sat in a chair for a week and then joined her.

'One day Edward *did* come home, wheeled to the house in a barrow by two more pigs like those. Crippled, he was, useless. They turned him out and left him to die. He'd lost his foot in an accident in the rigging, hung upside down for hours. The ship's surgeon could of saved him. They took a week to get him to shore. You could smell the rotten meat clear across the street. I'll never forget the sound of the gulls screaming as they chased after it. When I saw him, pitiful as he was, saw what they had brought him to, saw them laugh at his agony, I was in such a rage: white hot with it I was. It was as if all sight had left me. I couldn't scarce see nothing except these two ugly men's laughing faces. When they came in, I had the poker by me in the fire. Well then, I kept it in the fire, while they stood and laughed their fill, and mocked him some more, and jeered at the tears in my eyes.

'I kept my poker toasting nicely at my side and asked them who the ship belonged to, as if to pass the time. They mocked me for wanting to know, but they eyed me, too. With that poker glowing by me in the flames, down behind my skirts, I simpered at them, and they told me. I swear that as long as I live I will never forget that name. The owner of the ship was the same name as the one on that paper: *Koros*. That was the murderer's name. He served the West Indies, a roaring trade, by all accounts. Slaves and sugar, that's what he did. Theocritus Koros, and his younger brother, Mehmet. The younger one was the London end of it and took in the goods. He was known as the Turk. Their name has burned in my brain all these years since: Koros. A name I vowed never to forget.

'They said that my brother was no use to their master no more, so they were returning him. Damaged goods, they said. Ought rightly to charge for it, they said. They laughed as they heaved him all stinking on to the floor. He fell with a thud you don't never want to hear. He called my name in agony and tried to look at me, but he couldn't. They dropped him on the boards to die as if he was a side of rotten beef.

'When they had done that, they stepped over him and came toward me with a look in their eyn that I won't never forget, neither. After that, I couldn't see anything more, except flashes of flame, and as they tried to take me, I went at them with the poker.'

Lily watched her, aghast.

'And in return, they blinded me with it.'

Both women sat silent, staring out to where the flat-bottomed ships lay idle, waiting for the tide to fill and turn.

Half in the shadow of the open doorway, half in the woman's skirts, Lily kept her head down. If the watchmen came back she was finished, certainly if the woman chose; but there were still people about, and those who were stuck to their business, not giving the foul-looking old woman and servant-boy a second glance.

'*Koros*, you say?' Now it was Lily's voice that was strange, hardly more than a whisper. 'You say that Theocritus Koros was the owner of that ship. Are you quite certain? Sure beyond a shadow of a doubt that that was the name? For indeed, a great deal of time has passed.'

Elizabeth turned to her over the arm of the chair, and Lily saw that the eyes, shaded by the battered hat, were fixed upon her in a way that was surely impossible. 'Means something to you too, doesn't it? *My girl.* You think I couldn't tell? What do you take me for? These eyes were burnt, that's true; I was on the heap along with my brother. Except that this one sees well enough, in its own way. They didn't get it so good as the other, maybe the rod weren't so hot or they didn't hold it so close or so long. It don't matter why. What matters is that I often sees out of it better'n most.'

At this she almost poked herself in her right, blinded eye, in a sort of proud contempt, her voice so bitter that, to Lily's surprise, it wrung her with pity.

'Most people sees too much, that's what I've concluded. Many see without understanding what they see, but I see what I need to and no more, and then I think on it long and hard and proper. Take now for example: I seed what you were the minute you come in. But I seed something else, too; that you were in straits. There i'n't much to occupy my time, except for studying the oddities of persons, so I decided to wait to find out what sort of trouble it might be before deciding what to do about it. Make no mistake ducky, I'm not soft. I would've turned you in to them constables quicker'n a morning fart if I'd felt like it. It was a whim is all it was. You're a misfit like I've become, I was curious to hear your tale. And I didn't have to wait long, for it seems that God has sent you to me for a purpose and stayed my hand for the same reason.'

She leaned closer.

'I don't care whether you done it or not.' The words tumbled out rapid and low. 'If that animal Koros is after you, I'll help you, and more besides. I've devoted my life to waiting to cross him and those like him, to helping any in trouble to get out of it, whenever I could. Don't matter to me who they are if they've been wronged and I can help them. I do if for my brother.

'If I could get these hands on him, I'd take a burning brand to him myself, just as his men done to me. Weak as I am, I'd burn his eyes out one by one and I'd spit his entrails and set fire to them, too, until he pleaded with me to finish him off. I'd do to him what he done to my brother and me. No more, no less. Stand up, stand in the shadow of the door frame and let me get a proper look at you.'

Shuddering, Lily did as she was told.

Unable before now to look into the damaged face without discomfort, as she studied it she realised that the woman before her was probably no more than fifty. Then she saw the left eye glint and move, half open, while the right remained motionless and almost shut.

Observing Lily's change of expression, Elizabeth laughed. 'I keep it closed so fools can't tell the difference. I've told you, most people only see what they want to.'

Speaking more to herself than to Lily, her voice became brisker. 'Yes, I think it will work well enough. Help me up, now.'

The fearful bustle she made brought a chill to Lily's heart. 'Help me inside.'

After easing herself in a chamber pot at the back, the woman settled in a high, narrow-winged chair in the small parlour. Light seeped from closed, barred shutters pierced by two openings like fleurs-de-lis cut neatly in the top leaves, which the light outside made glow with gilt intensity. When Lily had first seen them from the street, they had shown as bold black shapes against the faded shutters.

'My father's sign,' Elizabeth said, catching Lily's quick glance. 'Silk from the Fleur-de-Lis was something to be proud of on both sides of the water.' It was as if she was about to recount more of her story, then her voice sharpened again.

'That bundle of yours. There's women's things in it, en't there?'

Lily looked at her in surprise.

'Don't argue,' Elizabeth countered. 'I had a peep while you slept. Didn't disturb nothing. This is an honest house if ever there was one. Put them on. Yes, now. In here. I'll help. We must make a plan.' While she fastened and smoothed Lily's crumpled jacket with surprising dexterity, she talked, half to herself, half to Lily.

'I will give you a bit of bread and cheese, and some of your coin to hide about you. Keep it close, mind, where they dursn't look. At soon as dusk falls, you go out from here and start walking down the street. Don't run mind, just stroll and look about a bit as if you're nervous. However idiotic they are, that ought to tip them off.'

Lily gasped. Surely Elizabeth was raving. She had been a fool to come and a fool to stay and listen; evidently the old woman was completely mad. Involuntarily she glanced in the direction of the bolted back door, calculating a dash for it.

Elizabeth chuckled. 'You could have drawn them, you know. They may look rusty but I keep 'em slippy as fresh fish for them as what need 'em. They're not pushed home to keep my boarders in, but to keep them sods out. Now set back on your horse for a moment and listen, young lady. It won't worsen your outcome to set a while longer. You might even learn something.

'That devil Koros has got men everywhere. Everywhere! Those bills are slapped up on every wall. They told me they were putting two hundred up in these parts alone. He must of believed that this is where you'd run to, and it seems he was right. God knows how he knew, though there's sense to it, and he's no fool, whatever else he may be. He's got men all over. He knows his mark and he's got money to back it. Cross over the road and down them river stairs and they'll scoop you up before your feet touch the slime on the bottom one. There's not a rowboat for a mile that isn't primed to take you in for a handsome reward. Everyone with skin your colour will be taken and turned over, mark my words. So forget the water.

'Then, too, what if you try to walk away, those limping lugs won't get you far, don't think I didn't notice that, neither. Where would you go? How far would you get? Because he ain't going to stop. You'll always be looking over your shoulder, you'll never breathe free. Not in London. Nor any bit of England neither. Never. Never!'

Lily was paying attention now. The woman was no fool after all.

'What shall I do, then?'

'Exactly as I say. Slip out as soon as it is just dusk, so the fools can still see, even in the middle of their intoxication. Stroll along the lee of the houses until they spot you. Whatever you do, don't offer no resistance, nor no provocation for them to hurt you. In the name of God, don't run. There's a reward so they want you alive, but they'll be a pack of rabid dogs if a chase starts. Nothing will save you then. If you do as I say, it shouldn't take too long. You'll be in Newgate before you know what time it is.'

At the young woman's expression of horror, Elizabeth laughed again, holding her side.

'My, my, whatever happened to the trust of the young in their elders, eh? Soon as you arrive, get a message to this woman.' She wrote a name in a tidy hand on a slip of coarse blue paper. 'Make sure to do it the very moment you get through them gates, do you hear me? There's some in there will aid you. In my time, I've helped many get away from trouble, and they know it. I've favours to call that would astonish you. I will send my own message, too, ahead of you. Leave the rest to me. I will take care of you, child. That monster will not harm you, I will see to it if it is the last thing I do.'

'But what will they do to you if you help me?'

At Lily's agitation, Elizabeth smiled for the first time. Lily supposed that under the wreckage she had probably once been comely, before her looks were destroyed and her hopes dashed.

'Even if they see you leave my house, what *can* they do? You tricked me, that's what I'll say. I'm stone blind, don't forget, an easy target, a stupid old woman and poor into the bargain. At the very bottom of the heap. Everyone about here believes it, from the parson down, not just the watch. I don't do things by halves. Where's the sport in charging a blind old fool who was gulled? Even if they strike me down where I sit, I'll thank them with my dying breath. I've prayed for it often enough.

'Take a pleasant meal with me to pass the time and tell me everything you know about him – Koros, that is; the older one. I've no interest in the other. I heerd he was a makeweight whose ship sunk when he tried to flee the plague, God rot him.' She shrugged.

'Omit nothing. Trust me, we will play Theocritus Koros at his own game. His men took my brother's life and mine too, come to that, but he shan't get yours, you have my word on it.'

The intensity of the manhunt Koros ordered was unprecedented. So many handbills were pasted up that it was impossible to walk more than a few paces without coming across the crude image of Lily's face, in alleys and coffee houses, on brick walls and in brothels, and all within twenty-four hours. Not only in Hatton and Covent Garden, but especially around Wapping and Ratcliffe, where Koros believed she would head, to board a boat or hire a skiff down-river and onwards, perhaps to France. Samuel paid for it, because Koros told him to.

It was Lily's great misfortune to have a black skin. Koros knew as much, and that the size of the reward would make people finger any black woman they saw, irrespective of how ridiculous the accusation. Even a few men were manhandled in and forced to don a cap or a woman's wig, in case Lily had been male all along. Koros did not care. Among the whole proceedings, this unexpected turn of events amused him, who had so little sense of humour. But he was determined to get her back into his custody without delay. Abusing his position as magistrate, he put considerable amounts of his own money behind her recovery, and promised a bonus to whoever brought her in.

And it was a great misfortune to the world that the qualities that would have advanced Koros in any career, and which might easily have been pressed into the service of goodness and charity, were entirely negated by cruelty, sadism and acquisitiveness. Of those, cruelty amplified his overweening desire to own and dominate. Since Lily's escape both challenged his sense of mastery and could hamper his possession of Zenobia, on which he was fixed like a viper on a vole, it stood to reason that she had to be annihilated. Yet even this logical computation did not explain the violence of his determination. His behaviour was erratic: that of a man thwarted in ambition or one who had lost a prized personal object and stops at nothing to get it back. Even, it might be said, that of a jealous lover. He behaved as if he was possessed.

Although shaken by her encounter in his robing room, Zenobia was in no position to judge the depth of those tendencies. Unlike a stone veined or blotched with striations or patches, whose imperfections often enhance its beauty, Koros was anthracite, black through and through.

When she arrived in Chick Lane in the magistrate's imposing sedan at the exact moment Lily stood across the street, the house she had left a few hours earlier was in uproar. Unburdened of the cloak and stained shoes, which Koros had kept to burn, she slipped quietly into the hall.

Servants ran to and fro and up and down the staircase, while Butter tried to instil calm. Having discovered where her father was from a new footman who did not recognise her, she ran upstairs to find out what was happening.

Samuel was in the drawing room, a place he reserved for greeting important clients. He was unpowdered; unheard of at nine in the morning; and his hair stuck up where he had been pulling at it. All the windows were open, their orange silk curtains ballooning as if they too were in mental disarray.

From his expression when she spoke, Zenobia might as well have flown in on one of his feared comets, rather than parted company after supper the night before.

'You ask me that, child?' His voice reeked of disbelief. '*You* ask what the matter is?'

Without warning he clasped her so tightly that she smelled the dressing on the silk of his morning gown. He began to sob and Butter, who had just come in, rapidly waved the other servants out again. Puffing himself up to block the view, he retreated and closed the door.

'You are alive! Praise God!' Samuel collapsed on to a high-backed settle. 'Come, let me look at you. Butter!' he bellowed, at which that man came in again with such speed and one cheek so pinked that it was evident that his entire fat body had been jammed against the door, which breach of etiquette Samuel overlooked.

It is curious that once the habit of mastery has been acquired, even by the most stupid person, it encourages a sense of mental superiority; an attitude Samuel had developed without noticing. It had crept up so slowly over the years that he was under the impression that he treated Butter as his equal.

'Have the search called off,' he said. 'She is found.'

'Indeed,' Butter remarked.

'Father.' Zenobia was more than a degree exasperated by her father's behaviour. 'Surely you received the magistrate's note? I saw him write it.'

But according to the hallowed preserve of parents, he did not listen.

'We thought you were dead,' he rebuked. 'Taken hostage in some dreadful place to be sold into slavery.'

At this she started and almost called out to Butter, standing in a corner like an oversized gargoyle.

'You said "we", father. Do you mean Butter?'

'Butter? Of course I don't!' he shouted and stamped his foot.

'Why on earth would I mean Butter? I mean Thomas! Good heavens, child. I am so overwrought. Thomas is going to live; his fever has broken. The moment the dear fellow woke, he sat bolt upright. God's elbow, I thought he would die on the spot, but instead he cried out that you had been kidnapped and that some ruffian was attempting abominations!'

At this, he took a big gulp of Geneva instead of water.

'The language he used – I cannot repeat it,' he added when he had stopped coughing. 'What he said was terrible. He pronounced the name of an inn, where he said you had been taken.'

Throughout this extraordinary account her mind raced. Surely she had smothered her uncle?

Too exercised to notice her discomfiture, he coughed again, and went on.

'I saw that he was feverish – that he must have overheard conversations while he slept and absorbed them as fact. But when I sent your maid to fetch you, the bed had not been slept in and you were not there. Then I began to believe that what he said must be true, a presentiment only granted to those on the verge of death. I was at my wits' end.'

Calmed by the fact that Zenobia was alive, buoyed by copious gin on an empty stomach, he paid her attention at last.

'But my dear child, whatever is the matter? You look deathly pale.' His joy turned to alarm. Since Butter had left the room, he rang for a fresh decanter and forced her to take a small glass, fanning her while she drank it.

'Then uncle Thomas is . . . alive?' Slumped down in order to avoid looking at him, she was studying him from beneath her lashes when Koros's footman came in with a fold of paper with a black seal. He had set out before her but could not tell right from left. He was only kept for his towering presence and running legs.

Samuel took in the contents at a single glance, let his hand fall to his lap, and shot Zenobia a most peculiar look.

PART FOUR

CHAPTER ONE

*J*ohn Crace was having one of his increasingly rare better days. As winter deepened, his health and strength had rapidly declined, but he strove to hide it, particularly from Zenobia. His physical demands became more frequent and prolonged, although they took their toll more on him than on her.

When he woke that morning, his back did not ache as it so often did, with a wincing intensity that sapped him and turned him queasy. He had told his physician, Stoddart, that it must be the fault of the bed, so was having a new mattress made. In this mood he even contemplated returning to magistracy, from which he had retired shortly after marrying Zenobia. Nothing could stop someone who had achieved so much, neither god nor devil, and he was damned if he would be thwarted by something as base as illness, let alone death. He was determined to live to see another son born – one with more spine than the fop Balthasar.

Meanwhile, in an attempt to patch the rift between them, he had summoned the boy for a visit. As the days passed, it was an event the household expected with increasing frequency.

But that would have to wait while he attended to more serious business.

His manservant had just left with a cloth-covered shaving bowl, careful not to slop. Despite Crace's tendency these days to stay in bed in a padded and furred night-gown and cap, now he was dressed, wigged, floured and perfumed, with an overmantle of smooth brown marten, wool-lined, snug against the December cold, next to a roaring fire in a high ebony chair that still smacked of the courtroom. Beneath the over-mantle, his black wool suit and plain, well-bleached linen hung looser than he remembered, and his stockings, when they had been rolled on, had wrinkled unusually. He discarded these oddities as a failure of his wardrobe-keeper, whom he decided to sack.

His man had given his face and neck a steaming rub with hot cloths, and after Crace pondered the effect in a hand glass, worked in a little rouge – something Crace had never had done and violently detested requesting. Those Englishmen who made themselves up to look like women were, to his mind, both abhorrent and aberrant and should be buried under the foundations of houses, or blocked up in walls like cats, to ward off effeminacy in others. At the time of their falling out, it had been tempting to have Balthasar disposed of like that. The moment Zenobia produced a replacement he might well do it.

Having prepared himself, feeling more exerted than he wanted to admit while in this ebullient mood, he took a gulp of fortified wine and glanced approvingly at the marble benches that Zenobia had so carefully prepared for him outside, vivid under a sharp blue winter sky. The plants round them had grown into strong stands whose shade beckoned. He repressed a sudden urge to sit there instead. The tallest group with its huge hand-span leaves and attractive seed-cods looked particularly welcoming. But with the wind biting and ice ridging on the stone terraces, it was hardly the time of year. Unless unexpected heat came to match the sun, he would have to wait until spring. He turned away.

The great doors to his chamber were opened and the Dutch painter shown in.

The man crossed the room with a swinging step. Crace examined him with disdain. A different breed, a different generation. A different race, probably, though it was hard to tell which, for his skin was still so bronzed from summer that he could easily be Italian or Spanish. Unlike his own flesh, Crace thought morosely. His mirror showed a face as sodden as mutton fat, in direct contradiction of his lying fellow of the bedchamber, who assured him that he was in rude health.

The Dutchman was as tall as he had been at the same age. Where Crace's costly brown furs were sober, this fellow sported lavish spotted lynx, almost as if he were effete. But although he wore his gleaming, curling black hair long, Crace was under no illusions; he had been closely informed about every aspect of the man's extramural activities. The servants that the painter had had: he knew every detail. By all accounts the man was as voracious as he was – but that was all that they had in common.

Apart, that is, from Zenobia.

'You desired to see me, milord?'

The bow was elegant, he had to give him that. Calm, too, leisurely, as if he had no concerns in the world.

Full of loathing, desperate to crush him to powder, Crace motioned genially at the chair beside his, a plainer, lower version, with no raised back. The Dutchman was attuned to theatrics, so there was no need to labour the point; but, that insult once passed over, the wine he was offered, the sweetmeats, were all the best. Money could not procure better, not even at court. Crace was certain of this, for he staffed his kitchens with the cream of Europe. He waved the attendant away, noting that his guest took nothing, merely sipped his wine and looked pleasantly interested in whatever might ensue.

'How does my ceiling progress?'

Crace felt warmer than he had for a long time, but not in a pleasant way. 'You have been here almost six months. It is surely complete, unless you intend to vie with the master of the Chapel of the Sistines for length of execution?'

'You honour me,' Hendrik replied in the accent Zenobia admired. He inclined his head with a modest bow that was anything but.

'It is complete but for the figures in the central cartouche, which must be done with my own hand. The work of a mere month. No more,' he added casually.

Crace could not detect a trace of insolence. Not a jot. Earnest. It infuriated him. He struggled to maintain outward calm.

'A month,' he echoed, scarcely touching his wine. He tried to look thoughtful. But, by God, any more of this and he would knock the wretch out of the chair and trample him to death, crack his spine and dance on his shrieking face, mash him to a pulp and suck his lights out with his own lips. He was sure he could do it. What a pleasure, what an insane relief! Then drag his bitch of a cheating wife in to see the last twitchings, force her to look at the broken thing, exult at her despair. Make her lick the blood and brains up, like a dog. And when she had had her fill, when her world was destroyed, when she could see that there was no hope of mercy, kill her too. Wring her neck with his bare hands and burn the corpses for a last dance together. A bonfire at the sundial. This man, this creature, this . . .

'A month, you say,' he repeated, carefully, as if the word was a supremely valuable jewel that he took in and out of a specially crafted box, to enjoy from every angle.

Without haste he put his glass on the table between them, its lustrous top arrayed with untouched delicacies, and wiped his mouth with the edge of a starched damask cloth.

Without warning, almost without visible movement, he swept his still-powerful hand, the one with the ring, under the lip of the table and violently upwards, turning it over, sending crystal and gold plate crashing with a catastrophic din.

As it hit the floor a great majolica stand worked in relief with glistening grass snakes and heaped with preserved fruits exploded into two halves, while three gilded dishes whose broad rims were decorated with gambolling cupids bounced and clanged, scattering nuts, little seeded cakes and a few pairs of porcelain buttocks in all directions. The enamelled drinking glasses and crystal wine jug splintered into fragments in glittering puddles around their feet.

Hendrik Snyders drew his left leg a few inches out of the bloody wet, but otherwise did not move.

Looking at his host all the while, he bent down slowly, plucked a dried half apricot off the plum-coloured velvet of his breeches, and set it cut-side up on a small table that had escaped Crace's fury.

Crace turned white. Despite his dignified pose, the pink salve on his cheeks stood out as if it floated. He clasped the arms of his chair, as if to prevent himself from leaping up to commit murder.

'A month!' He steadied his breaking voice. 'You will complete this work in a week. In less than a week, if you wish to leave my house upright. During this time, you will live and sleep in the hall and never leave it. You will speak to no one and see no one. Is that clear?'

'Ah,' Hendrik said.

Apparently undisturbed either by the preceding racket or by Crace's ragged voice, he neatly peeled a small blood orange that he had rescued from next to his Morocco-booted foot. His manicured fingers removed the skin in one twist, which he arranged next to the apricot. It sat on the black wood, a still life.

'Ah, how I applaud your keenness to enjoy my finished work. It speaks of great discrimination and honours me more highly than I could ever hope. Such admiration from one who commands the attention of princes – nay, kings and emperors. It is my dearest wish to agree on every point you so amiably suggest. However, keen as I am to concur, in one small thing your suggestion is impossible. Despite my heart's clamour to satisfy your request and go beyond it as a mark of gratitude, it cannot be done without help from at least one of my men. To grind pigment and move the scaffolds. That is all I ask,' he finished with a shrug. 'Such is life. Such practical details cannot be avoided.'

He put the entire naked orange in his mouth and chewed, his bulging cheeks reminiscent of the smashed putti, smiling with an air of complete enjoyment.

Crace returned his look with an expression so glowering, so calculatedly evil, that no one but a fool or someone longing for immediate death would sit a moment longer. His hands, gripping the chair, had turned purple, blotched red over the knuckles, while his face, beaded with sweat, was appalling to behold.

Orange swallowed, fingers meticulously wiped, Hendrik suddenly noticed the odour Zenobia described rising from Crace.

He is afraid, he thought, careful to keep smiling, working out how fast he could move should Crace suddenly lunge, for it was possible that the older man wore a dagger. As long as he could see his host's hands he felt safe, but should either move he was ready to move himself, and quickly, too. Though where could he go, he wondered, in his opponent's house? So close to slaughter, the only card left to play was outward calm. If Crace saw that he too was afraid, all would be lost. His life, Zenobia's, all smashed to pieces.

'Of course, should it please your lordship, I *could* do it in the time you request with one man,' he continued pleasantly, as if nothing unusual had just passed between them, nor that they were surrounded by glittering carnage worth more than a hundred ordinary men earned in a lifetime.

'Very well.'

To the unexpected reply, Hendrik inclined his head and welded the pleasant smile to his lips. Beneath his doublet his heart pounded. He took a deep breath. Crace must never understand how close he had come.

'One man will stay.' The words came through gritted teeth. 'Neither of you will leave the gallery, not even if the house burns down around your worthless heels. No one will come in and no one will go out. The work will be done within the week or you will wish you had never set foot in this country – certainly you will not leave it alive. My servants will guard the door. They will feed you and deal with your necessaries. Do not try to bribe them, it will only do you harm. Believe me, sir, I will only tolerate your continued presence in this house as long as you work in a way that you have never done in your life. The moment it is finished you will go, taking leave of no one. I shall decide which assistant stays. The other will be sent off at once. Do you understand?'

'Most perfectly, sire,' Hendrik executed a second immaculate bow, with no apparent trace of insolence. 'A well-considered plan, with not a detail neglected.'

As he straightened up he picked up two candied figs and tossed them as if they were sugared dice.

'You will not be disappointed in the fruits of my labour.' He bowed one final time.

Howsoever those who have risen to the rank of princes delude themselves, nothing stops news from travelling in a large household. It permeates cracks, flits on the wings of flies, sifts in with dust, hitches on hems, transmits in a nod or a glance and ricochets between panels. It travels in more prosaic ways, too. Zenobia found out what had happened the next morning while Agatha dressed her, after a rare night during which her husband's demands had not broken her sleep.

The assistant sent away was Agatha's lover, Lukas. Before he was bundled out of the house with a slab of black rye and no coat against the icy wind, he risked a thrashing to leave her a note, flicked into a fire bucket. One of the maids, the only person to notice the rapid movement of his wrist, brought it to Agatha, having first satisfied herself that it contained nothing worth selling to Crace's spies.

Agatha's unhappy face, even longer than usual, told Zenobia how bad things were.

Indifferent to convention when it suited her, Zenobia wasted no time learning the truth. She sat on the edge of her unmade bed, her stays not yet laced nor her stomacher stitched in, which was a relief, for she had recently suffered uncharacteristic wind.

'He knows.' She spoke softly, as much to her lap as to Agatha. 'Without a shadow of a doubt, he knows.'

Agatha produced the note, scribbled in ink on a triangular scrap of linen, all Lukas could get hold of in the rush. The bit of mousy cloth hacked off a corner of another piece was hard to read, but she could just make the message out. Half-English, half-Dutch, Lukas was not literary, but he was eloquent. Agatha brushed away tears as Zenobia read aloud:

> *'Gone.* Ewald is hier voor en week aan de meester te helpen. *Problemen. L'*

'Not even a kiss.' Agatha made a bold effort to stop Zenobia putting two and two together. 'Don't these ignorant foreigners even know how to write *that*, madam? How much effort would it have cost him, the parsimonious bastard?'

'Why does he say a week?' Zenobia interrupted, puzzled, threading the scrap through her fingers like a cat's cradle. 'The day before yesterday Master Snyders told me they needed a month, probably more. He thought it would take until the end of January. Have you seen him this morning?'

The way Agatha avoided her eye caught her attention.

'What is it, woman? Speak up!'

Agatha took a pace back, her face, if possible, even more gloomy. Then she came close enough for Zenobia to catch a whiff of the fish glue that stiffened her bodice: 'For the love of God, madam, take care. There are spies everywhere. I have wanted to tell you for so long but dared not, in case you rebuked me. Master Snyders and Ewald have been locked in. His lordship has given them a week, on pain of death. The moment it is done he will send them away. They are allowed to see no one. Not as they work and not as they leave.'

'*Death*?' Ignoring the tears rolling down her woman's face, Zenobia pulled her beside her on to the bed.

'Death? What on earth do you mean? Have you lost your senses?' She shook Agatha.

'Madam, speak lower, I beg you.' Agatha's voice was the one she used to address Zenobia in private colloquies, late at night in bed, in the moments before Lukas – she tried to push the thought away, but it would not be pushed – before Lukas joined her, exhausted from painting on scaffolds all day, cramped and stifled below the freshly plastered ceiling, his neck and back bent, his shoulders racked by fire, the muscles in his arm inflamed, trembling so badly that he wept. She must not think of that, not until later, when she could weep.

The emotion in her voice made Zenobia, who had been on the point of slapping her to bring her to her senses, sit, suddenly, silently, head bent, and listen intently as the older woman went on.

'It is no idle threat and it is not just them he has threatened.'

'Explain.' Zenobia's voice was dull.

To make sure that she was not mad, that she would not take the wrong course, Zenobia had to hear the words running through her own mind from the mouth of someone she could trust.

'He has known almost since the start, madam.' Agatha waited for blows to rain down. She was no stranger to her mistress's temper, knew it better than anyone. Better than the master, from whom Zenobia concealed so much pent loathing.

Nothing happened, no blow fell; her mistress sat quietly beside her.

'He has spies everywhere, they inform him about everything you do. Every single one of them, as far as I can tell.'

'Except you?' Zenobia touched the back of Agatha's hand so lightly that it startled more than a slap. 'Why should I trust you not to betray me? Why not take his money?'

It was Agatha's turn to fall silent.

'I asked a question.' There was anger in Zenobia's voice. 'Why? How do I know that my words do not go straight to him? Perhaps it is you who betrayed me; you, the closest.'

In reply Agatha raised her tear-stained face, in which such love and pain mingled that Zenobia almost had a presentiment of what she was about to say.

'Because of Lily Boniface.'

If the name had not been so frequently alight in her own memory, Zenobia might not have caught it, whispered so low.

'What do you mean?'

Once Agatha began, nothing could stop her. 'Lily Boniface was my previous mistress. Before I worked for your husband. I was not always in the master's employ.'

'You were with Madam Boniface?'

Agatha nodded. 'Yes. If only it could have continued forever.' She paused. More tears welled, which she controlled with difficulty.

'I know that you tried to save her life, madam,' she went on. 'But I watched her hang.'

'I was determined to bear witness, to do her that last act of friendship, to be a loving presence when truth and justice had forsaken her. However fiercely my heart begged me to stay away, sure I would not be able to stand it, I had to go.

'I arrived just in time, but right at the back of the crowd. It was hard to see anything because of the throng. She was the last of a group, hanged one by one, so the crowd had worked itself into a frenzy. Most were men, taller than me, out for a jaunt. How I loathed them. They were drunk, yelling obscenities against her, egging each other on, calling her a black whore and much worse, leering and exulting at her distress. I wanted to kill them all. More than that, I wanted to kill whoever had brought her to it, for I knew it could not be true, that the allegations must be false. It struck me that by going I might hear something, discover something that would lead me to whoever had committed such a foul crime.

'A few moments later, an awful roar went up. I managed to glimpse her as she mounted the scaffold. Then I was shoved back and all I could see was her cap. Oh! My heart nearly broke at what they had done to her. I hardly recognised her. She was in old clothes, not her own fine things. Bowed with shame, her chin on her breast. I was glad I couldn't see her face; she would have hated the indignity. Then . . . she fell. The crowd went beserk, and I fainted. If only I had been trampled to death and died with her. But God made me live to tell the tale.'

Zenobia said nothing and motioned her to stay beside her.

The meaning of Agatha's words dawned on her. Could Agatha have been in Lily's service in Covent Garden when Zenobia first met her? Why, could it even have been Agatha who delivered the dress and domino to Samuel's house?

For during the times that Agatha attended her after an unwilling visit to Crace, Zenobia sensed that the woman hated him too; that her disgust mounted at every fresh injury. But she never asked why. It did not occur to her that the woman had a life or thoughts beyond service. Moreover, Samuel had always told her that a servant privy to private matters was a liability. Agatha was experienced, with skilful hands, so however tempting it was to unburden herself, she did not.

But Agatha's revelation could not be left unquestioned. If she knew that Crace was responsible for Lily's death, why would she serve him? There was something else, too. Why would a respectable, intelligent woman capable of a position in a household like Crace's work for a black madam? Any of the great houses would hire her, not only for her abilities but for her impeccable demeanour.

Zenobia ordered her to sit. 'Tell me how you came to be in Madam Boniface's service.' She leaned forwards to watch Agatha's eyes. 'Leave nothing out.'

Agatha began to protest that a maid had been needed, but Zenobia interrupted. 'If you don't tell the truth I will send you packing. You will never get another position, I will see to it. You will starve. I cannot have a liar in my household. Do not be afraid. Speak freely.'

Agatha wrung her hands in her skirts, trying to hold them still, so Zenobia changed tack and spoke softly. 'Whatever you say is a confidence and will stay so, I swear. You have tended me well, I do not overlook it. I shall not betray you. What you tell me now rests between these walls. Speak without fear. But do not keep me waiting,' she added, unable to conceal her impatience.

Contemplating Agatha's tormented face, Zenobia realised that she rarely looked at her directly, for she always stood to one side, head lowered.

Now she saw that Agatha was about the age Lily would have been. Her grey eyes were alert, she had a clear forehead and well-shaped mouth, and her thick hair, just beginning to grey, was dark blonde. She had a good figure. She could be made to look beautiful, but all was obscured by her position.

'Speak, trusted Agatha,' she tried again. 'How came you to serve Lily Boniface?'

Halting at first and then with more confidence as she forgot where she was and how perilous her situation, Agatha talked as if to an equal.

'I was not always as you see me now. My life began differently, but it pleased God to change my path. I was raised in the country, two days' ride from here. My father was older than my mother, his second wife. We were not wealthy but we had land to feed us, so we survived the plague. When I was small my mother began to waste. One day my father brought a girl back from London as a companion for me. We took our lessons together and since my father was so often away and my mother bed-ridden, we became inseparable. I loved her from the moment I saw her, and that love deepened with time. You know that I can read, madam, but I also play. I was raised a lady – though only in the country.'

She shot a nervous look in case she had overstepped the mark, but Zenobia waved her on, too keen to hear the rest to take affront.

'If my life had continued on its intended course I should have married and lived much as my parents had done. I was an only child, so would inherit the estate, which brought an income. However, when I was twelve, I noticed that my father paid my companion a great deal of attention. At first I did not understand. Then one day I passed a room and saw something that caused me great distress.'

She bit her lip and her hands became restless again.

'Surely you sent the vicious girl away, for leading your father into sin?'

Sparks darted from Agatha's eyes before she resumed her familiar passive expression. 'Send *her* away? She did nothing wrong.'

The passionate account sent shivers down Zenobia's spine. She wanted to know the outcome and hoped John would not send for her until the story was finished.

Agatha rose and faltered a few steps, but remembering where she was, sat down again.

'You promise, madam, that this will go no further?'

Zenobia nodded.

'Very well. My life is in your hands. My companion was suffering, so I tended her, just as from time to time I tend you. Her horror knew no bounds. It was pitiable. There was nowhere to turn, nobody but me would have believed her, and if she swelled with child she would lose her place. Her situation was ghastly, while I, loving her, could only watch the nightmare unfold. My father was brutal, but I was helpless. With no one to check him he became worse. He treated her like an animal.

'All that time my mother stayed in her room. I could not turn to her, she would have renounced my friend rather than accuse her husband. There was nothing to be done, and I was afraid of what he would do if I spoke out.'

'Go on,' Zenobia urged. The drumming of her heart made it difficult to speak.

'A month after that he became very ill. He died not long afterwards.'

'How so?' Zenobia asked at this unexpected turn of events, eyes burning on her servant as if she cast a light upon her. 'What did he die of?'

Agatha's reply was only just audible. 'Things could not go on as they were. We studied together, as I have said. We read a great deal. We –' She tailed off, then came to a decision. 'Do with me what you will, my life is meaningless.'

'Go on,' Zenobia urged once more.

'My friend poisoned him.'

At Zenobia's astonished expression, Agatha continued with greater urgency.

'We did not intend it, not at first. We read his books to discover what herbs would kill any infant that tried to nest inside her, and in learning about those we came across plants that could do the same to an adult. So, as any inquisitive child might, we explored further, and found numerous plants that can end a life with ease. They thrive in the most ordinary gardens, madam – if one knows where to look.'

She reeled off a list of flowers, leaves and seeds that could cause violent sickness, wasting fevers, hideous eruptions and scourges, or kill in all manner of subtle or sudden ways. The list was long, and her face was so passionate and illuminated, so spellbinding, radiant, that Zenobia could not take her eyes off it.

'As much God's creations as we, madam; every single one.' The light in her face snapped out. 'She used one of those.'

Perfectly calm, any sign of trepidation gone, Agatha met Zenobia's gaze squarely: 'I did nothing to stop it. Some might say that I murdered him as surely as if I had prepared the poison with my own hands; and, before God, if she had asked me to, I would have done. Once he was dead, we learned that he had gambled the house away, including the servants, among whom my friend was especially singled out, on the same terms that my father had enjoyed her. Her appearance was carefully noted, so there could be no doubt.

'He had thrown the land in, along with my mother's jewels, even her clothes and shoes. There was nothing left . . . just my mother and me and the clothes on our backs. He intended to leave us destitute, while my friend would be handed from one man to another. There was an engraving among his papers to identify her. When my mother understood that she had been deliberately made a pauper, she died. Neither death was questioned. The estate's new owner was keen to take possession, so no enquiries were ever made.'

'What happened to you?' Zenobia asked.

'When my friend grasped that she had been won at a game of cards and belonged, like a chair leg, to a man in London, she ran away. I did not stop her. Nor did I see her go or say goodbye. She just disappeared.'

Agatha wiped the back of her hand across her face and sighed deeply.

'As for me, nobody would marry me after that. All I could do was to go into service myself, so I followed her to London. I was certain she would go there. I could not face the county once my destitution became common knowledge, or that I might be offered a position out of embarrassment. All I wanted was to find her, my only friend.

'For a year, I worked for an apothecary on the Bridge. He knew my mother's family name and took pity on me, asking nothing in return except help with his work. He was an old man, and kind-hearted. He allowed me to sleep in the attic. My botanical knowledge impressed him, I was apt to learn more. I ground medicines, roots and herbs and delivered packages – all the time looking for her. Eventually, I learned what course she had taken. In the path she chose, the services of an apothecary were often required, and this man was the best. A certain type of woman often came to his shop. Just as I found out where she was, she discovered me, too. So I stayed with the apothecary and learned a trade. As soon as she was able to support me, I joined her.

A curious blandness came into Agatha's face, the smoothness of a mask.

'Because of the colour of her skin, her path was different from mine, but both were set by my father's actions. I willingly take responsibility for what she did, for, as God is my witness, I have never stopped loving her, not for one single day. She would not have become what she did if it had not been for him. I did not blame her and never have. He paid for destroying her life, but she paid more.'

Agatha sat as if carved from stone, waiting for a sword to strike.

When Zenobia finally spoke, her halting words were not what Agatha expected.

'My husband betrayed me on my wedding day. He lied to me and murdered Lily just as well as if he placed the rope around her neck with his own hands. Tell me, Agatha: which plants did Lily use – and how did she use them?'

PART FIVE

CHAPTER ONE

*A*fter rapid negotiations, Zenobia's marriage to Theocritus Koros was set for a fortnight later. According to Samuel, who did not show her the note, her suitor urged the much swifter arrangement of a day. As a magistrate, he could obtain a licence at a moment's notice. But, for one of the very few time in his life, Samuel asserted himself. Even though he knew no living relative except his brother and could ask neither his clients nor his tailors to witness the ceremony, which meant that from his side it would be a very small affair, the thing he *could* do was make a trousseau fit for his adopted daughter's marriage to a rich and powerful man. On this basis he calculated the time.

His enquiry into the magistrate's family met with a blank. Koros informed him that both his previous wives were dead. His brother had been lost at sea; and his son, Balthasar, was abroad and unable to return for months; therefore the nuptials should press ahead.

Samuel countered that Thomas wished to attend and would need time to recover. This argument was disingenuous, for as he read the extraordinary note scratched in Koros's impatient hand, Samuel remembered the promise he had made to God to give Zenobia to her uncle if he lived. Now he found himself gripped by a dilemma.

On one hand, upstairs lay his brother, who had survived an attempt on his life, who surely deserved the reward of the person Samuel loved best in the world, an arrangement that would also keep Zenobia in Samuel's orbit. Moreover, elevating this selfish motive, he told himself that he had made a pact with God, so reneging would invite all sorts of horrors.

On the other hand, he pursued, sucking the tassel of his Turkish cap, no one knew he had made that promise, and he had been distressed at the time. If he did not know his own mind, nothing he said to anyone, including God, would count.

He glanced at the note again. Improbable though it seemed, there was the demand in black and white. On a fresh side of the argument stood the imposing magistrate, who owned so much property, including land gifted from the King, and who could raise Zenobia as far as the court just by making her his wife. She would live entirely beyond his own paltry purse and connections. Surely God, understanding the advantage of such a union to the entire family, would back him up.

For, contrary to what Zenobia believed, Samuel *had* seen the way the magistrate looked at her. When he took it for mere lust, it had made his blood boil so hard that as he prodded the fire he had toyed with the idea of branding the lecherous goat; but the guarantee of clothes, jewels, carriages, houses and preferment was a different matter. If only Zenobia could learn to play the role of a meek wife (which he doubted), unforeseen riches were hers.

Moreover, Thomas's liaison with the Boniface woman had tarnished his standing as a husband. Indeed, in order to distance Zenobia from the scandal, Samuel had already had a paper drawn up that insisted Thomas revert immediately to using his real name: Welkin.

Before this, Samuel's ambition for Zenobia had never gone further than marriage to a gentleman. But now that worldly success was within her grasp, Thomas's false claim, for so Samuel now considered it, dwindled at astonishing speed. It was no more troublesome to remove than to brush a thread from a table. How could such a vague promise stand in Zenobia's way?

Koros's note was characteristically blunt:

Give me your daughter in wedlock at once.
As long as the whore Boniface is recaptured and tried with speed,
your brother will not be prosecuted.
I will call on you later today.

Though the words stamped themselves on his mind at a single glance, their meaning slithered, eel-like. In an effort to calm his heart he reread the note, but that organ did not calm. What on earth did the second sentence mean? What crime could his brother possibly have committed from his bed with a bullet through his thigh? The magistrate was mad. Throwing off his banyan and ignoring his hair, Samuel told Zenobia to go and see her uncle, then wait in her best gown for his return. After which he rang for a chair to take him to Hatton Garden.

Believing that she had smothered him to death, Zenobia did not know whether she felt horrified or terrified by the idea that Thomas might be alive after all. The servants had gone back to their duties and the house was calm.

But Thomas sat wedged upright by bolsters, his freshly dressed leg thrust out, very much alive. The slashed night-gown had been replaced by a brocade banyan and cap like his brother's, but brighter. Fresh linen concealed his neck and his face no longer looked sweaty. Most strikingly, he had crimsoned his cheeks and was smothered in scent.

'How good of you to come. I have been severely troubled in case you had not found your way safely home.'

Zenobia's heart leapt into her mouth. What did he mean, had he lost his mind? She had been brought home by Koros's runners; only a lunatic could get lost over such a short distance. Could he possibly mean after their fateful carriage ride? She settled herself in the chair.

'I was so thoughtless not to take better care of you.' His puny hand groped towards her and came to rest lightly on her sleeve.

She tried not to shrink away. How could that hand have gripped so hard in the carriage?

'I accept my fault, but I thought Lily would look after you. I never dreamed she would send you home alone. I have been anxious ever since leaving her house yesterday evening.'

'Yesterday evening?' Zenobia stuttered.

'Yes, yes indeed,' he repeated. 'I was so caught up in play downstairs that I did not appreciate the lateness of the hour.'

'But, your leg . . . You do know, uncle, that you have been shot? We thought you would die.'

'Just so.' Patronisingly. 'Samuel has explained it all. I am astonished that the woman to whom I gave so much tried to murder me, but I must believe it, my leg stands witness. If it could speak, it would howl murder from toe to thigh; it would fly at her and beat her to paste. I count my blessings that we came home separately, so that you escaped unharmed.'

Mawkish tears edged gingerly down each cheek and he dabbed them with a tiny lace handkerchief, darting a piercing look at her through its delicate edges. However, when flakes of pinkish-red stuff came off, the tears stopped, leaving him streaked as a slice of ham.

He patted his thigh and groaned, though Zenobia observed that his fingertips hardly met his leg at any point.

'The insane creature who did this must be found.' His voice rose and his eyes flashed. 'Your father told me that a search has been mounted, and not before time, for she is mad as well as deadly.'

Baffled, Zenobia determined to find out what was going on as soon as she left the room. But he went on, oblivious. 'Oh! That I nursed such an asp at my bosom! She must hang for such a dreadful crime, if not burn, which would be preferable.'

Fanning himself with his cap, revealing his greasy, black-fringed pate, Thomas's breathing became rapid and he turned pale once more. If he had not been a charlatan, she would have had the impression that his life still lay in the balance.

Impatient to discover what he meant, she ushered Mary back in. As she did so, she saw the eyes that had seemed drowsily closed fixed on her like gimlets.

Back in her own room, Zenobia lay down for a moment. But when she awoke, the light had moved right round the walls; she had slept all day. Bells pealed six times. At once, the troubling thoughts of the morning returned.

Could Thomas really have forgotten what happened? If so, then only her father and Pentreath could accuse Lily of anything, though with no evidence; while she herself was cleared – or would have been if she hadn't rushed to the magistrate to blurt out her crime. If she had stayed at home, all would have been resolved, and even if Lily was found, there would be nothing to charge her with. Zenobia was deep in this train of thought when Jane came to dress her, ready to go down to the two men who, the girl informed her, were waiting.

It felt as if a lifetime had passed since she went to Koros's house that morning. Had he told her father about her visit? Surely not, what good would it do? She was certain he only did things to his own advantage; that while supposedly acting in the public interest, his true ambition was power, and he would use any means to achieve it.

Jane stitched her into a plain bodice and threaded ribbon through her hair, letting it curl on her shoulder.

In the face of the magistrate's obvious attraction, Zenobia wanted to look demure. But when she studied herself in her long mirror, she made Jane spring a few curls round her brow, and bit her lips to pink them. Even if she did not care what Koros thought, it was rude to look slovenly. She pinched her cheeks. Only because she looked wan, she told herself; not to taunt him. For though just days ago she had wanted to marry her way into the world, for which Koros was an ideal candidate, now the idea horrified her. He had called her a liar and discounted Lily's life. He considered himself master of life and death, it could not have been plainer. If she ever married, he was the last man she would accept.

Candle flames bristled on a great iron candelabrum suspended above them. Still dressed in the same sombre black, the magistrate's eyes reflected the fire. Those gleaming eyes followed her as she sat.

Agitation came off Samuel in waves. 'His lordship wishes to marry you,' he announced abruptly. His voice sounded strained. The fire spat and crackled beside them. 'And I have agreed.' He looked away from her. 'It is an excellent match that does this family great credit.'

He bowed in the other man's direction, as if she was an afterthought.

Clearing his throat, still avoiding her eye, he continued: 'His lordship has informed me of your visit this morning.' Though she could hear that he tried, with a degree of success that might have fooled anyone but her, to suppress it, there was outrage in his voice.

Koros's impassive eyes bored into her. His gaze engulfed her, she felt undressed. With one bound he could cross the short distance and crush her. She was certain that he had not told Samuel their true conversation.

Samuel wiped his forehead with such despair that she wondered what he could possibly say next. When he finally spoke, each word was as awkward as if it had a bad taste. 'For most of your life you have been without motherly guidance, and these past days have made me painfully aware of my error in not remarrying.

My work took me away from you, for which I curse myself. You have become wayward and bookish, and developed fancies inappropriate to your sex and years. Your uncle warned me, but his wisdom came too late.'

He trapped his hands between his knees to stop them trembling, and with astonishment she realised that it was rage he trembled with; rage that made his voice harsh and unfamiliar.

'His lordship has told me that you shamelessly offered yourself to him this morning.'

At the ghastly lie, Zenobia rose to defend herself. 'Father!'

But he silenced her. For the first time, she saw his brother in him.

'Nothing can redeem such behaviour. Further lies will only make matters worse. It confounds me that his lordship wishes to know you. If he were not so magnanimous, God knows what would happen. I should be forced to put you into a nunnery as an abnormality. There is no earthly explanation.

'However, his lordship believes that you cannot be held responsible for your actions, having no one to temper them, for which I accept the blame. It is your great fortune that he perceives enough merit to take you off my hands and break your spirit himself.'

With this pronouncement, he rose.

'A private ceremony will take place in a fortnight. Until then you will stay in your room, repent your actions and adopt a frame of mind suitable for a wife. The only persons you will see are your uncle, your maid and a clergyman. That is all.'

Zenobia rose from her curtsey swallowing tears. He had put her into a position she could not fight; deserted her; thrown her away like a rag. Against her judgement, she glanced at Koros.

His eyes still dragged her towards him with magnetic force, but what she saw was impossible to forget: anticipation, greed, open lasciviousness. No scruple, no remorse. In that moment, she knew what it must feel like to be sold and terror took hold of her.

The magistrate held up his hand. 'Wait,' he said to Samuel. 'I will speak in private with Zenobia before I leave.'

With a look that made her father flinch, the magistrate added: 'Now.'

Even though they were now engaged, the impropriety of being left alone with him struck her. But she was as surely bound to him as she would be in two weeks' time, when he could do whatever he liked, and a great deal more than Thomas had attempted. The thought left her mute, glancing at him like a caged animal, wishing she could die.

He examined her from a distance, as if she were some trifle he had just bought, and rubbed the thumb with the ring on it.

'I trust the bargain pleases you.'

At the unexpected words, she broke out in dismay: 'Pleases me? I do not know you, sir, and the lies you have told my father –'

With surprising agility, he sprang forwards and dragged her upright.

'Take care not to say anything you may regret. It has always been my policy in life and has served me well. I have made an offer far above your station. I have ignored what you told me this morning. By making you my wife, I make you inviolate, immune from any further challenge. The harpy Boniface –'

It was Zenobia's turn to interrupt. 'For the love of Christ, sir,' she cried, 'we both know she is innocent. It would be a grave injustice to punish her for my sin. And Uncle Thomas mends! I beseech you not to pursue her further.'

Without warning, he pulled her to him so hard, forcing her head back, that she could scarcely breathe. Held fast, she looked into the eyes that glowed on her. He bent his face towards hers but, though trapped, she turned to avoid his mouth. His grip suddenly relaxed a little. In his grasp she fluttered, as if before a great cat that bides its time.

He licked his lips, tasted her words. 'Beseech me? Yes, you will do that and a great deal more. Resist me and I will hang the Boniface woman.'

He gazed at her. 'Hang her from the neck, until she is dead.'

He paused again. 'A horrible death and an agonising one, make no mistake; but an avoidable one. It is in your hands. What say you now?'

His grasp had become as light as air, yet she did not pull away.

With hopelessness that made her want to be trampled, she understood what he required.

'If you save her,' she started slowly, knowing there was one chance, 'if you save her,' she continued, vomiting the words like pebbles, never taking her eyes from his, 'if you do that, then I will be honoured to be your . . . wife. Sire.'

'*Honoured*?' His great paw still on her breast, his breath hot on her cheek. 'Come now, Zenobia, tell me that you *desire* it. Show me that you do and all will be as you ask. I will not take less.'

'I desire it above all things.' She waited dully for whatever he would do next, but instead he released her.

'Very well. I shall hold you to it. In that case, you have my word. The very day we are married, the Boniface woman will be . . . let go.'

With a brief inclination of his head, he walked out.

CHAPTER TWO

$\mathcal{T}$he arrival at Crace's mansion of his only living son, Balthasar, and the hungry retinue who accompanied his every preening step, was badly timed.

It was freezing cold; lividly cold at Temple Bar and the new houses south of it near the river. In the eerie absence of cloud, stars grated at the thin black sky and the moon poured an icy wash over the badly cobbled street, a street so cumbered by snow that it had lost its form. Snow-covered carts stood abandoned where exhausted horses had stumbled out, fetlocks frozen. Here and there, mounds covered corpses of animals frozen to death. The previous day's fall had set hard. Fresh snow on top made the blanketed road, now mud frozen with ice, treacherous and slow.

With arrogance inherited from his father and honed at court, Balthasar had not sent word, and since his appearances were so rare, his father had given up expecting him. Just before midnight, he arrived with a jangling retinue of eight. Because of the snow, he had ridden almost three days from the estate Crace had given him, his exhausted wolfhound, Fog, at his heels. After thawing out and inspecting his new mother-in-law, he intended to go on to the brighter blandishments of court.

Had the weather been less dismal and the dog less weary, or two of his servants not suffering from such an acute complaint in their stomachs that they kept voiding themselves, he would have reached London earlier and ridden on without pause. He had done it many times before, but this time, nature forced his hand.

In the middle of the night, Zenobia was woken by insistent hammering, then the bolts on the nail-studded front door shuddered. Crace kept a well-armoured entrance. At the muted noises of servants running to and fro, she did not leave her chamber. There was a flurry of activity that stopped, then briefly renewed; then the footsteps quieted. All sounds died down, and the household slept once more, wrapped in deathly whiteness.

The snow continued to fall without pause, slow and strangely sticking. When the thud of a small log slipping from the hand of a new girl rebuilding the fire woke her, it still fell beyond the leaded windows. Despite the growing flames, the room was freezing. Cocooned under her covers within the heavy curtains round her bed, she peered through a crack at the sheeted skies flying outside. Pulling back the thick fabric, she blew an experimental breath, which clouded at once.

Knowing that Agatha would bring honeyed bread steeped in hot cream to break her fast, she decided to stay put until the chamber warmed up, but when Agatha arrived, she was asleep again.

Agatha drew back the bed curtains. Usually she admired her mistress's beauty for a while before waking her, but this morning she roused her.

One look told Zenobia what she dreaded, for although Agatha had wiped her face, it was obvious that she had been crying, and for the same reason that kept Zenobia in bed.

Busy at one of the cedar-lined chests that held linen-wrapped furs, Agatha drew out a heavy over-robe of embroidered camlet lined with stoat and laid its shimmering mass near the fire to warm. From another chest, she lifted a padded petticoat and a burnt-orange skirt and bodice.

Zenobia toyed with the dish of posset. What did food or clothes matter, for this was the day Hendrik must leave, and she would not be allowed near him. Although Crace had not accused her of anything, his actions were enough. Everyone in the house understood; it was as if he had denounced her.

Until that morning, her one relief had been that Balthasar had not made his promised visit. The boy was known to be idle, full of hot air. If only he would wait until Hendrik had left, there would be less danger of gossip and scandal rocketing through Whitehall. The thought had buoyed her all week while her lover painted to save his life. But the commotion during the night could mean only one thing: the prodigal had arrived.

'I must dress you, madam,' Agatha urged. 'Your husband requires you at once.'

Zenobia put the two-handled dish down. She had hardly touched it; the cream made her liverish and the cinnamon tasted strange. Had Crace decided to have her poisoned?

'Madam.' Though her head was bowed, Agatha did not cede an inch. 'Delay gains nothing, it will only anger him. He requires you most insistently.'

Zenobia swung her night-gowned legs over the edge of the high bed. Her instantly cold toes felt for the broad oak steps as if she were about to kick away the support under a gibbet. In the yellow-white light the room swayed. She clung to a post, scared to move in case she fell. Her life toppled around her or she toppled with it; one way or the other it was the same thing: the hand of eternal, cold death.

What did it matter what she did for the rest of her life? She was certain that she had been deceived, that Hendrik and his assistant were long gone, bundled out at dawn, sent off to freeze – or worse, hacked down from behind and buried in the snow. No one but John Crace would turn a dog out on such a day, but he would revel in it. He possessed no charity, no heart; his concern about his soul was a false gesture to dissipate damnation. His only passion lay in furthering his own interests; she had grasped that before she married him.

Since her visit to his house, she knew he exploited his position. Although she had hoped that his attraction to her might allow her to control his excesses, from the outset he had bent her to his will as if into an iron maiden. He had outwitted her. She wished he was dead.

Hailstones pelted devil's claws at the glass and made her shudder; then came the gentler crack of the fire and the step of Agatha to steady and comfort her.

And to pass a fold of paper small enough to hold between two fingers. She remembered the scrap of linen from Lukas.

'I managed to say farewell, madam. Nobody paid me any attention.'

Agatha waited for the chambermaid to go before continuing: 'The two men were to leave at midnight. But late last night I heard the servants whispering. The master had given special orders to do it earlier than planned, the moment you were abed, so there could be no fuss.'

Zenobia looked up. That meant no fuss from her. She clung to the bedpost. Short of killing Hendrik, or her, how could he have been more cruel?

'They were about to leave when there came that knocking,' Agatha continued. 'His lordship's son had arrived without warning. Master Snyders and Ewald were in the passage, bags in hand. His lordship had set four men on guard, including the thugs from the coach house. Once that was done, he retired.

'The plan was to go down through the gardens to the river gate, that's what I heard. But so much snow had blown against the back that it was blocked, and the path, too, as far as they could tell, for the door couldn't be opened more than an inch – and then on to a wall of ice. The delay digging through it would give them a chance to escape, which was the last thing he wanted. Even if they cleared a path, who knew if the skiff would be able to put out? The river was freezing clear across. They were to be taken as far as the estuary, and then drowned. That's what I heard. I know it isn't my place, madam, but –'

'It's all right,' Zenobia said dully. The same thought had tortured her all week: why let them live when he could murder them so easily? Drown them down-river and pass it off as an accident on the way to freedom. No one would dispute it; Crace could not be blamed. She was certain that had been his plan.

'Since that failed, they were just about to be taken out the front instead, when his lordship's son arrived. It wasn't in his lordship's reckoning to let Master Balthasar see them, in case it provoked questions. I've heard it said that the King himself has taken an interest in Master Snyders' work. Because of that, they were pushed into a chamber to one side while the young master and his men came in.'

'Did you *see* him?' Zenobia 's listlessness was gone, though her eyes were still dull.

'Yes, I was determined to be your eyes and ears. Before anyone could stop me, I went straight up and clasped his hand to fare him well. Why would those dolts bother with an unimportant woman? What harm could I do? I saw their faces. They could see that his hands were empty, and mine too, so I kept moving before they concocted a thought between them. They think like snails. If they belonged to me I would stamp on them. That's when he gave me this. It was so quick that I felt nothing till we parted. His eyes were eloquent, but all the same, it was only when I was ushered away that I felt it. I have not opened it. On my life, it is just as he gave it to me.'

The bit of paper had been folded in four to slip between two fingers. When Zenobia opened it, she recognised her own writing. Of course, she thought, he would not have had any opportunity to write anything himself, Crace had made sure of that.

It was the opening words of a note she sent Hendrik at the start of their affair, telling him to come and find her. Her first private note, and her last, for he said it was reckless, fatally foolish, and insisted she never write such an incriminating thing again lest it fall into the wrong hands. Now she knew he had kept it.

Her heart leapt. He had kept it so close and secret that he could find it in an instant and tear this piece from it before anyone saw. It must have been in his doublet, next to his heart.

'*Come to me*', it said, in her imperious, small hand. Neatly written – she had been in no rush when she wrote those words, idling over composing them, forming each letter as carefully as a caress; never dreaming that their affair would be found out. She had been delirious, desirous, happy; in control of her own destiny for the first moment since her betrothal to Crace. It seemed like the start of a light-hearted game, and how could such joyful feelings possibly be wrong? What a fool. What deathly folly to underestimate John Crace. Yet there they were, her own words, each as true now as then: *come to me.*

As for the remaining part, he must have it still. Every bit as incriminating, since it was in her hand and she remembered what she had written so teasingly. She shuddered. More than enough reason for Crace to kill Hendrik, and her into the bargain if it ever came into his hands.

Zenobia's heart somersaulted. Hendrik had risked his life to tell her he loved her. She clasped the precious thing. His were the last fingers before Agatha's to touch it, his last eyes to read it; and he held the other part, whose edges exactly fitted her own. A pledge which, put back together, would fit perfectly.

The thought made her burn with longing. However cavalier his behaviour had been at times, she was assured of his love now. Pushing the precious token deep in her petticoat pocket, she allowed Agatha to finish dressing her, before joining her husband to meet her son-in-law.

The snow's sullen persistence turned to renewed fury, so it was decided that the spoiled boy would stay a few days. In truth, he had no choice.

Zenobia struggled to detect a likeness between father and son. Where Crace was powerful, wide and swarthy, Balthasar, in his pompous red heels, was pale, slim and slightly bent, as if he might sway or break, with a habit of standing on one leg while the other traced the opening of a pavane. One be-ringed hand rested on his waist in a studied gesture, a waist emphasised by a narrow belt studded with square diamonds and cabochon rubies. In the height of French fashion, he was beribonned, dagged and slashed from every angle. He looked as foreign and Catholic as one person could look, and reeked of perfumed oils.

The only saving grace was that beside him her husband, who in his restrained way normally looked elegant, appeared clod-hopping and puritanical.

A great deal of work had gone into Balthasar's outfit. Even though her father had never created Frenchified suits like this, she could estimate it. Yet its exuberantly decorated surface made the youth inside seem insubstantial, a glittering puddle that would dry out at a harsh word. His long mouse-brown wig was as gently curled as if it had just been lifted from a travelling box, and so well done it looked real. It perfectly matched his small, crossed, calculating eyes. His cravat was cutwork, his one earring a large pearl and his moustache his own work, a wispy thing that could belong on his face or someone else's arse.

Having concluded this in a second, Zenobia executed her deepest curtsey, admiring the fluffy lemon pompoms on his shoes, the only coloured note in his black suit apart from his rubies. She had never seen a more pointless person in all her life – the most repulsive yet dangerous marvel, barring Uncle Thomas, that she had ever clapped eyes on.

'Your food, sir, is filthy,' Balthasar growled, legs out like his father, ignoring Fog, an affectionate, mangy bolster on whom his stacked heels rested. 'What sort of plague-riddled kitchens do you keep? One of my men has already died, yet we have been here but a handful of hours. I'd only had him a month. Given decent victualling, *certes* he would have recovered. Had I got him to court, upon my eyes, all would have been well. You should run a sepulchre. That's my advice to you, sir.'

Crace glared at the silly court language. Raised up, wrapped in furs, his chamber's ever-present stink masked by the equal stench of his son's perfume and of steaming dog, he considered this exudation of his loins thoughtfully, clasping his hands to hide his irritation.

Balthasar got up, stretched his legs like a hound and farted so voluminously that his breeches bellowed. He strutted to the window with his hands behind his back. The hound followed, a misty and malodorous tail.

It was no surprise that the servant had died. Two of Balthasar's retainers had arrived slung over their horses, and Crace expected that the other would soon follow his companion. It didn't bother him, unless they carried an evil miasma that could pass to his own men or even to him. Balthasar's fellows were ordered to dump the corpse outside, which they did with alacrity.

Although Crace suspected a simple case of putrid bowels, anyone who had lived through a plague had learned to be careful. It might always return, for 1665 had not been the first and would not be the last. On the basis that suspicion was the friend of longevity, he told his doctor to examine the yet-living man and report back. Meanwhile, surely this wind-blown idiot of a son could tell him something he did not already know. Had he not spent enough money on him to benefit?

Because of illness, Crace had not attended the court for a year and was aware that the fop's star had risen at his own expense. His palace spies informed him that the boy embraced Catholicism as if he wanted to wed it. But surely, he thought, Balthasar's newfound conviction could not be sincere, for throughout his lazy childhood, the boy had shown only cursory interest in God. Crace believed his conversion to be an affectation. Now that burning for heresy had fallen into disuse, why risk it? The prudent thing was to keep your head down, be temperate and resolute, and let the wheel turn. Why showily embrace a religion that could fall from favour as fast as a king?

Crace sighed. He believed in conducting politics and personal matters the same way as business, where wavering was untrustworthy. Better the man who stuck to his beliefs, even if they opposed one's own, than one who turned. Turn once, turn again.

In general, this principle had served him well, but not, he had to concede, in his public role, for there he was required to follow the religion of the King. But since the only god Crace truly served was self-interest, his resulting vacillation was no hardship. Perhaps, after all, the boy was more like him than he wanted to admit.

He studied him with distaste. Scratching a buttock through the breeches, gawping through the glittering panes, the dog a-quiver against him, farting competitively. God Almighty, in those huge billows of cloth and preposterous heels, he had the calves of a woman. He belonged on the stage. Had he not been his own fruit, he would have dispatched him with a shovel and put him under the snow.

Which explained why, had Hendrik Snyders not crossed the one uncrossable line, Crace would have been more inclined to own him for his son than this imbecile. Snyders was talented, opinionated, steadfast and bold, even when his life was at risk. That was when men stuck to what mattered, though sometimes they died for it. Crace saw it in Snyders' defiance, and it was the reason he had let him live.

From what Crace's informants told him of Whitehall, the King, while exhibiting some of the zealotry of the convert, was generally both fair and equable. He had never required pledges of faith from Crace beyond professional ones; for which confidence Crace held more than grudging respect. Besides, the ageing magistrate's influence was over and the King knew it.

But he was certain that this crackpate son would do anything to increase his own lustre, even by falsely tarnishing his father, which could be dangerous.

He paused to cough a bolus of soot-stringed snot on to the kerchief in his hands. Folding it quickly away, he wiped his mouth.

'How do you find the King?'

'His Majesty has expressed great interest to see your new ceiling.' Balthasar turned from watching driving snow in time to see the stained cloth disappear under the bed covers. He made a mental note to interrogate Crace's physician. It was high time his father died.

'For, as you would expect, His Majesty has heard of it,' he went on smoothly, 'and how remarkable quick it has been completed. Miraculous quick: that is what they say, sir. Surely not rushed for my benefit?'

Crace considered this fresh insolence. If he had not felt as sick as a dog, he would have leapt out of bed and boxed the boy's ears. 'We will look at it together this afternoon,' he said, rage making him ignore how faint he felt, his too-rapid heart. 'But now I shall rest.'

'Visit with my wife,' he instructed, sleepily aware that Stoddart had still not come to tell him the condition of the corpse. The fool's report would have to wait. Another candidate for a sharp blow with a shovel.

In the painted hall, Zenobia had stared so long at the ceiling that her neck ached. She hated to imagine what it must have been like for Hendrik this past week, working by candlelight, twenty hours at a time. The result was spectacular and the cartouche, the part he had done so fast, its crowning glory. There was no evidence of haste. On the contrary, speed had given the main characters' draperies, limbs and expressions fluidity and grace, a breathing vividness that she had never seen in a painting before.

Adam and Eve were tumbling from the Garden of Eden, which in a daring reworking, he had set in the heavens. As a girl, she had often wondered whether those magical gardens resided in her father's attics.

The couple's bodies twined about each other and almost touched, yet in their helpless hurtle towards hell they did not quite meet at any point, suffering together but alone. Hendrik's achievement was remarkable, as if they flew straight towards one. Adam plummeted like a burning brand, while Eve turned an Archimedean somersault around him, with back, buttock and breast exposed in a breathtaking spiral of a twisting fall, blonde tresses coiling like flying straw, glinting gold. Above them, their drapery flashed vertical towards the heavenly paradise forfeited forever.

How on earth had he achieved this heavenly magic? But now he was gone, leaving only a tantalising glimpse of paradise, plus a small piece of paper that burned in her skirts.

She had been afraid to look at the finished painting in case he had done something foolish, such as making Eve resemble her. But, apart from the blonde hair, this fat-buttocked temptress bore no resemblance, nor did Adam look like Hendrik, or even Crace.

How could she have credited him with so little intelligence? Had he done anything of that sort, then from the moment he pricked it out on the plaster, there would have been no chance of leaving the house alive.

Satisfied on this point, she turned to the great room's four corners, walking slowly, rubbing her back, determined to see all of it before the light faded. Perhaps there was some reference to their love in a detail only she would understand, so subtle that her husband's dogged intellect would not pry it out – for without doubt he would search for it. Certainly, during the preceding months, she had seen no such thing. But Hendrik might still have found a moment to add a touch that would speak only to her.

She began her patient examination.

Immersed in this activity she missed the subdued click as Balthasar tiptoed the length of the gallery.

'Does it please you, ma'am?'

Startled, she spun around and almost lost her balance, eyes and nostrils flaring.

'You seemed so rapt that I dared not interrupt,' he continued, his squinting eye that of a rock-lizard in a gap in a wall. 'You appear to be at your devotions. Yes, quite as if that were so. *Worshipping* at the altar of art.' In his sprightly manner, evil smoked. 'And who would not, faced with such a vision?'

Overwhelmed by the pungent scent that poured off him, she took a few steps back. Where had she smelled something like that before? Civet, mixed with cloying violet, a little amber and deep rose. Perhaps cloves, too – each one beautiful on its own, but melding into a stink as vivid as dung. She had married into a fetid family. She cursed herself for not smelling him coming.

Testing his calves like a dancer, he stepped delicately into the exact place she had just relinquished.

'What is it that held you so spellbound?' Though this was spoken in a dreamy tone, his eyes were sharp as pins. 'What held you so firmly that you did not hear the tarantella of my approach?' At which he rose, clattered like a doxy in a sort of plié and settled into a stance of affected contemplation.

'My father, though unable to partake of this marvel as we do, will surely want to know what binds you so fixedly. Shall we bring him in a chair so that we may all enjoy it together? Will that please you, madam?'

Giving a brief curtsey, Zenobia stood quietly to one side, hoping he could not see how her breasts rose and fell. Mustering strength, she smiled. This shrivelled turd would not outplay her.

'It pleases me vastly,' she managed, steadying her voice. Not that Balthasar was as attuned to its nuances as his father – although she wouldn't bet on it: a snake from start to finish. Had Hendrik known him, he might have given the boy's face to the serpent.

Thinking of Hendrik bolstered her confidence. 'The entire ceiling is wondrous, with a biblical tale in each corner,' she began.

'*This* corner in particular,' Balthasar interrupted, scrutinising it, 'is most unusual, surely? For here are Adam and Eve in the garden, enjoying their innocence before the serpent corrupts them; and here, high up in that tree laden with tantalising fruits is a most unusual dream, showing what appears to be a Protestant church, where they are being married . . . if my eyes do not deceive me. Is that not so? The figures may be small and have their backs to us, yet the woman with such fine blonde locks could surely only be Eve? Despite the *great pity* that we cannot see her face?

What say you, my lady?' He stared pointedly at Zenobia's hair, an evil smile on his lips, while his twisted eye darted here and there, impossible to follow or hold.

Under her breath she cursed him, but she held fast.

'Ah, sir, I commend your acuity and am certain that it must be she, even though, as you say, this scene is not in the Bible.' Pretending to look keenly at the painting, she held the smile to her face as if clinging to a rope in a river. 'But to my eye it is not possible to describe the church's disposition, since all we can see is the base of an altar, and that, at best, indistinctly. To my mind, sir, *altars* have no denomination?'

He wiped off a glare and changed tack. 'Then consider Adam.'

From inside his doublet, a double nose-pinch edged in thick black steel appeared, which he perched in place, his little finger out like a squirrel cock. 'Adam, if indeed that is he, turning around from the parson's blessing, looks different from the Adam who tumbles from grace. Dost thou not agree?'

Before she could reject his insinuation of a Protestant parson, not to mention of Hendrik himself, he dragged her, with unexpected strength, towards the central cartouche.

'Look thee up, madam! Do not hang thy head.' Hard as steel, the voice of an interrogator. His pointed fingernail under her chin, and the proximity of his person, made her want to scream. But she did as he asked, teeming with rage. Before she could reply, he dragged her back to the corner so roughly that she almost lost her footing.

'Look again at *this* face of Adam. Quite different, is it not? How is this marked discrepancy to be accounted for in so gifted a painter?'

Releasing her, he assumed a posture of reverent attention.

Good God, if she had had a sword, she would have smitten him to tiny pieces. This was no moment to be fainthearted for, like a sparrow-hawk, he would not hesitate to plunge at anything weak and rip it to shreds. There was no doubt any more that the tricked-out carcass before her was his father's son. Puny he might be; weak he was not. If she wanted to live, she must be careful. Her heart and lungs pounded; it was all she could do not to tear away in fear, but she did not flinch. He would not beat her at this game.

'Ah, but yet, sir, it is a most amusing convention, is it not?' The glassy calmness of her voice surprised them both.

'I agree that the painter has put himself into the picture instead of his signature, and I believe, master Balthasar, that among great artists it is a common jest; one that both Leonardo and Rubens employed to entertain their patrons. You who are so familiar with the court must recognise the honour the painter does your father by it. For does it not align him with the greatest patrons – the Medicis, the Strozzis?' It was no time for half-measures: 'Even, perhaps – though I tremble to be so bold – with the Papal Father himself?'

Desperate to move away from Hendrik's face, she went on at reckless speed. 'I feel confident that if we continue our search, we shall discover an image of your illustrious father himself, to complete the conceit.'

Eyes on her opponent she beamed, praying that he would believe her. This self-satisfied stinking toe-rag did not care about art; such monumental vanity was never interested in the achievements of others. Much as the light of a candle does not blaze beyond its circumference, so his focus would never penetrate far beyond his own sphere. She risked her life on it.

Balthasar suppressed a scowl.

'It appears that you know one or two very small things about art, madam. But more pressing concerns than female fancies occupy me, therefore I must leave you to them. I trust however that we shall meet at dinner, when you can present your *proofs* to my father.'

With which ominous word he clattered out.

Zenobia unclenched her hands and headed to her own chamber. Proofs, indeed! Something must be done about Balthasar, and without a moment's delay.

She rang for Agatha.

Crace did not come to the painted gallery that afternoon but slept until dinner. Shortly before the meal, since his master was still sleeping, Stoddart brought Zenobia the news that Balthasar's second servant was close to death. Each man, he said, had fallen victim to a despotic disorder of the bowels, refused food and water and become weak and hot, before succumbing to a profound sleep from which it was impossible to rouse them. He held no hope of recovery.

Before Zenobia sent Agatha for refreshments she took her aside to ask her opinion of Stoddart's diagnosis, for she rated Agatha's medical skills a great deal higher than those of the physician.

'Join us at dinner,' Zenobia told the doctor, 'and tell my husband of your findings. Meanwhile warm yourself. The fire is just fresh-made, it is a shame to spend it merely on my servant and me.'

A loping fellow, accustomed to being treated with abrupt disdain by Crace, who ignored his advice and regularly threatened to discharge him or force him to take his own medicine, Stoddart happily accepted a second glass from Agatha, who stood at a respectful distance, waiting to re-pour or bring more sweetmeats.

As the warmth and wine and food, not to mention pleasant female interest in his business, suffused him, he became more expansive. It struck him that he should talk to mistress Crace more often, she was remarkably perceptive and it was an error to think that just because she was young and blonde and lissom she must be stupid. It was evidently not the case. How good it was to be listened to so appreciatively.

'How do you find my husband's health, sir?' she asked sweetly, an imperceptible blink at Agatha keeping his glass brimming. 'Please be frank, I shall do my best to follow, complicated though these matters are for the female mind.'

He basked at her correct assessment of his superior mentality.

The firelight showed her bosom to pillowy advantage. This was a pleasant place to be. He could get used to it. Of course, should Crace die . . . He shook himself. If such thoughts ever came to his master's attention, it would be a death sentence.

'It is an imbalance between his inner organs and his skin,' he droned. Something trapped in his nose since birth resulted in a nasal twang that, he felt, had blighted his career. It often made him sound as if he was snorting, and at the point of orgasm he emitted a high-pitched whistle.

'He suffers from a disorder of elimination. What should come out in one way appears, mysteriously, to come out by another. He has what I shall call, so that you may follow, an overactive skin. I have never seen it, but I have read of it.' (This was a lie; he had done neither.)

Easing back, he bit into a plump little cake filled with cooked sweet custard and brandied cherries, with one cherry pert on top, and stole glances at her bosom between bites. The delicacy was delicious. Mistress Crace must have a wonderful pastry cook. What a relief it was to get away from the perpetual bad temper and smell that hung around Crace. If only this happy state could be made to continue.

'I struggle to follow your intelligence,' Zenobia said.

She pretended to look confused, though in fact there was no need for pretence, since the man rambled like a lunatic.

'Do you refer to that . . . *odour* . . . that comes now and then from my beloved husband?'

'Exactly so, madam,' he said, admiringly. 'You have grasped it.'

Ignoring his tone, she continued, 'Much as a river, if dammed in one direction, shall inevitably seep forth elsewhere?'

It was difficult not to laugh at the dumbfounded look on the doctor's face.

'Then, having studied all this, as you say, surely you can help him overcome it? He grows weaker by the day; listless, which is not in his nature. If I may put my innermost self in your hands, sir, I must confess that it makes me fearful.'

Stoddart was enjoying his fourth glass even more than the first. It was annoying to be brought back to her moribund husband's health. There were so many more interesting things to contemplate, such as her innermost self in his hands, and how they could sit a great deal closer together while they did so. He would much rather think about that.

He sighed discreetly and put his glass down. As long as he was employed by her husband he must also answer to her, but when *he* was her master, she would talk a great deal less. There were much better things for her to do.

'In such a case, the outcome is never clear,' he said assertively, 'nor whether he will recover, given his age.'

'Surely you cannot mean that he may die?' She brought the final word out with tremendous effort, clasped her hands and looked beseeching, rose prettily but then staggered, clutching at her chair-back.

'Sir, you cannot let him die, because . . .'

Looking about wildly she tailed off, pressed one hand to her stomach and held the other out fetchingly towards Agatha, who somehow just caught her as she toppled over.

'Father in Heaven,' proclaimed Stoddart, 'what ails your mistress?' He rose to lend a hand, though to his irritation Agatha, who was a great deal stronger than she looked and quick on her feet, somehow blocked his path to loosening Zenobia's bodice, which he insisted was an immediate necessity.

'Surely she cannot be touched by the sickness the men have brought?' He took a step back.

Agatha hesitated. How *could* this maggot have qualified as a doctor? On the other hand, it might be useful that he was as blunt as a spoon. One should never discount the gifts God gave.

'Ah, sir, you have prised it out of me,' she said, straight-faced, 'though it is not my place to reveal. My livelihood hangs on less, which a man of your brilliance will understand. But since you insist, my mistress is with child, I am quite sure of it. These five months at the very least, by my calculation, and more than likely six, sir.'

Crace lost no time announcing a feast, for with characteristic economy he realised that he could use it to celebrate both the new ceiling and the impending birth of what he declared would be a son. Zenobia stayed constantly at his side, brushing off any enquiry into her own health and supporting him when he tired, which was increasingly often. She attended to his every need with widely remarked solicitude.

Balthasar, still housebound by great clumps of dirty snow turning to ice outside, spent most of his time with his six living men, carousing, dicing and upending any maid or groom who went near them. Otherwise he sulked and did not hide it. His attempt to poison his father's mind against his stepmother had failed for, having staged a miraculous recovery from her fainting spell, Zenobia leapt out of bed the moment that Stoddart, who told her to stay there for a week, left and immediately took her husband to show him the parts of the painting that did him such credit. Just as she had hoped, Hendrik had painted a small likeness of Crace as patron into a scene in the corner diagonally opposite the dream of Adam and Eve.

On a pallet carried by four sweating bearers, whatever Crace really thought of the vast ceiling above him, he felt too bone-weary to be combative. There was certainly no doubt that the Dutchman had painted him well; one might say handsomely. There was nothing to find fault with, indeed it was regrettable not to have included a full-size portrait in the commission, given the man's skill. But it was too late for that now.

Crace never dwelt on failure, on which strategy his success was partly based. Nor did he think for a moment that the child Zenobia carried was anyone's but his. Not only because he combined overweening arrogance with a striking ignorance of reality, but because of Stoddart's relayed prediction that the pregnancy was so far advanced. Stoddart had not troubled himself to investigate further, which was fortunate for Zenobia, since he never washed his hands and had just examined the putrid corpse of Balthasar's second man. And Crace did not so much as consider the idea of Zenobia lying with Hendrik Snyders the very day they met. Those of extreme sexual voracity rarely countenance the possibility of a similar appetite in others.

More than that, once he had been told that she was with child, he reversed his impression of what had taken place between his wife and the painter, and concluded that his spies, in their wish to please him, had made over-zealous reports. For although there had been accounts of potentially clandestine conversations, he had not received any actual evidence of their lying together or anything remotely approaching it.

With good reason, for after their first satisfactory grapple behind the tapestry, they had been circumspect. At Hendrik's insistence, greatly helped by hot weather, they only met at the temple. This made it impossible for the most eagle-eyed spy to say anything beyond the fact that they *might* have met, for they came and went at different times and by different routes. And Zenobia's rapidly escalating interest in gardening had made sure that no trees or shrubs spoiled the view from the folly, which also meant that no trees were near enough to be used to spy into it either.

Crace's reappraisal did not diminish his loathing of the painter but did increase his desire for his wife. Certain that the child in her entrails was his, he would have lavished a great deal of physical attention on her if he not begun to feel increasingly weak and nauseous.

The evening after the announcement, Zenobia and Agatha spent much of the day with the cooks, discussing how to dress the boar that would be spitted, how long to roast the various furred and feathered meats, from venison to the smallest quail and locally netted moorhen, and what other delicacies to prepare. A hundred people had been invited, with musicians brought in and all manner of seasonal delights that included, along with sweet and savoury pies and tarts, spectacular ices made with dried and preserved fruits and gloriously coloured syrups, all of which were laid up in the enormous pantries, using ice cut from the ice houses, as well as snow.

Crace kept the house fully lardered so that he could entertain the King and his retinue at short notice, so little needed to be sent out for, even though the snow was at last beginning to thaw.

Invigorated by planning a dazzling event with the happy prospect of feasting and dancing, Zenobia was relieved to draw on these plentiful supplies. She and Agatha spent hours cloistered in the preparation rooms and cellars, examining and tasting, mixing and muddling. They kept the cooks and pastry chefs busy from dawn until dusk.

One evening Zenobia told Crace that she would like to involve Balthasar, and ask him to stay until the celebration, rather than going to the palace, as he planned.

'This is the first time that he and I have met . . . my love,' she urged, sitting close and petting Crace's hand in a way she had never done. 'I fear that as soon as the snow finally clears he will set out. It will not be long now. God knows he has not concealed how dull he finds life here. Once diverted by the amusements of Whitehall, will he return? Therefore, may we persuade him to stay until the feast? I should welcome his help.'

Crace replaced his now habitual grimace of pain with a smile, a rare event these days. He had not expected her unfamiliar softness. Nature was evidently working from within, readying her for the role ahead. Stoddart had said as much. It struck him afresh that once she gave birth to a son, Balthasar would be far less important, which idea he greeted with more than equanimity. He agreed at once, only in stronger terms: he would inform the boy that his assistance was both desired and required, taking on some of the responsibilities of his father to support his stepmother.

'All will be as you suggest,' he pronounced. 'I will tell him at dinner. Rest assured, my love, he will guide you in all things.'

He had never before called her 'my love', either.

But Balthasar did not appear for dinner. After waiting less than ten minutes, furious at the boy's contempt, Crace gave a signal to begin. Next to him, to help, and to pour his wine, Zenobia laid her jewelled fingers on his. 'We should enquire after his health,' she said gently. 'Yesterday he seemed out of sorts, and unlike yours, his constitution is delicate.'

Tempted to brush her charitable gesture aside, flattering though it was, Crace agreed, though it annoyed him to wait. At her insistence, he began alone. His stomach hurt, but he hoped that warm broth would soothe it.

And it was not Balthasar but Stoddart who arrived five minutes later, at a trot instead of his usual lazy amble. 'Forgive me, sire,' he snorted, hovering uneasily as Crace continued to spoon up nourishing mutton and barley.

'Forgive me, but Master Balthasar exhibits signs of the malaise that took his men.'

He crossed himself and blinked nervously. Crace rubbed a piece of bread around the slops, let them sink in and ate the sopping pieces. Finally, he laid the spoon down.

'Speak straight,' he said. 'Do not mince. Will he mend?'

Stoddart glanced uneasily at Zenobia. 'It is too early to say . . .'

Zenobia straightened her spoon beside her plate of untouched soup. 'I shall go to him, John,' she said, 'he cannot lie alone.'

Crace's fury was palpable. 'You shall do no such thing, not with my son swelling your innards. Great God in the Heavens, madam, are you gone clean mad?'

'Do not leave his side,' he bellowed at the physician. 'Do whatever can be done. Spare no effort. My wife is not to go near him, do you understand? Not even to stand at the door. On my order.' He glared from one to the other.

Once the physician had left, Crace stared at his empty bowl, his arms slack. He looked puzzled. 'I do not feel quite well,' he said, his brow sheening with sweat. 'Damnation on the boy for bringing pestilence upon me.' He tried to rise, but faltered, at which Zenobia signalled for help and John Crace was carried to his bedchamber.

Balthasar's death two nights later surprised no one. His symptoms appeared the same as those of his stricken men, a tormented stomach and continuous purging from both ends. He died, the servants whispered, contorted, crawling around under the bed looking for his dog. Unlike the wasted bodies of his men, however, his was not dumped outside in the rapidly vanishing snow.

Alas for Balthasar, as he futilely sought a shred of comfort from the one creature who was actually fond of him, Zenobia ordered Fog brought to her. She said she had taken a fancy to its mournful face, and woe betide Stoddart if she was not humoured. She was adamant that the shambling animal could not transmit human sickness. Despite its dolorous expression, it abounded with health.

Even more unfortunately, as Balthasar lay dying, the focus of the household swung towards his father. Stoddart immediately abandoned the sick boy to his men. The well-being of John Crace was far more important. Given that an atmosphere of constantly voiding guts was intolerable, unobserved by the last vestige of Crace's household, Balthasar's men set about drinking in the antechamber and left their master to die alone.

Stoddart was not a complete fool. He knew what a pathetic doctor he was and that he lacked the slightest medical qualification. He suspected that Zenobia either knew or guessed it, and if not her, then certainly her sharp-nosed woman.

If only he could keep Crace alive just a bit longer, he thought, he would retain his credibility and after a brief interlude make a play for the widow. Whereas if both son and master died in rapid succession under his care, he would be very unlikely to secure another position, let alone live, unless he could persuade Zenobia to marry him – which even then he still did not rule out. If that plan failed, he would have to try his luck far from London and perhaps abroad. It struck him even more gloomily that he might have to return to Scotland, where he had been born. This was a dreadful prospect, given that there was a charge of fatal incompetence outstanding that could destroy if not hang him. Therefore, he vowed fervently to Zenobia that he would do his very best to save her husband's life.

To himself he admitted he had never seen anything like it. When he entered the chamber that evening, Crace was vomiting into a shallow bowl, though the vomit looked normal enough, with no blood. Stoddart prescribed warm water mixed with a little wine to ease his stomach. It was his fall-back when he had no idea what to do, since it rarely caused harm and occasionally helped. Crace refused. Between moans he described burning pains, as if someone were taking a red-hot poker to his innards and scraping his guts out with it. His eyes as he described his anguish were haunting.

Despite Stoddart's entreaties, Zenobia would not move from her seat next to the bed, but dropped her eyes when Crace spoke.

'Is it the same malady?' she asked quietly when he dozed for a moment.

'It would appear so,' Stoddart snorted. In fact, he was utterly uncertain, but had no better idea.

After a while, Crace fell into a deeper sleep.

The doctor diluted strong wine in a pitcher of water. 'He must take something,' he said. 'He has lost liquidity. This will soothe and replete him. It was the same with his son. It is most vital that his liquid is replaced. Desiccation would be his downfall. His humours are entirely out of sorts; he burns horribly and must be cooled. I will leave this pitcher. It must be administered whenever he wakes. He must be liquidated. You also must take some fortification,' he continued. 'I insist that you retire to your chamber to rest and take nourishment. This is no place for anyone in your condition. As your husband's physician, I command it.'

Making him promise to summon her if there was any change, Zenobia reluctantly agreed, saying that she would shortly send Agatha to assist with Crace's liquidation.

The household waited. What was left of Balthasar lay freshly embalmed in the painted gallery, with Adam and Eve heading for a direct collision with the herb-stuffed body. The mason cut a monument. On the side, in his workshop he also blocked out a much bigger piece for Crace. Word got about, even to the mason's yard.

Crace was still fit enough to emend his will. Striking the boy out, he made the whole estate over to Zenobia and through her the unborn child, including the house that Balthasar had recently set out from on his fateful journey.

Balthasar's death met with little more than formal expressions of sadness. Even his father, bent on staying alive, mourned more in appearance than fact.

The feast was cancelled.

Balthasar's remaining men set out at once with a letter from Crace to King James. Crace expected little to come of it, and he was right. Absent from court for so long, his reputation destroyed by his son, he could not expect royal interest in his deteriorating condition. Even so, with a flash of the tenacity that had not yet deserted him, it crossed his mind that the royal physicians would do a better job than his own and wondered whether they could be bribed to come.

Zenobia stayed a great deal in her chamber and spent the rest of the time by her husband's bedside. He was making a slow recovery, which perplexed Stoddart even more than his affliction had, though he hid it well. He had been certain that Crace would die. But after three days he sat up, to find Zenobia, as so often now, dozing next to the bed.

Crace looked down at the girl he had married four years earlier. She had grown lovelier. Pregnancy had enlarged her beneath her bodice and buskin, swollen her breasts and given her face rounder contours. Her bright hair, the first thing he noticed when he met her, shone, and was fashionably dressed. She had never worn a wig. The black gown she insisted on wearing to mourn Balthasar enhanced the almond tones of her hair and her peerless skin. As she rested, cheeks flushed, her parted lips showed even, pretty teeth that were so unlike his own. He wondered whether he would live long enough to see his child born or to engender another.

He brushed the foolishness aside. He was determined to live and felt better than he had for a while. He would dress and dine; a good piece of meat would work wonders. Perhaps he did not have the fatal malaise after all, or perhaps – which struck him as more likely – his robust constitution had put paid to it. If Balthasar had not been so feeble, he too would be alive yet.

He looked at the black silk clothing Zenobia's belly and wondered when the child would come.

As he looked, her hand, clasping a handkerchief in her lap, slipped off her skirts. A small phial fell to the boards and disappeared under his bed. He heard it roll. The dark little bottle looked like smelling salts. Since he could not get out of bed unaided and had no wish to wake her, he rang for help to retrieve it, but in doing so knocked over the full water goblet that she kept constantly renewed and to hand by his bed.

Zenobia's black eyes flew open like startled crows. For a particle of a second she seemed as shocked as if he was a ghost or she had never seen him before. Then she smiled.

'My lord, have I deserted you and slept? Can you forgive me?'

'It is of no consequence,' he replied. 'Nothing has happened, but you have dropped your salts.'

She looked puzzled. 'There,' he gestured impatiently, 'look there, it must have rolled near your feet, a small flask.'

She bent and retrieved it quickly, though with a little difficulty because of her expanding waist, and dropped it neatly through her pocket slit. 'You think of me even when you suffer yourself.' She reached out and kissed his ring. 'What would I do without you?'

One hand still in the pocket, she waved away the servant who had just come in. 'Let me refill your water glass with my own hand,' she said, 'and help you drink.'

CHAPTER THREE

*L*it by candles in sconces on one cool stone wall, the pastry cooks' preparation room in the bowels of the kitchen wing was so cold that breath hung in great clouds as an uneasy mist. From the high, unadorned windows, from the smooth marble slabs for working chocolate and pastes, and from the stone floor, dampness crept. The fire was out to ashes. Empty pie cases made of cold-water dough stood in rows like abandoned sandcastles, gently decaying, spotted with mould. One that had fallen in resembled an ancient cheek. All forgotten since Balthasar's death and the abandonment of the feast.

From her pocket, Agatha took a twist of paper that held a dozen ovoid seeds like small, striated black pearls. She looked at their near roundness, at the faint patterns on their shining surface; they almost resembled a sort of beetle. Gently, she ground them in a white marble mortar, adding drops of sweet almond oil one by one to make a black paste. It was hard to imagine anything quite so black.

As she worked unhurriedly with repetitive twists of her wrist, the grinding released the smell of the almonds and nothing else. In a bigger mortar, she pounded handfuls of roasted cocoa beans into fine powder, to which she added thick cold cream, butter, plentiful orange zest and honey. The result was smooth and glistening. She tasted it, added just a little more honey, and mixed it again.

Putting a third of this into the small bit of silky black paste, she blended them thoroughly. She divided this mixture between four crisply baked pastry barques almost the length of her thumb, scraping every bit out as if it was black gold, working neatly, never sullying the filling with the touch of her fingers. Not a drop fell on the slab. To finish, she smoothed their surfaces and decorated each little boat with a large piece of orange peel preserved in sugar.

Having put the used pestle and spoon in the stone sink, she washed them using water from a tall jug, dried them, then thoroughly washed and dried her hands, before replacing the pestle on its shelf and the spoon in a drawer. Returning to the table, Agatha deftly filled twelve more pastry boats with the larger amount of plain chocolate paste, scooping a little less glossy chocolate mixture into each shell than before.

She tasted the mixture again with her fingertip. It was rich, deeply aromatic from cocoa and orange, and honey-sweet, so that one craved more. She cut some pieces of orange peel in three and decorated each of the dozen new barques with one of these smaller pieces.

The larger group looked much less enticing than their four companions.

She set the pestle and spoon in the sink for the scullery boys, arranged all sixteen pastries on a large majolica dish and put the leftover orange in a handkerchief to eat later, because she was fond of it.

After a final look around, Agatha extinguished the candles, making sure that they did not reignite. John Crace had often said that what he prized her for was thoroughness. As threads of smoke twirled upwards, she carried the plate from the room and shut the door firmly behind her.

A week had passed since Balthasar's death. At the evening meetings with Zenobia that Stoddart enjoyed so much, he grew daily more confident that Crace would survive. There was no doubt, he twanged, that her husband's vitality had been sapped and that he suffered exhaustion and nausea, but he was not worse.

However, alone with his books each day, Stoddart panicked. He could find no symptoms that matched Crace's and had no idea what was wrong or what had caused the violent sickness. If it was the same thing that killed Balthasar, why hadn't Crace died? But in the light of Zenobia's unstinting admiration and gratitude, he would as likely have admitted his ignorance as sawn his feet off. Besides, Stoddart also believed in the indomitable quality of Crace's will.

The day following Balthasar's interment in the Crace vault was gloomy for everyone from the lowest pan-scourer upwards, since no one dared to appear cheerful.

'We must lift our spirits or we shall all decline,' Zenobia announced firmly that night. She put her needlework aside and, apparently absentmindedly, tucked a cutwork fichu into her bodice, aware that its whiteness immediately brightened her skin. Covertly she watched Stoddart's expression.

Just before he came in she had flamed her cheeks with a spirited amount of rouge. 'Dolour does us no favours,' she cooed softly, quickly checking her reflection. She poured Stoddart a large glass of metheglin.

'I have instructed Agatha to prepare the sweetmeats that my husband loves above all others,' she went on, as if announcing a strategy for storming a stronghold. 'It is hard enough to bury a son when one is hale. Even he is not made of iron.

'Yet,' she went on, sounding anxious, 'do you consider that his stomach will be able to digest them, given his recent malaise, for though dainty they are undoubtedly rich. I should not wish to do anything that might harm him or cause a reversal. Better that we all sup on stale bread and water if you think there is any chance, however remote, of that being the case.'

She smouldered appealingly from under pale lashes.

Stoddart enjoyed being asked for his advice. Anything that kept him in her company a little longer, leaning towards him conspiratorially, showing the deep rift between her breasts to tantalising effect.

'I am sure so,' he soothed. 'He has shown marked improvement recently and we all need our spirits raised. As long as he does not overindulge.'

The oily, creeping sound that came from his throat as he said the last word made her want to nail his tongue to the bedpost.

'Very well,' she replied, ignoring the way the fool looked at her. 'Very well, sir, I knew I could put myself in your hands. I shall limit him to just one or two. Though as you are aware he is not a man to be checked. You must taste them too, doctor, but only if you have a mind. My husband proclaims them to be most delicious. Agatha!' she called, 'shall you attend us shortly with a flagon of honeyed wine, and afterwards, the sweetmeats.'

Leaning her warm weight on Stoddart's arm, Zenobia left the room, her wide skirts rustling along the flags of the cloister. Gracefully, slowly, Zenobia walked. Flaming sconces turned her diamond-twined hair into a halo. From the darkness outside came a sudden blade of moonlight, a dart so bright it would pierce the most corrupt heart. In the silent garden, under a cloudless sky, moonlight bleached the marble benches and plants intended to shade John Crace. Glancing in through those glittering windows, it was as if an angel hovered; but whether of life or of death was impossible to tell.

The group around the high bed had already drunk half the metheglin when Agatha arrived. Warming and sweet, fermented from home-grown honey tinged with the rosemary Crace loved, it fortified the heart and calmed the senses. Zenobia smiled as she freshened his glass. This was no time to stint, she said; who knew what the future held. They should toast happier times; the birth of their son. In her soft hand the viscous liquid glinted and danced like a golden articulated bird.

From raised pillows Crace looked on with appreciation. The wine mellowed him, made him consider afresh whether he could bed her yet. Across his drawn face came a hint of colour.

Seeing it, she stroked his hand and, observing how her touch moved him, continued. Delicate against his coarser skin, her fingers evidently awoke hope.

'My husband is well tonight,' she declared proudly to Stoddart, her breast quivering as if she might explode with pleasure. It was as much as he could do not to dribble.

'We are grateful to you for your constant attention,' she went on, stroking with her voice. 'You have saved my husband's life and will be richly rewarded.'

The intense look she gave him confused him; he was almost sure that he saw the lustrous depths of her eyes flame, though it was surely only a candle flash.

'Give me the platter,' she commanded Agatha, seizing the dish so that Crace could choose a sweetmeat. When he had taken one she took one herself, then offered them to the doctor, who took the nearest. Crace demanded them back and helped himself to another two.

'My husband, I delight in your appetite,' she purred, 'but the doctor will certainly forbid you to have any more.'

She smiled on Stoddart in such a way that he saw her swimming in a red haze, naked, her breasts tipped with tiny raspberries that he would gladly lick and eat. Who knew what violent carnage would follow. He shook himself. The wine must be very strong.

'I am sure it can do no harm,' he got out hoarsely, basking in the warmth of her eyes, helping himself to two more succulent aromatic treats, daring to hand her one with his fingers. As if she did not notice the impropriety, and which sent him into a further rush of desire, she swallowed it whole, and picked the last crumbs from her lips with the tip of her tongue.

'If you are quite sure, doctor,' she said, 'though so much rich food may not be wise? Nor for me, either – although from your hand it is irresistible. I would assuredly make myself foolish if I had more.'

He bridled, goatishly.

Meanwhile, since the plate had somehow been left on his lap and no one was paying attention, Crace was on the point of tucking a fourth little boat, brimming over with its dark cargo and large orange sail, into his mouth.

Zenobia snatched the plate playfully away, although not in time to retrieve the pastry from his fingers. 'My husband,' she scolded, leaning over and kissing his cheek as he swallowed it, 'for your own good, I beg you, desist.'

The next morning passed uneventfully. Crace kept to his chamber; Zenobia, as instructed, kept to hers, with a new maid in attendance.

That afternoon she rang for Stoddart to complain of a stomach upset by rich food. She remained in bed the rest of the day, constantly attended by Agatha, but rejoicing to the doctor that her husband was, as ever, more stalwart than she – and how glad too that she had prevented him from eating any more, for even a man of his prodigious constitution should not be reckless.

Stoddart attended them both. He expected a first pregnancy to have queasy episodes, so was certain that nothing serious afflicted her except fatigue and indulgence. He had eaten the same amount and felt perfectly well. He was sure she had worn herself out looking after her husband instead of leaving it to the servants, which had made her susceptible to a disturbance of her humours.

Against her laudable wifely wishes and constant enquiries after her lord and master – which was how she put it to him, while he marvelled at her subservience and fantasised about its application to himself – he insisted that she keep to her rooms.

That evening Crace complained of nausea. Given that it had become common these past days, Stoddart settled him with his usual panacea of watered wine and platitudes. Reassured by Stoddart's account, Zenobia did not set foot in her husband's chamber, and the household went to bed.

In the morning, having told one of the two maids who had been with her all night that she felt refreshed, Zenobia went to pay her respects to her husband.

The doors to his chamber stood wide open, which was unusual.

Doubled up in a spasm over the edge of the bed, Crace let out grating noises, while Stoddart and a manservant stopped him falling. Dreadful sounds ground from his innards. His face was ashen and beaded; his nightshirt, transparent and sticking, gave his massive body the frailty of a pupa after the butterfly has flown: a husk.

Zenobia had spent an hour being helped into a new gown to please him, but faltered in case he vomited over her. She approached with doubtful steps, holding her stomach to protect it from whatever afflicted him.

'Is it safe to go nearer?' she asked. 'What fresh ailment assails him now?'

Stoddart did not miss the reproach.

'I do not yet know, ma'am.' Rebuffing her accusation, he contemplated his patient from an equally safe distance. Awkwardly propped, the sick man looked deranged. His weight made him difficult to move.

The full hideousness of his condition became apparent. Blood-grained vomit had spewed across the sheets; his eyes were coagulating like coddled eggs. His face was puce, and from his half-open lips, which were as black as his tongue, came sooty drool.

The room was filled with a stench more horrible than any yet, a mixture of urine, vomit and excrement, and a metallic tang that struck at the back of the throat. It was all Zenobia could do not to clap a handkerchief to her face.

'His heart races as a snared rabbit,' Stoddart confided hoarsely. 'He burns and strains to pass bloody stools. He has been contorted with fever and purging these two hours. I did not wish to wake you, hoping that the crisis would pass, but it has become more savage. It is as if his body is dissolving into itself, as if it melts.'

Zenobia staggered, but rejected his offer to help with an angry look. He felt her accusation once more.

Righting herself, she fixed him with searing black eyes. 'Then you will save him.' All softness was gone. 'You have done it before and must again. I forbid you to let my beloved lord and master die. Is that understood?'

It was not a question.

She began to push him towards Crace, noting that he resisted more strongly than one would expect.

'I fear there is no hope.' He pushed back.

After plucking his sleeve from her grasp, Stoddart gravely led her to a chair far from the bed. Wedging her into it, he stood behind.

'I do not advise remaining here. The purulence is insinuating and devious. Who knows where it may next fly, what orifice it will sniff out. This is no place for a woman; it could seep between your thighs and thence into the child in your womb.'

Zenobia spun around and glared at him.

Throughout this exchange Crace stared at his wife in her new velvet gown as if he had never seen her before. Without warning, he painfully raised one arm. Slowly, terribly, damp linen clinging like a shroud, he pointed a shaking forefinger at her.

'Dear God in heaven, what on earth can he mean?' Wrenching herself from the chair she rushed to the bed and pressed the accusing hand to her face, sobbing.

Making savage gargling noises, Crace struggled to free himself, but she clasped his hand tighter and sobbed louder.

He began to double up again and his grip slackened for a moment. Zenobia threw herself to the floor and lay writhing in helpless abandon. At which Stoddart, ignoring Crace's renewed attempts to speak, rushed to her and urged her to leave, telling her that he would let her know through Agatha the moment there was any change.

'He tried to accuse me,' Zenobia moaned as Agatha mopped her brow. 'He pointed, like this. He could hang me!' Her eyes darted, as if to pry out spies in the corners.

The room was almost dark, lit only by a newly laid fire and single candlestick on a low table. Zenobia and Agatha gleamed black and red in the unequal flames. Agatha's shadow, ten-foot tall, flickered up the wall and across the ceiling. Across the room the new maid crouched on a stool to listen for approaching footsteps.

Agatha stroked and stroked Zenobia's hair. 'There,' she counselled, smoothing with blunt passes, as if the younger woman was a cat. 'Stay stalwart. All will be well. He knows nothing. A stab in the dark, that is all. No human hand can save him now. Be steadfast and hush. Let not fright betray you.'

Zenobia looked into the darting tongues as the strengthening fire belched sparks. Agatha's words steadied her.

A knock came at the door.

At Stoddart's approach, Agatha calmly lit an extra candle and held it to guide him.

His face was terrified, bewildered, all colour drained from it, leaving only shock.

'Then it is over,' Zenobia said tonelessly, twisting to bury her face against Agatha. Stoddart heard the loud sobs that broke from her, but missed the jubilation in her eyes.

PART SIX

CHAPTER ONE

*Z*enobia contemplated John Crace's face. Every line was commanding and cruel, but in death it was more hawk-like, the features sharper: the true image of the man. Such a man did not die easily and it satisfied her that he had not. In the end, she thought, gluttony not power had been his abiding passion, whether for wealth or women. Gluttony was his life force, gluttony his downfall. She was glad that his fate had been terrible, that he had tasted some of the horror meted out to Lily. If he had not murdered Lily, if he had not betrayed *her* with his promise to save Lily, he might be alive yet. He had reaped as he had sown. Three long years had passed since Lily's death, but at last, justice had been served.

The doors of Crace's former bedchamber flew open and Hendrik Snyders strode in. 'Rise, my dearest. Agatha arrived from the country a full hour ago and waits impatiently to see you.'

Zenobia dragged her glittering eyes from the new ceiling painting above her, from which fading whiffs of turpentine still came. John Crace's face, mounted on the serpent's body, writhed in Paradise. She laughed and held out her arms.

'You have got him to the life!'

Lit by mid-morning sunshine, she was beautiful, exulting from the lace-decked bed. 'Short of his head on a spike, you could not have pleased me more.'

High above, in the just redecorated bedchamber, a new Adam and Eve, who bore more than a passing resemblance to the humans beneath, twined in a close embrace, while on the serpent, caught fast in a tree, Crace's face boiled.

'Just a few moments, then.'

He vaulted the steps and landed fully clothed, a spur tangling in the covers.

'I told Agatha that the delay was from dressing, but she knows you better. I will paint that thing out when our daughter is old enough to ask about it. However vastly it amuses you, it is not seemly. I refuse to lie beneath it forever.'

'Never,' she retorted. 'This face is his monument. I promised him one and here it is, higher and far more memorable than he expected. It captures his soul. Sheherezade will never be forced into a marriage like mine. She and her girls after her will be so wealthy, thanks to him, that they will never answer to anyone – but it is your name they will bear.'

Her words were so cool that silence fell between them.

Hendrik felt his way slowly. 'You know that I fully expected to die at his hands? And what Agatha told me about what he did to you justifies your hatred. But even so, the depth of it surprises me, given that he has been dead for months, and you have a great fortune, a beloved child and our happiness. What more do you want before you consign him to hell? If only you would tell me, it would be easier to understand.'

She settled into his shoulder. 'You do not know the half of it.' Her voice vibrated with remembered rage. 'However badly he treated me, it wasn't enough to die for. But the day I married him, he had a woman falsely hanged. The very day. She was innocent, and he knew it.'

As if some fierce debate raged within her, she paused, and silence hung like an invisible weight.

'Then who was she? What was she to you? Not your mother?'

She shook her head and relaxed her clenched fists. 'No, she was long dead. He knew this woman's innocence because I had told him. And there was no doubt of the truth, because it was me who committed the crime.'

Before Hendrik could speak, she went on in a determined rush.

'Her name was Lily. We only spent one evening together, but I liked her and expected to see her again. I never knew my mother, and Lily was the only person who ever behaved like one. She tried to save me from making a terrible mistake; she saw my stubbornness and tried to stop me. I will never forget it.' Her face had softened, but immediately sharpened. 'She didn't deserve to die. He murdered her as if he released the trap himself. She must have cursed the day her path crossed mine, for it was my idle curiosity that killed her. He hanged her to prevent it coming out that it was me who shot my uncle. He could have let her escape; it would have been so much easier. He forced me to marry him by vowing to let her go on the day we were married. I only learned that he had had her hanged three years later. Every day of my marriage had been a betrayal and a lie.'

Appalled, Hendrik asked how she knew.

'As a girl, Lily was Agatha's companion, and Agatha was at the execution. Lily died because of me and though I can never change it, I owe her an irredeemable debt. I thank God every day for ending his life, for if God hadn't, I swear I would have done it myself.'

Hendrik shook her. 'Never say such a terrible thing, not even in jest! You are no murderer, even if he was. You are just overwrought at remembering.'

'You say that because you love me.' She buried her face against him. 'But I exulted when he died, and as God is my witness, I *would* have done it. I'd worked out how. There were certain plants in the garden. I knew which ones they were, and I was going to –'

Hendrik put his hand across her lips. 'Hush, speak no more of this. Never. Whatever dark thoughts he drove you to, you did not do it. Whatever terrible ideas you had during all the time that he mistreated you, they were just that – ideas; thoughts. Thoughts are not a crime. He died of natural causes, he was ill; he was an old man, and God took him. That is what his physician recorded, and that is all. Why have you borne this anguish without telling me? Come here.'

Swinging long legs over the bed, Hendrik sprang up and embraced her, dashing tears from his own eyes, though she did not see. 'Now, beloved, dry your eyes. We must not keep Agatha waiting any longer.'

CHAPTER TWO

*D*agbert Oliphant Esquire, Keeper of Newgate, took an interest in some of his prisoners that went further than the usual sphere, an interest he considered beyond speculation; something that would offer the world great psychological and scientific insights, and immortalise his name in centuries to come.

Although the prison had burned down during the Great Fire, it had been rebuilt, and by no less a genius than Christopher Wren. In the new gatehouse, the Keeper's rooms were comfortable and commodious, warmed by generous fires and illuminated by numerous sparkling panes in the high, leaded windows. Standing at the window of his office provided Oliphant with an excellent view of those traversing the main gate and entering the master's yard, both prisoners and public alike. Closing his eyes, tipping back his chair, a small glass of porter and a neatly tamped pipe within reach, he folded his arms behind his head and contemplated with great satisfaction the rich purple wall-coverings that had been hung last week. It was true that in such quantity the colour was strident, but afternoon sun lightening a section of giant ogees on the thick silk helped a great deal. And it looked very expensive, which since it had been brought over from Italy, was consoling. Besides, he had only himself to please, for he was not the marrying kind and the cost would go through the prison's books and be borne – as was only fitting – by the wards themselves. What did it matter if their victuals were short for the next few months? It wasn't as if the majority of them did anything except stroll around the yards taking pleasant exercise, for which they hardly needed food at all. Some of them arrived distinctly fat from crime: he was doing them a service. As for those chained in the airless cells below, they were beneath his consideration.

Oliphant himself was thin to the point of emaciation, though not for the sake of trying, for he had a prodigious appetite and never stinted himself or his guests, eating copious rich food. But somehow nothing stuck to his ribs, just as kindness and compassion never stuck to his heart. He was made dry, his humours were dry, his hands were dry, and his spirit, not content with matching his baser parts, was desiccated.

As a boy, he could not possibly have foreseen the position of importance and authority to which he would rise. Young Dagbert, raised at Islington, was a zealous trapper of live flies and wasps, which he mounted on pins in a neat felt-lined boxwood tray that he constructed for the purpose; and then he watched them die. He liked to watch from start to finish, leaning on his elbows; becoming sullen if his mother, who took in piece-work and mending, interrupted or had him run an errand. After the first few creatures had lived their last on one of Dagbert's carefully acquired steel pins stolen from his mother's counted collection, and turned into dull insect-shaped husks that he eventually threw out of the window, he decided that other humans should benefit from his ingenuity. In the name of science, he began making meticulous observations, neatly recorded in a little book that he stitched together himself. As time passed and Dagbert grew from seven to seventeen, these became a series of larger books, more carefully bound. He observed every twitch and turn, every distressed buzz or fatal flutter, minutely, and made tiny, insect-scaled notes in an insect-like hand. He soon discovered that depending where he stuck his pin, the outcome varied a great deal. He learned how to do it to prolong the dying creatures' dance for the longest possible time.

He had no feelings, let alone remorse. Flies and wasps were unnecessary, unattractive, distracting and at times vicious. The world was better without them and he was convinced that he performed a useful service. He was also confident that one day his little books in their paper and later leather bindings would be published to great acclaim. Soon his range of enquiry and victims extended to include birds, reptiles and eventually mammals, progressing from lizards and sparrows to rats and cats.

As he grew older and worked for his mother during the day, he deviated into petty crime by night to fund what he now saw as vital scientific work. He took copious notes on any process of death he came across, such as a dying beggar. Though more than once it crossed his mind to accelerate the – he felt – merciful end of such accidental subjects, he never summoned up enough courage to do it. For Dagbert, like so many killers, was a coward, extraordinarily unable to tolerate the mildest pain himself. And although he relished observing the fatal suffering of others from a safe distance, he was far too scared of reprisal to inflict it with his own hands. He hated the wetness of blood. Insects did not have it. Nevertheless, when his mother fell seriously ill, he found himself close to making the transition to murder, for alone in their small dwelling in her weak state she was a pathetically easy target. From the first, Dagbert found the duties of the sick-chamber irksome, which he did not make the slightest effort to hide. After a month, if she hadn't thrown herself out of the window to escape his bad-tempered neglect, he might have committed a very serious crime.

As it was, in losing his provider he also lost his lodging, which had never crossed his self-serving mind. But the seventeen-year-old homeless Dagbert was lucky: after just two days he secured passage on a slaver bound for the West Indies, in the dual role of medical orderly and scientific recorder. He talked himself into the job by spouting a lot of scientific claptrap, falsely claiming a surgeon for a father, and opening two of his little books in rapid succession to ink-drawings of dissections. But even as he did so, it struck him that actual medical qualifications must be a very low priority, since the pictures he showed were of a wren and a rat. The ship was owned by two Turkish brothers, Mehmet and Theocritus Koros.

On returning to London five years later with some money in his pocket, Master Oliphant, Esq, as he now styled himself, got a job as a prison warder. During his spell abroad, along with studying rare creatures that he had never seen before, he had also learned a great deal about victualling, living and dying – not to mention many other aspects of human nature, all of which he now applied with enthusiasm.

One day twenty years later, out on a daily stroll, Oliphant spotted Theocritus Koros in a coffee shop.

Koros was unmistakable, though heavier. Dressed in good-quality black clothes, there was nothing of a ship-owner about him now. And in his thin dry way, Oliphant was also distinctive, his still-youthful head slightly on one side, always observing and appraising, as if humans were a species quite separate and apart, to collect and display. Over the two decades past he had risen to the position of senior warder, and when not on duty, dressed neatly and well.

Koros had accurately assessed Oliphant's unusual proclivity for disinterested cruelty all those years before. Now he invited him to join him for a pipe and a share of his jug of wine. Over the course of their conversation, the latter discovered that the magistrate, who was also the head of the Board of Governors, was looking to appoint a new Keeper; one who, in return for being allowed to run the gaol in his own way, would be amenable to suggestions. 'Pursue your studies,' Koros suggested genially. 'Enlarge your mind. There will be ample time and opportunity, and congenial accommodation. It will interest me to see your ideas and experiments when I visit now and then in my role as Governor. All I require from you in return is occasional cooperation, and an open mind.

'Cooperation and advancement', Koros went on, 'go hand in hand.'

Oliphant's eyes gleamed. By the end of the jug, the advancement was his.

'In you go, and don't give no trouble, or else.'

Having been roughly handled a great deal over the past days, Lily ignored the warder who ushered her into the Keeper's room, but instinctively smoothed her coarse second-hand skirts and the lavender coif that fitted close over her cropped hair. It was cooler than the familiar exuberance of her wigs, sparkling with jewels.

'New prisoner to see the Keeper. Sir!'

Oliphant glanced up at the short woman in grimy servant's clothes.

He made a habit of scanning the list of incoming prisoners. Any who took his fancy, either because of their name or crime, or perhaps because of a note by the arresting watchman, were brought up under guard. Occasionally someone caught his attention as they entered the yard. He called up a great many more men than women. Depending on their disposition and appearance, he made notes in his book. Six months earlier when he accepted the position from Koros, it struck him that an examination of the criminal mind and personality could be a glorious culmination to his life's work, garlanded by plentiful opportunities to observe death in all its permutations. Indeed, he thought pompously, God had singled him out for this singular reward, for how else could such a perfect job have become his?

Generally, women prisoners scarcely interested him: they became emotional, sometimes they begged, or used female wiles to throw themselves on his mercy, the misguidedness of which ploy filled him with disgust before they were dragged out. But he did like to take a look at those females who were rich enough to stay in the Master's Yard, or those sentenced to death. The first entailed the possibility of personal profit and the second made his spine tingle.

Lily, motionless, glared and remained silent. An unremarkable creature, he thought, notable only because of her colour, which was no novelty to him; and rather squat of figure. Her unflattering clothes smelled, which displeased him: in women, he took it as a deliberate affront to his dignity. He scanned the trial notes before him. The accusation was attempted murder, which was rare but not uncommon. She wasn't even a murderer, just an inept harlot. In his mind, he sentenced her in seconds and without a thought. Such a humdrum career of botched crime held no scientific interest at all for him; he waved his hand at the warder to remove her to the ordinary yard and dipped his nib: his entry on this creature would be very brief indeed.

'Come 'ere, you!' the coarse voice roared triumphantly. 'Come wiv me, I've been expecting yer!'

With the dismal clang of the gate still ringing in her ears, Lily, who had just been shoved into the ordinary women's yard through a side chamber that held two recently boiled heads in a basket ready to go up on spikes, started as the big face leered into her own. Standing her ground, she glowered back ferociously.

The large woman was covered in rags so filthy that they made Lily's sorry garments look almost new, in layers that must once have been different colours, with puffs of flesh between. Her face and hands were as dirty as her clothes, her skirts so bulky that in outline she resembled an overgrown infant. She rocked from one dirt-crusted foot to the other, a battered cup pinned to one waistband, took another few menacing steps and snarled at a huddle of prisoners creeping up behind. Emitting a growl, she lowered her head and swayed towards them, showing her teeth.

The group's drunken, wavering shuffle petered out. Those with enough money drank raw gin to avoid the water.

'This one's mine! Keep off of it!' The woman spat on the ground, at which the others broke apart and drifted sullenly away. Lily began edging away too, but the woman pushed her against the high wall with one big flat hand in the middle of Lily's chest.

'You're the one from Elizabeth, ain't yer? She sent a message to look out for you the moment you come in. Not to miss you on no account, *she* said. Hard to miss, *I'd* say. You got something to show me, ain't that right?'

Lily nodded, at which the woman's mad look and voice instantly disappeared. 'Oh,' she shrugged. 'Do what you have to if you want to stay alive here – Bett taught me that; she's the master of it, as you prob'ly know already. It could keep you alive too, if they doesn't string ye first. Show me what she give you, so I know there's no trick.'

Lily handed over the slip of sugar paper on which Elizabeth had written a sentence.

The creased old face relaxed; the woman's expression was almost normal. 'Yes, that's her way of writing, indeed it is. Sainted woman. Goodest person I ever met.' Having kissed the scrap, to Lily's surprise she prodded it between her lips and swallowed. The sinews in her neck stood out.

'I don't leave no crumbs for them other birds to follow. You can't be too careful. Bett's helped me give the law the slip many a time and may again. Your trial's in a week from now most like, that's the word. My mate Sally's been tupping a gaoler, he told her that a black whore'll be added in, special. Can't mean no one else but you, no one fit the billet till you come in. From what I heard it sounds like you've got on the wrong side of whatshisname, the magistrate that done for Bett's brother.'

Lily looked at her sharply. 'Magistrate Koros, you mean?'

'Whooh! Don't *never* say that name in here.' The woman's face darkened. 'Magistrate my arse! Murderer! That's the on'y word for that one. If I could kill just one person in the name of humanity, snap him in two, it would be him. Evil through and through. Slaving, it was. Then building after the fire. Misery and death, everywhere he went. You can't count the deaths on his head and you can't count the money he made from it neither. A trafficker, that's all he is, however hard he tries to hide it. He might think it's in the past, but blood like he's got on his hands never washes off. Never. May God drown him in it yet. You know him?'

She spat.

Lily's expression said enough.

'Then I'll help you. Bett asks me to, but I'd help anyways, just on account of that. Keep your money close and follow me.' The woman tugged her sleeve impatiently. 'Don't pay no attention to how I look, just trust me. 'Sides, what choice have you got?' Her laugh fell between a cough and a bark, and she paused, panting, to catch her breath before going on. 'Stick close so none of them gets another look, they've seen more'n they deserve. Pull that cap down and get a move on. When they're asleep, we'll talk some more.'

One sunny morning almost a fortnight after Lily entered Newgate, Dagbert Oliphant had an unexpected visitor. He had not seen Koros since taking up his post and did not expect to. The new Keeper had settled easily into his comfortable surroundings and new role, and once a month had passed, he began to assure himself that since he was evidently ideal for the job there was no need to be overseen or interfered with, and the governors must keep their proper distance. Moreover, he decided, Koros's hint about favours from time to time had simply been a demonstration of authority rather than an actual intention. After a further two months, during which period he was left entirely to his own devices, he had begun to consider the very idea of intervention as unwelcome meddling that he would not allow, not on any account.

He was writing in one of his notebooks, peacefully enjoying a dish of tea and some slices off an excellent ham sent in by a prisoner's relation, all neatly arrayed on a newly acquired silver salver that had come by a similar route, when Koros entered unannounced, though as the door opened the guards below could be heard calling to him to wait.

As Koros strode in the square room seemed instantly smaller, and Oliphant's cat, Lucia, shrank next to her master's leg. The magistrate took in the gleaming silk walls with an expression of distaste, strode noisily to the window in his stout boots, strode back, and sat without being invited.

With his own distaste, Oliphant noticed some dry mud clinging to the magistrate's sole, but said nothing.

'Your notebook for the past few months,' Koros began without preamble, 'your records of individual prisoners: is that the volume before you?'

Oliphant's hand rested lightly on the open book with its fine paper and beautiful, if small, calligraphy. From the loving delicacy of his touch, it could have been the rosy cheek of an only child. He laid his starched napkin neatly across his unfinished food.

'Yes,' he said noncommittally. He poured tea, but Koros waved it away.

'Give it to me,' Koros said.

Oliphant began to stutter that these were his private records, to be read only by himself. But as Koros's eyes burned into his, and as the large, powerful hand that was held out did not move, his courage eddied away like dead leaves scuffling in a gutter. Lucia trembled against his stockinged calf.

'I do not intend to be kept waiting,' Koros added.

He rose, leaned over, removed the book from under Oliphant's motionless fingers and crossed briefly to the window, flicking through the pages as he went, then laid it back on Oliphant's desk at an entry speared with his finger. 'Have this one brought up.'

Minutes later the man in question was blinking in front of Oliphant, unaware of the magistrate who watched from the depth of the window embrasure. After the prisoner had stood for a moment, Koros signalled for him to be taken away again. The whole time, Koros leaned motionless against the stone stanchion, deep in its shadow.

'What is all this about?' Oliphant failed to control his voice. It was intolerable to be interfered with in this high-handed way. 'I insist –'

'Do not ever insist to me,' Koros said pleasantly.

Oliphant could not judge the other man's eyes where he stood against the sun.

'You will expect me to examine your records from time to time. It is only reasonable. From this brief inspection, I am satisfied that you write with accuracy and discernment. Perhaps that fellow's wish to die should be granted, but so be it. Make sure that your records are always kept in order; your position depends on it.'

He walked over and rested his hand lightly on the chair.

'There is to be a hanging next Wednesday afternoon, is there not?' he went on. 'A group of felons from the most recent sessions. Among them, the harlot Lily Boniface. I would have it that she is hanged last. Ensure that it is so. Once the arrangements are made, you will report to me in person that same afternoon with all the account books, for my inspection. I observe that you have installed new decorations. Make sure that they too are fully accounted for.'

Unable to conceal his dismay at being excluded from the hanging, Oliphant broke in. He had been looking forward to it with increasing excitement, for he had designed a new style of gibbet with a variable plunge that he longed to test. It had a crank that altered the length of the prisoner's fall, thus prolonging or curtailing their agony at the turn of a wheel. He was sure it would prove entertaining, and possibly useful. But he was damned if he was going to try it out if he was not there to gloat at his own cleverness.

'It is my duty to oversee – '

'Nonsense.' Koros dismissed him. 'The chief warder will oversee it. It takes no skill to pull a lever. That is all.'

Calming himself with Lucia, Oliphant quivered with rage at the confident thumps of stout leather descending the new stone steps. Not because he had been told what to do and pleasure had wilfully been plucked from his grasp, which was bad enough, but because his magnificent treatise had been referred to as – what – an ordinary *record*? Some dreary, practical account of prisoners, something which could be set down by any drooling idiot, rather than the great work of literature that it patently was?

His hands shook, his legs trembled, and tears blurred his eyes so badly as he looked at the particular entry which now, as a final insult, bore a large grease-mark made by Koros's gigantic thumb, that he was unable to read it for a full half-hour, during which time he sat stonily at his desk, the cat pinned to his doublet.

Had he, instead, gone to the window, he would have observed Koros emerge into the yard and make his way into the warders' private office on the south side, where he stayed for a good twenty minutes, before reappearing with the chief warder, who pumped his hand as if it was a water spout and bowed him grovellingly out. He would also have observed that same warder congratulate himself with a brief jig, then set off across the yard towards the woman Lily had recently met, whom the warder escorted towards his room with the promise of a flagon of ale and a coin.

Above in the gatehouse, to reassure himself that he alone ran the gaol, and to soothe himself, rather as a baby might by sucking its own familiar thumb, Oliphant at last reread the following meticulously inscribed entry, now marred by the oily exuberance of Crace's skin:

A man going by the name of ***Jug-Eared George***, whose true name is not known, is an *African* Felon. He is of some intelligence and ingenuity compared with the general run. Of unusual appearance, his face is small and round with a ready smile. To the eye, he appears diftinctly more like a woman than a man. His ears stand out wide to either side and he wears his hair growd and tied in a crinkelled knot on top of his head. In stature he is short, with delicate hands and feet, which *neatneff* he has put to use in a long career of breaking and **thieving**. He is known to be wery partial to wear women's clothes to commit these thefts, the skirts being most *Capacious*, in which to conceal STOLEN GOODS. However, since being incarcerated, to his fury he has been required to wear trowsers.

Jug-Eared George is a singular character who constantly demands attention and Indulges in fantaseys regarding his owne importance. To this end he has made repeated and Urgent appeals even to my **S**elfe, the **K**eeper of this Gaol, to be hanged apart from the others, quite alone. In order, he sayes, that he may leave the world with every eye fixed fast upon him, without his exit being marred by what he terms the clumsy diftraction of *those leffer, and worfe-dressed mortals* than himself. He has, further, made repeated requests to be hanged in women's garments. He has become alternately tearful and abusive in purfuit of this aim.

As the illustrious **Keeper** of this Gaol, who am most cognisant of the heavy burden of the King's Duty that is fixed by His Sovereyn Grace upon me, as much as of the **Eye of God**, it is my pleasure to record in refpect of this Felon that *each and all of these several requefts has been denied*.

How the devil dared Koros even *hint* that the man's whim should be indulged, Oliphant asked Lucia indignantly, feeding first himself and then her a large piece of ham. He noted with approval that she was a dainty eater. A wise cat, aware of the sharpness of his dissection knives, Lucia made sure to agree with him in all things.

CHAPTER THREE

enobia cancelled Crace's monument the very moment the vault had been sealed, saying that she would create something more fitting.

Next, she granted Stoddart a very large pension, whose only condition was that he left the country at once and never returned. Agatha let it be known that Zenobia forgave him.

Now the last of the servants had finally left, after laying fires ready to light, along with other necessaries. Agatha intended to interview replacements in the morning. The dark, empty house might have felt forbidding, but to Zenobia its wide oak corridors, lit by carefully guarded sconces and unpeopled by the suspicion that always surrounded her while her husband lived, were roads to freedom. With no one to see her she lifted her skirts and skidded along the polished planks. It was good to feel alive; she did it again.

'Madam!'

In the gloom, Agatha emerged from Crace's chamber clasping two strong boxes balanced on each other, a squat candle in a holder resting on top.

'You asked me to tell you when I found them.' She led the way into an alcove next to the bedchamber, which had been Crace's office. With its shining black lacquered cabinet and the severe ebony chairs he favoured, it still smacked of a courtroom.

But there was also a tray of rosemary-spiked roast chicken, stewed dried apricots and a flagon of wine and Agatha had lit a snapping fire. As the birth grew close, Zenobia was constantly hungry and felt the cold. Her feet ached, too. She eased off her slippers. Swathed in furs despite the flames, the women peeled roasted chestnuts as they worked.

Crace had been meticulous in business. The boxes were in good order and showed that his holdings, each matched by one of the papers in the first box, were far more numerous than Zenobia had guessed. She now owned property across the city that would bring a vast income. Agatha jotted everything in a small gold notebook on a chain at her waist and Zenobia decided to work out what to do with it all later, once the child was born.

Perched on the edge of Crace's high bed, a leg of crisp chicken in one hand, Zenobia leafed through the smaller box. Not even half full, it had not only been locked but sealed, and several traces of wax on the iron showed that the seal had been broken numerous times.

A clatter made Agatha swing round from where she sat at the desk totting up her list. Bolt upright, motionless, skirts trailed with grease, Zenobia sat clutching a sheaf of tightly written documents.

The court transcript of Lily's trial, which Agatha prised from Zenobia's rigid fingers, was straightforward and short. It was the last of twenty cases at the sessions held the day of Zenobia's betrothal. Lily was charged with shooting a certain bondsman named as Thomas Welkin in his carriage, with the express intention of killing him.

Slowly, Agatha read out loud: 'The charge has been brought by Samuel Severin, royal tailor, and endorsed by a powerful magistrate.'

'Why would he endorse it?' Zenobia interrupted. 'He was the magistrate, not the jury.'

Biting her lip Agatha read on:

The accused, **Lily Boniface**, entered a plea of not guilty. The accused is a notorious prostitute and madam, of African extraction, formerly a slave, known for depravity in Covent Garden and beyond. Her carefully chosen victim was a man of unblemished reputation, good family, and prospects of advancement in the City. He was also her patron, who owned the house from which she conducted her sordid business, and which she liked to call her own. Beyond her initial plea, the accused made no further representations. The grand jury found against her. The verdict, of guilty of attempted murder, was unanimous, and a sentence passed of hanging by the neck until dead.

Agatha gave the paper back, but Zenobia left it on her skirts. At last, with a sigh, she studied it.

On a bit of parchment attached to the front, which looked as if it had been addressed to the presiding judge, Koros had scrawled: *'Extend session to include. Guilty verdict. If needful override jury.'*

'She was added at the last minute. He couldn't have got it in any quicker if he had tried,' Zenobia finally said.

Agatha screwed the paper up and cast it into the fire. The flames spat as if embracing Crace himself.

'Let me take the box. We can go through the rest tomorrow.' Agatha was certain that any further upset could damage the child that must be very close to being born, for Zenobia was larger than anyone she had ever seen.

But Zenobia leaned back and stroked her furred stomach. 'Not quite yet. We must discover whether any other horrors lurk.'

Agatha sat quietly as the younger woman shuffled through the remaining small pile, rapidly handing over one sheet after another to burn, until only two sets of papers remained.

Zenobia frowned. 'These look like another set of deeds, so why did he keep it apart? See what they say, dear woman. I'm too weary to look.'

Shielding their skirts from the candle-holder she held up in one hand, Agatha peered at the writing on the outer paper. It was the hand of a professional scribe; a legal clerk, not that of John Crace.

'There is also this appended letter.' As she spoke, Agatha unfolded the packet, smoothing out the layers it contained. She stopped with a gasp. Papers and wrapping fell from her hand, along with a small object which, before Zenobia noticed, she quickly plucked from the floor where it had fallen outside the candle's small pool of light.

'What is it? Do not keep me in suspense.'

Agatha was pale, more than pale, as if the letter would bite. 'It does not seem possible, yet I know this hand as well as my own, even after so many years. It is my father's. These are the deeds not only to the house I was born in, but to everything within it, including Lily. My father clearly names her here, as a slave and chattel to be enjoyed in whatever way the new owner chooses.'

It was the story Agatha had told Zenobia, what seemed like a lifetime ago.

'How can that possibly be? Surely you are mistaken?'

Shaking her head, Agatha showed her the object, a gold-edged oval miniature with a hooked golden tongue to catch to the neck of a garment. Instead of handing it over, she prised gently at its edges with her nails, and continued as if she talked to herself.

'I haven't seen this for a lifetime but would recognise it anywhere. As a girl, it was the most valuable thing I owned, a rare gift from my mother. I'd promised it to Lily as a proof of our friendship while we were apart; a token of my love; but she ran away before I could give it to her. I'd forgotten about it.'

From behind the painted copper miniature within, Agatha carefully removed a second, thinner, even smaller copper oval. Side by side on her palm, one had a gleaming gold binding, while the other, unframed, was no longer than a thumb nail. The first bore a still-recognisable likeness of Agatha, done at perhaps thirteen, the work of a professional miniaturist. The other, badly painted, showed the face of an African girl.

Agatha threw herself against Zenobia and although her words were muffled, they were still audible. 'I painted her when I was twelve. Our blacksmith cut me the copper, without my parents

knowing. But she would not sit still, and I couldn't do her justice.'
She shook her head in bewilderment. 'I don't know how this
ended up here. It must have been taken, along with everything
else. But it proves that your husband was the man who won our
house at cards, the man who acquired and owned Lily Boniface.
It can only have been him. He was the man she fled from, to
avoid becoming a slave again.'

Zenobia ran her finger gently over the tiny painting as if
caressing it. 'Then imagine his fury when he discovered her,
years later, an independent woman – when he realised who Lily
was. Under the law, he owned her; but how could a magistrate
take such a woman into his household? She was widely known,
it would have been a scandal. He could not bear to be crossed
by anybody, certainly not by a woman. No wonder he tried to
destroy her.'

They stared silently at the small objects in Agatha's hand.

'We will talk about this tomorrow,' Zenobia said. 'My back
aches, the day has suddenly become too long.'

Without another word she rose carefully, every movement
painfully slow, and left the room.

Agatha banked the fires and collected up the scattered
papers. The crumpled pieces that had been wrapped around the
miniature had fallen under the bed hangings. Catching them up,
she saw that the inner sheet was closely covered in writing that
she immediately recognised as Crace's.

As she read it, a frown gathered. She read it a second time,
then a third. The frown deepened, mixed with something else.
Horror – perhaps doubt. Glancing behind her to check that she
was quite alone, Agatha put up the desk's writing flap and pulled
out the shallow supporting drawer below. Glancing round again,
she gently prised up its thin wooden lining and laid the papers
beneath it. Replacing the slip of boxwood she tamped it down
carefully. Holding the locket as if she would never let it go, she
locked the drawer and attached the small golden key very firmly
to the chain at her waist.

CHAPTER FOUR

'Mind your step there!' The boatman's sharp alarm boomed out of the rapidly descending darkness and brought Lily to her senses just in time. Catching hold of a thick iron ring pounded deep into the stone wall, she regained her footing. Pickled Herring Stairs were unlit, the glimmer of near-obsidian water slapped at the lowest step as it foamed evilly in and out of the greedy water. Light from a small closed lantern on the craft's bow picked at the rough flanks of the granite stair and helped her find her way. Where the tide rode them, the lower steps were thick with slime from which a smell like manure rose and fell with the tide.

Agile and sure-footed, one thickly muscled leg parrying the rocking of the boat against the slap of the river, the man held out a strong hand. 'I shan't drop you. Come, hop in. Best to move fast if you're afeared.'

Lily grabbed the outstretched calloused fingers, which closed hard on her own and yanked her violently towards him. She landed clumsily in the small boat. 'Hold the sides,' the man commanded, already settled and drawing on one oar, pushing off with the other, talking sideways as he looked for his way. 'Stay low, you'll feel safer down. Wrap that cloak about you.'

Against the force of the water he rowed with strong silent passes, breathing through a half-open mouth in time with the slice and dip of his oars. Lily, who could not swim, sank down as instructed on the wet plank seat, afraid of the strange glimmer and plash of the oars, or an occasional run of phosphorescence mid-stream, where currents met in oily masses that licked and rolled. She felt the sullen water push them back every time he lifted and swung for fresh purchase and was troubled by the pool of water around her feet. Then she became accustomed to the movement and felt the fresh soft air, cooled by the river, on her cheek. She looked about with greater interest. Far across the wide expanse rose the familiar, horrible shapes of the Tower, cut out dark against a streaked sky. She looked away, breathing hard. On the nearside they still hugged the bank, running along Pott's Fields; but soon the oarsman reached New Stairs, where the river narrowed, and swung the prow out towards the middle of the river.

Now he bent to his work in earnest, pulling with a hard, short stroke, his chest curling and unfurling, snorting with exertion, and inched them out to where the current ran strongest, glancing back to check that no unlit smuggler sped into their path. There was little traffic, but as they crossed the mid-line and began the haul towards Wapping, it was as if the traders' ships moored there rapidly swelled, rearing their immense bulks high up from the water, masts lacerating the sky. Wet wood and fresh tar filled the air.

Lily shuddered, remembering the ship that had brought her to London as a child, the loss of her mother, the horror of that passage. She had been too young to remember where they disembarked; there was no reason to think it was the same place; but she shut her eyes as the boatman pulled around a great curved oak flank, cursing and pushing off once where he ran in dangerously close under the lee of the ship's side. Then with a sudden bump and ugly rasping sound he tucked the craft in at Wapping Stair.

At the exact moment they drew close to the stair, an indistinct, cloaked figure came swiftly forwards, deftly seized the rope-end and caught at Lily who, half-fainting, stumbled once more. The cloaked figure paid the sailor and helped Lily up the stairs. She turned to thank the boatman, but he had already swung away.

The stranger helped Lily into a small, narrow old coach drawn by an even older horse with a white nose, its once-black sides specked with hoar frost.

'It isn't far.' They settled opposite each other and he drew back his hood, observing how Lily shrank away from him into her corner. 'You are exhausted. Rest. You are safe now. Have no fear.'

As the iron wheels struggled on the lumpy, rammed dirt road, Lily studied her saviour. She was quite certain that she had never seen him before. Though he seemed kind and had a gentle demeanour, his face was worn and lined, and his oily grey hair – he wore no wig – thin, lanky, without any attempt at fashion. What she could see of his clothing in the gloom was poor but neat. Aged like his horse, the once-black wool had a rusty cast. Perhaps he was an impoverished gentleman. Yet – and this contradicted her assessment – his finger pads and nails were ingrained with dark stains, as if he worked in a mine or a tannery. Even in the darkness, lit through the open window by a thin wash from a just-rising sliver of moon, she saw it. Catching her expression, he made no attempt to hide his hand, but smiled. The smile held no judgement.

'We are here.' He sprang out first to help her, agile for his age. 'Forgive me for not introducing myself. My name is Joachim Knapp.'

The name meant nothing to her, and before she had asked him who he was and where they were, he ushered her through a narrow door into a small two-storey house that appeared to be in darkness, bar a faint glimmer from the shutters over the ground floor's single window. The front door was rotted along the bottom and the shutters themselves bore cut-out fleurs-de-lis, from one of which faint candlelight bled into the darkness.

'My girl, home at last!' In her customary chair in the front room, next to a small fire and a sputtering tallow candle in a battered holder, the ravaged face lit up. 'I've made a new hat to celebrate.' Elizabeth indicated her old shapeless one, spurting a clump of red-dyed, battered chicken feathers.

'Come, sit, quick, there's drink aplenty, and food; and a clean bed below. I've been waiting these three hours past, you must have a hunger.'

Under her watchful eye, Lily devoured boiled mutton, tearing it with her fingers, followed by a thick slab of fruit pudding peeled from the cloth, washed down with a pitcher of ale. Finished, she wiped her mouth on her sleeve. Knapp picked at his food with the tip of his knife, never taking his eyes from her.

At last, as Elizabeth smoked and Knapp drank brandy, Lily told of her escape.

'You saved me.' She kissed the older woman's hand. 'That is all I know; but by what miracle – that I don't know.' But Elizabeth merely nodded and smoked contentedly, so Lily went on.

'It was time to be taken out and strung up. That's what I expected. I was the last in the day. The others went in two groups. Nobody explained why. All I knew was the horror of it, penned together in the heat, waiting. There were murmurs that I was a special show. We could hear what was going on, how it was being dragged out. After the first group, the roars were terrible, all around me were fainting. We had no water. It must have been five or six by the clock.'

'But Margaret?'

'Yes, she met me when I arrived and said she would help; but that it was better that I knew nothing more. She spoke well of you.' Elizabeth nodded; her one eye glowed briefly under its lid.

'Then, as the second group . . . ' Unable to go on, Lily drank the brandy that Knapp quietly proffered.

'The second roar went up, even louder, and more awful. This time I heard it quite alone, waiting my turn. Then I gave up all hope and knelt on the damp straw, waiting to be taken out after them. I could not pray. All fell quiet around me, yet I could still hear and feel the restless crowd not far away; felt them grow more so by the second, moving and shifting like slaves crushed in a hold. As if hundreds of men pressed down on me, forcing the life from me, so that I could scarcely breathe. I knelt with my back to the door, waiting for the key to turn, unable to steady my heart, knowing that shortly a rope would choke off my last breath. I thought of those who had loved me and to whom I should never be able to say farewell.'

Moved by her words, Knapp, who turned away for a brief second to brush a speck of soot from his eye, watched with a mixture of horror and pity. A man he had once called his friend – too long ago to imagine now – had brought her to this terrible pass, waiting to die like an animal in a trap. He looked at Elizabeth, whose brooding, ambiguous gaze never left her young friend. As he did, with a shock he remembered a once-comely face, a girl with light hair and sparkling eyes, whom he had nodded to and smiled at, so far back that it seemed like a dream, when he delivered some trade bills to her father, beautifully engraved, to sell silks at the proud sign of what would be the new Fleur-de-Lis.

Unaware of the change in his expression, Elizabeth cut through Knapp's memory. 'Tell us the rest, quick now. It cannot be worse than this.'

'The dreadful sound of the key came at last and I sank to the ground, hoping it would swallow me or that my heart would stop, but someone strode across the room, pulled me up and dragged me out backwards. I was fainting, my feet would not move, so he almost carried me. But instead of going left to the yard, we turned right. He shoved me along the same corridor we had come down, which led to the street. As we turned that way, a woman was led quickly past, towards the screaming herd, a woman in a cap. I hardly saw her before she vanished and the greatest roar of all went up. Then, I just wanted to run.'

'Who was it?' Elizabeth leaned forwards, gripping the arms of her chair.

'I had never seen her before. She was black; older than me,

though about the same size. And as she passed, she grinned at me as if she went to her wedding. But much stranger than that . . . '

'Go on, child,' Elizabeth urged.

'If I hadn't known, I would have said that she looked like a man. But I only saw her for a second. Then I was pushed into a chair waiting close by the door. It was black, the runners in black too. Like shadows. The blinds had been fastened down tight. It was stifling hot inside as if it had been waiting a long time. Someone banged the side and the runners took off. I must have collapsed, because that's all I knew till we stopped at the stair and one of them told me to get out. They had to pull me out. I didn't know where we were and didn't want to move. I don't know how much time had passed.'

Knapp brimmed their glasses and for a while no one spoke. The single flame sputtered and sprang, the smell of grease and smoke hung in the warm air, mixed with Elizabeth's tobacco. The poor fire drew and crackled companionably.

'And you, sir.' Elizabeth broke the silence. 'How came you to be waiting for her?'

Knapp rolled his glass gently between his palms, savouring the sweet odour that came up. Brandy this good must be contraband, for it was better than any he had ever tasted.

He saw that she did not remember him. Wryly, he supposed that just as she had altered, he was much changed from the young man full of hope, dark-haired, not bad-looking, a talented draftsman, the whole world speared on the sharp point of his burin. She was the girl he might have married, or so he had thought then. Despite her disfigurement, flashes of that long-lost girl still hovered and glanced somewhere in the damaged face. He would tell her; he wanted to, but not yet.

'I run a printing press,' he began quickly. He was not used to making speeches. 'Someone put a note under the door last night. I found it this morning.'

He did not add that he had instantly recognised Koros's hand; it did not seem important.

'It told me to wait at that spot from a certain time and to meet the occupant of a certain chair and to bring that person here. It described them as I found them, no more, no less. The directions were good enough to find this house. There was no name,' he added, seeing her mind working behind the half-open eye.

She sat bolt upright. 'To bring her here? Who can have written that note? Most assuredly it was not Margaret.'

The letter had said to burn it after he had read it, to reveal its author to nobody unless he was a fool. He knew what the threat meant, he had heard it too many times and he was tired of it, but he still believed that Koros could destroy him with a snap of his fingers. He ignored the question.

'It said that this place had beds to let and was close to where she was arrested. And that from here, if I gave her some money, she could go on her way. Leave London. That was all there was. There was no name,' he asserted again – after all, that was the strict truth.

To avoid Elizabeth's piercing gaze, as if she knew he was not telling all he knew, he felt around in his breeches pockets. He had almost forgotten the money; he had put it somewhere. Not a large amount, but enough to leave the country, should Lily choose. It was his own, there had been none included with the letter, though there was plenty of room under the door to slide it. He tried not to dwell on Koros's meanness to the last.

He found it and gave it to her. The same little bag Koros had once given him.

But Elizabeth's good eye, open a slit, was fixed on him as if she burned him into her mind.

'I still cannot understand, for I do not know thee, although there is something familiar about thee,' she pursued, probing. 'Were you ever in silk stuffs? Or the navy? Did you know my brother? Is that how I know your face?'

Knapp shook his head. He had heard the story of her brother. Another person destroyed by Koros. Yet without a doubt it was Koros who had written the note. Even to him it did not make sense.

'I saw you once, when we were both young.' He told her about the trade card he had made for her father in preparation for their move to the new shop. 'I winked at you across the counter when your father's back was turned. You were standing in the room beyond, by the open back door, with a big fold of heavy silk in your arms. But it wasn't as lustrous as you. When you saw me, you stopped and stood quite still. You looked like a painting. I have always thought that you must be the lily in the name over the door; in my mind that is what I have called you, all these years.'

Sucking on her pipe, Elizabeth pondered this, still glancing, but hesitantly, almost coyly, as if uncertain whether to believe him or not. But Lily noticed a faint flush on the less-damaged cheek.

At last, Elizabeth told her to open the corner cupboard where the remains of the pudding congealed on a thick, chipped plate, and bring out a small box that had been pushed right to the back. The sort of ordinary box a sailor whittles to pass the time, to bring back to land for a loved one to hold keepsakes in. It was covered in dust.

Elizabeth rummaged through its few contents: several bits of pasteboard, a sailor's buckle and the ribbon from a queue. Replacing the last two with a sigh, she brought out one particular card and held it up to her eyes. There, under a fine drawing of a spacious shop with broad counter and folded bolts of cloth stacked proudly behind it, in the smallest print that could be struck, was the name of the person who had engraved and made it: Joachim Knapp.

She moved the card to and fro in front of her good eye as if she crawled all over it or drank it in. At last she laid it down in her lap, and kept it there, patting it gently, with an expression Lily had never seen.

Elizabeth shook herself. When she spoke, it was in her familiar tone of command. 'You will sleep here and get away at first light. Don't worry, my girl, this time you will not oversleep, I'll see to that. Clothes are laid ready downstairs. You will travel as a maid, there's no reason to call attention to yourself until everyone has forgotten the story, certainly in London; but there's another set as well, for when you get there. I will travel along with you. I've long been minded to visit my brother at York, after so much time, but it's a hard thing to travel blind. A sitting duck for thieving coachmen. With you at my side, I shan't be afraid of losing the way. You'll be doing me a favour in return for the one I done you. After a year or so you can come back, if that is your wish. Perhaps start up the old business again – '

Lily was about to speak, but Elizabeth's dry laugh sounded.

'Not that business! Never again that business.' She laughed again, this time a derisory bark. 'Consider, in that one regard, however you curse him, he did you a favour.'

They all knew whom she meant.

'But my brother might like the benefit of a London shop. Who knows? And in such a case, our friend here – ' She shot him an almost soft look, although in the uncertain light, and given the rigidity of her burned features, it was hard to be certain – 'might agree to draw up a fresh card. Go to bed now, and rest. Mr Knapp and I – ' again, stronger this time, the faraway look, in which the years seemed to fall from her hard face and the blighted skin soften – 'Mr Knapp and I will sit on together, just a little while longer.'

EPILOGUE

Three years later

*A*gatha, Zenobia and Hendrik stood in the courtyard, outside the massive nail-studded door. As a mark of particular friendship, Zenobia wanted to see Agatha off on her return journey to Suffolk.

It had been a curious visit, Zenobia thought. Agatha had spoken little, as if something weighed on her mind. Sometimes while they talked, she had caught her friend looking at her and got the distinct impression that she wanted to say something and was deciding how to introduce the subject. Yet, whatever it was remained unsaid, at least for the time being.

For some reason, Hendrik too had seemed preoccupied. Handsome and genial as ever, he stood or sat beside her, apparently faultless in his attention; yet it was as if he was caught up in a strange interior agitation. Zenobia could not fathom it, but perhaps, she thought, she was imagining things. It was a searing hot day, after all, in which everything danced in a peculiar haze.

When she had at last left their bedroom that morning to join Agatha, they had all talked with pleasure together, but inevitably, when Zenobia showed Agatha the painted ceiling, the conversation turned once more to Crace. Laughing, Zenobia was about to repeat her droll idea that whatever glorious thing he had had in mind, the mural was his only monument. But as she opened her mouth, she caught sight of his great lacquer writing bureau, still in its old place in the small octagonal antechamber. Everything else of his, including his ornate, high-backed ebony chairs, was long gone. The lacquer was so deep and polished, the small figures on it painted with such skill, that in this midsummer light they seemed almost animated. She had hesitated to destroy it, and Hendrik said it was a handsome and very rare piece.

Yet, as the rich summer light continued to flow across its watery surface, it looked particularly black, almost sinister, a sleek pool that sucked all the brightness in the room deep into its murderous depths. Its bulk was so monumental that it could have been Crace himself standing there. Mute, yes; but arrogant and determined to be heard.

'I must get rid of that old relic,' she said, turning her back with a shrug. 'I have been meaning to for some time. I will have it done at once.'

Just as she was about to call her maid, Agatha spoke.

'Let me take it off your hands.' Almost carelessly. 'It would be useful in the country. I need just such a thing for the household accounts.'

'Indeed, but in this case, I would rather destroy it. It reminds me too much of him. He already has one monument.' As if the matter was closed, Zenobia gestured at the ceiling, expecting Agatha to smile at her quip. But to her surprise, the other woman's face remained solemn.

'Come, dear Agatha, do not be downcast. I will order you a much better desk; something light and fashionable in the very best Italian work. Elegant and gay. In fruitwood perhaps, inlaid with flowers. Not that gloomy monstrosity. Surely you would prefer that?'

Agatha gave a quick smile of assent. But as she rose to follow Zenobia from the chamber, the glance she cast at the bureau was anything but smiling; a glance that Hendrik, who was following, saw.

They took a long, pleasant midday meal together. The dishes were well planned and the wine the best that could be offered. Everything was remarkable. Yet Zenobia was perplexed by Agatha's distracted air and the way Hendrik's eyes sometimes fell broodingly upon her. She dismissed the idea that her husband had taken a fancy to her former servant as palpably absurd. Even so, an air of discomfiture sat at the table with them.

The meal over, they went outside. Standing in the sober but fashionable dark clothes that befitted her station as a country gentlewoman, in thick silk, her thick hair curled and twined with jet, Agatha was undoubtedly handsome, though her garments were modest compared with Zenobia's. Only a pair of fine pearls lightened the overall tone.

'Ah! I have lost a pearl,' Agatha said, suddenly, her hand to her ear. Its mate glistened from the other. 'I noticed its lack earlier but there was no time to search. It must be in the antechamber.'

Zenobia was about to send someone, but Agatha insisted on going herself. She said she knew the way, and where she had dropped it.

Outside in the sun, Zenobia basked in the simple pleasure of standing beside such a handsome man. After a few minutes, when Agatha had not returned, he bowed and went to help. Surprised by this, for surely it was more pleasant with her, Zenobia refused to allow misplaced jealousy to spoil the day: Hendrik had no interest in Agatha, he was merely chivalrous. She settled her skirts comfortably on one of the two lion benches, now flanking the door, to await their return, Fog panting on the ground at her feet.

Inside the waiting coach across the courtyard, Agatha's maid sat, obscure in upholstered gloom. She must be sweltering, Zenobia thought, fanning herself. The woman looked surprisingly elderly – perhaps a housekeeper acting as temporary maid. But now that Agatha was a woman of property, it was no concern of hers who she chose to serve her. On the coach door, a gold palmate leaf grounded a small black fleur-de-lis.

Her mind drifted to her daughter, who was cutting her first tooth, and often became fractious in the afternoon. When Agatha had gone, she might go to the nursery. Whatever could be keeping them? Imagining them scouring the dust under Crace's bureau, she lifted her face to the sunshine and closed her eyes.

❧

Whatever he had been expecting, the sight that met Hendrik as he trod softly round the doorway into Crace's antechamber took him by surprise.

Agatha was bent over the desk with her back to the door, so intent on what she was doing that she was quite unaware of his entry. The drawer that supported the writing flap was open and she was frantically prising up its lining with her fingernails. He caught a glint of something gold on the edge of the cabinet. Not her lost earring; not a large pearl. For he had marked it well; just as, with greater interest, during the meal he had watched her remove it when Zenobia was not looking. For Zenobia was only truly observant about herself.

He also knew that the drawer had been locked and that Zenobia did not know where the key was. Nor had she expressed any interest in finding it, beyond saying that Agatha might know. But the question was never put. He had intended to force the drawer one day.

Agatha was so absorbed in her hasty work that she only heard him when he was close behind her.

'Did you find it?'

She whirled around. In place of the guilt he anticipated, her face held something very close to a snarl. A wild animal that might snap his neck in two. He shuddered. He had never seen her like that.

One hand swept whatever the gold thing was off the top of the cabinet and deep into a pocket slit, while she backed smartly into the desk. Her skirts pushed the drawer shut with a loud click.

She looked flushed but quickly controlled herself.

'Thank you, yes.'

Both ears held beautiful pearls. Whatever was clenched in her pocket was not her earring. And whatever was so important to her in that drawer, he would certainly have it the very moment she had left.

He beamed and took her arm.

'Then let us return to Zenobia.'

Agatha did not move.

He pulled gently at her elbow. Beneath the silk, unlike Zenobia's soft, yielding flesh, her arm was rigid and almost as muscled as his own.

'No.' She remained stubbornly rooted to the spot. 'I cannot allow it.'

At her tone, Hendrik's hand fell to his side.

'What can you not allow?'

Biting her lip, Agatha brought her fist slowly out. Dwarfed on her palm lay a small gold key.

'I have had this since he died.' The words were quick and low. 'Every day since then I have debated whether to say anything. It has almost destroyed me. I was a fool; I should have destroyed the letter the day I found it. God knows why I did not cast it into the flames where it belonged, but I hesitated, and from that moment it was too late. If she reads what it says, it could kill her.'

Puzzled, unsure what she referred to, Hendrik did not take his eyes off her.

'I do not understand – ' he began, but she brushed him aside and went on determinedly. 'I cannot prevent you from reading it. You must decide whether to tell her or not. But there is no need to break the desk. Here. Take it. But I beseech you, whatever you do, think how much he made her suffer. He tortured her. He deserved his death. Think of her soul and burn it, I beg you.'

With which ominous words she gave him the key and walked briskly ahead, back to the still-open door and the bench where Zenobia dozed blissfully in the sun.

Final farewells quickly made, the short black coachman, impeccable in black velvet, wigged and powdered, leapt down from Agatha's carriage, pulled the steps smartly out and opened the door. Zenobia caught a quick, bright flash of gold among the puff of lace at his throat. Perhaps from a livery button, she thought, although the other buttons on his coat were jet.

Remounting the box, this lackey with finely turned legs cracked his whip in a flourishing salute as the horses struck eagerly at the gravel.

Zenobia broke away from Hendrik's side and ran to the carriage to bid farewell one last time, and to retrieve Fog, who had bounded over to bother the horses. Just as she reached the window, Agatha's elderly maid bent to arrange her mistress's dress with coarse, worn hands, of which Zenobia had the impression, no doubt an illusion caused by a fold of Agatha's skirt, that the tip of one finger was lacking. On the box above, the coachman turned aside to attend to the harness.

In the pink and cream-flushed afternoon, life hung and shivered deliciously on the scent-laden breeze. Agatha's carriage moved slowly off and it struck Zenobia, sniffing the air and picking up an unaccountable whiff of violet, rose and civet, that the short-statured coachman, glorious as a finial, cut a most distinctive and unusual figure.

As soon as Zenobia was asleep that night, Hendrik rose and crept into the antechamber. Once through the connecting door he breathed more easily, for there was no direct line of sight from the bed to the bureau. Even if Zenobia awoke now, she would not see him.

He gently unlocked the drawer and pulled it soundlessly out, scarcely breathing, uncertain what he would find.

Agatha had almost managed to prise the lining up. Had he delayed a moment longer, she would have done so. It only took him a second with a slim blade to lift it enough to find what lay beneath.

He left the antechamber by the other door and walked to the cloister. Hard moonlight came in from the garden. The sundial and the herbs and flowers around it were a field of white filigree, their bright colours washed to nothing. Most extraordinary of all, the stand of castor oil plants that Zenobia had planted, no longer shading the marble benches, held their hand-shaped leaves up to the sky like beseeching supplicants, while below on the moon-washed ground lay the strangest shadow, exactly as if the bulky form of a large man was stretched out dead.

Hendrik shivered at the repulsive impression. Under the wash of bleaching light, which mercilessly flattened his own features, glimpsed in a window pane, into a sort of cypher, he opened the paper and read the following words in John Crace's masterful hand:

For my wife, in the event of my death:
Aware of the doubts you have had of me, particularly regarding my former slave, Lily Boniface, I beg you forgive me for withholding what I tell you now. Had you not betrayed me with [the next two words had been scratched out so violently that the paper had disintegrated, but it appeared to be a name] I would surely have done so. Before that event I fully intended to, and should an opportunity arise before death claims me, I will tell you yet.

You believe that I had her hanged. As death fast approaches, I understand that it has poisoned your mind irrevocably against me. I do not expect you to believe that an escape was arranged for her, that I knew of it, and that I allowed, indeed assisted, what could so easily have been thwarted. However, such is the case. You have my deathbed word for it. What I promised you on the day of our nuptials was, and is, true.

So many and varied accusations of cruelty have accrued against me, so many deaths have been set against my name, for which I shall have to answer before God, that I cannot hope to escape damnation. But I did only what many others have done in order to succeed. It is not this that torments me.

In marrying you I made an unnatural liaison, for you are the only daughter of my brother. Your instinctive and immediate revulsion towards me before we married, and every day after that, was proof enough that you sensed what you could not possibly know. But I wanted you more than anything I had ever wanted, and since it was my impression that – at least at the moment you first saw me – you felt some attraction, I closed my eyes to it. I tried to bend you to my will, but your resistance made me cruel. I was your only living relative in the world. If I had become your guardian instead of your husband, you would have loved me. May God forgive me.

Yet, if just one righted wrong may be set against that score, and after my death ease the burden of hatred that you carry against me, I shall be glad of it, even if it cannot save me from hell. Therefore, I enclose a small miniature, bound in gold. Should God grant you grace to return it to its rightful owner and see her wear it, you will know that these words, *written by the hand of your husband – on this day –, in the year 16– are true.*

Hendrik saw no miniture, but perhaps, he thought, Agatha had taken it when she first found the letter, for it must have been of Lily. He read the letter several times, then refolded it carefully, exactly as it had been. Agatha's words troubled him deeply. What had she meant by Zenobia's soul? Or that Crace had deserved his death? Surely he had died of the same terrible sickness as his son, compounded by the illness he already had? That was what his own physician had recorded, there was no suggestion of anything else.

He stared out at the blinding garden. It was true that Zenobia had said that she wanted to kill Crace for murdering Lily and that she had worked out how to do it; but he had refused to believe it. Was it possible that she had really done it, as Agatha's words, he realised with horror, implied.

With shaking fingers he unfolded the paper and read its contents again. How could it possibly be true that Crace had spared Lily? According to Zenobia, Agatha had seen her die, had described watching her hang. Nobody could invent such a terrible thing, and there would be a record of Lily's execution.

His heart beat, his hands would not stop shaking, his mouth was dry. He could never show Zenobia the letter. Never! For then she might learn that she had murdered her own uncle. And, as Crace wrote, before the birth of Sheherezade he was her only living relative. Not only that, but however much Zenobia had hated him, under the law he was her husband. Murdering him was treason, for which the punishment was death at the stake.

Besides, how was he to know whether what Crace wrote about Lily was true? Was it just one more of the man's monumental cruelties, his final evil act from the grave? Even if by some miracle Lily had survived, she could have died in the past three years. Agatha believed her to be long dead. What vile cruelty to offer hope that Lily lived somewhere in the world, to reopen that wound.

Hendrik sighed heavily. He could not grasp what he had read, nor Agatha's words. Outside, the dreadful form still appeared to sprawl under the castor oil plant. If only he had stayed outside in the sunshine with Zenobia that afternoon, none of this would be happening.

Deep in thought he returned to the antechamber, replaced the paper in the drawer, laid the tiny key next to it and shut the drawer firmly. As it had earlier in the day, the lock clicked into place.

In the morning, he thought, and whether against Zenobia's wishes or not, he would have the desk sent to Agatha.

She should have destroyed the letter when she had the chance. Now she would understand the decision he had taken and could make her own.

And he would have that stand of plants in the garden cut down and burned. He had never liked the look of them.